# FALSE IMPRESSIONS
*A Megan Scott/Michael Elliott Mystery*

## SANDRA NIKOLAI

Published by Vemcort Publishing
ISBN: 978-0-9880389-1-2

Cover art and design by Carolyn Nikolai
www.carolynnikolai.com

*This novel is dedicated to the memory of my parents
who inspired me with a series of Nancy Drew
mystery books when I was ten years old.*

# CHAPTER 1

If I'd known I would be visiting the morgue just weeks after I saw my husband sitting with Pam at Pueblo's Café, I'd have gone over to say hello that sunny Monday afternoon in July and maybe changed destiny. But I was late for a five o'clock appointment.

Later that night, I told Tom I'd seen him at Montreal's trendy downtown café.

"Yeah...talk about weird," he said, undoing his tie and tossing it on the bed. "I was waiting for a client when this blonde comes over and sits down at my table. I didn't recognize her until she introduced herself as your boss and mentioned the Christmas party last year."

"She's also the friend I told you about. The one I go to the movies and have dinner with every week. Didn't she mention that?"

He nodded absently, as if it were a vague memory, then looked at me. "What did the doctor say?"

My eyes began to sting. I fought back the tears. "I'm not pregnant—again. Damn it! So much for those home pregnancy tests." I tried to rationalize the situation. After all, we'd only been trying for three months. Statistics showed it took most couples up to a year or longer to conceive. "The doctor told me to relax and not think about it. Same conclusion as the shrink. Easy for them." I wriggled out of my jeans and kicked them off, my frustration flying across the floor with them. "Neither of us had siblings. It's what makes having a baby so special. Is it too much to ask? I mean, what am I doing wrong?"

"It's my fault, Megan. I'm never home. All those business trips to dig up new clients—"

"It's not your fault. Besides, those new clients got you that promotion to senior manager. Maybe now that you'll be home more often, I can relax and—"

"Not really. I have to travel even more now."

My heart sank. "You're not serious. I miss you so much already."

He shrugged. "That's why BOTCOR pays me the big bucks—to sell their software."

BOTCOR Dynamics customized multimedia-training programs, to be precise. Way over my head. "Okay, so the upside is that we'll have more money to invest in the new house."

For three years, we'd pooled every extra dime into a savings account toward the purchase of a two-story brick home in the prestigious west end of the city—an area renowned for its tall trees and spacious parks. According to my calculations, we'd be able to leave the leased condo apartment and move into a house by next spring.

"What do we have so far? About forty thousand?" I asked him.

"Yeah...almost." Tom dropped his shirt on the bed, then unzipped his pants and stepped out of them. He walked over and slid his arms around me. "About the baby, it'll happen. You'll see."

I stood on my toes and wrapped my arms around his neck. "You know that trying to get pregnant is the most important part, don't you?" I kissed him on the lips.

He responded with a passion that made me want him even more and reminded me how much I loved him.

We lingered in bed later, my head resting against his back. Even in the dim light, I could see the small tattoo of two intertwining roses on his lower back—the same one we'd both had engraved on our lower backs while honeymooning in Nassau. "I wish we could just pack a few things and fly away to an exotic place. When was the last time we took a vacation? I mean, a real vacation. On our honeymoon?"

"Yeah." He turned to look at me. "Mmm...tell you what. I'll try to take some time off. We'll go away for a weekend. Okay?"

"How? You've been working every weekend for the last six

months."

"I'll make it happen. I promise."

I managed to get a seat on the bus to work the next morning—a rare occurrence on a weekday in this city of multitudes. I took it as a good luck omen on this hot, humid day and enjoyed the view of the majestic maples and historic sites along Sherbrooke Street even more.

Half an hour later, I got off and walked down the block to the fifteen-story building that housed Bradford Publishing. I crossed the lobby, flashed my ID card at Carlo at the front desk, and took the elevator up to the sixth floor.

Lucie, the fresh-out-of-college receptionist Pam had hired last month, greeted me with a wave from across her desk as she spoke into her headset. I made my way down the corridor and passed the glass-framed boardroom. Kayla Warren, the project coordinator, was sitting in a closed-door meeting there with a client and a woman named Helena who was a freelance ghostwriter like me. Next up was the admin assistant's office. Emily Saunders was tapping away on her computer while talking into her headset. Lots of giggling and weird lingo going on. Definitely not work-related, but typical for the twenty-one-year-old.

Minutes after I'd arrived at my desk, voices drifted in from Pam's office at the end of the corridor. Bradford's offices only occupied fifteen hundred square feet, so conversations flowed easily through the air when doors were left open. I couldn't tell who the other woman was, but her tone of voice grew argumentative as "bitch" and other slurs reached my ears.

I was wondering if it would come to blows when Emily tiptoed into my office. "Who *is* that?" she whispered, pointing a thumb toward Pam's office.

"I haven't a clue." I did a double take. Emily was wearing a white blouse almost identical to the one Pam had purchased last week at Holt Renfrew. Ditto for the red lipstick—

My thoughts scattered as the altercation in Pam's office escalated.

3

"I am *not* sleeping with him," Pam said. "You have me confused with someone else."

"I doubt it," the other woman said, her tone curt. "Keep this in mind: my family doesn't tolerate scandals. We don't get rid of people who disrupt our lives by paying them off either."

"Is that a threat?"

"Call it priceless advice."

Footsteps approached. A woman with a stride that said, "Get out of my way!" whizzed past my office. Well-coiffed hair, dark blue suit, lots of makeup, fiftyish. Old money.

I recognized her as Tricia, the wife of company president, Bill Bradford.

And so did Emily. She turned to me, her face a shade paler. "Oh my God! What's *she* doing here?"

The main door slammed shut.

I rushed out of the office, Emily on my heels, and almost collided with Pam as she peeked out into the corridor.

"Good. She's gone." Pam looked past me to Emily, her gaze taking in the blouse and lipstick, a flicker of perception in her eyes.

"What did Mrs. B. want?" Emily asked her, as if she hadn't overheard the conversation.

"Nothing to worry about." Pam waved a hand in the air. "Em, did you call the lab to find out if the photos for the cookbook project were ready?"

"Oops, I forgot. I got real busy." Emily twirled a strand of long blonde hair around her finger—a habit she fell into whenever she was caught in a lie.

"Call Ray now," Pam said. "If the photos are ready, run over and pick them up. We have to approve them ASAP."

Emily's eyes lit up. She'd been dating Ray Felton, photographer and karate enthusiast, on and off since he'd joined the company weeks ago. "Okay, but what about the clients we're meeting with in half an hour?"

Pam gave her a pointed look. "*I'm* meeting with them."

"But I need their signatures on the contracts the lawyers prepared."

"Bring me the paperwork. I'll take care of it."

"Whatever." Emily scowled, then gave me a side-glance and left.

I waited until she was out of hearing range, then said to Pam, "What an attitude problem! No wonder she got fired from her last job."

"She was laid off. There's a big difference."

I shrugged. Pam had believed Emily's tale about having lost her former job due to downsizing, but I hadn't. My phone call to Emily's last employer had proved she'd lied, but Pam had decided to keep her on anyway.

Her gaze softened. "Look, I realize she can be difficult to handle at times, but she wants to learn. She's just an ambitious girl trying to assert herself in this cutthroat world."

"She's incompetent. If it were me, I'd fire her."

"I can't do that! Where would she go? Companies are downsizing all over the place."

*She hired Emily and now she's trying to cover her ass.* I stared at her.

"I know, I know. I'm a real sucker when it comes to underdogs." She waved the topic away. "Come, let's sit down."

Entering Pam's office was like stepping into a different decade. The spacious room had recently been revamped in a black-and-white 60s décor theme. Two black-and-white pieces of optical artwork, supposedly worth a small fortune, filled the wall at the far back. The circular "op art" generated movement, if only through visual illusion, but it was enough to have anyone reaching for their migraine meds. In the center, a glass table with chrome legs provided a landing strip for three narrow metal sculptures winding their way up like tornadoes from hell—the creation of a local *artiste* whose book Bradford had published. Six black vinyl chairs with chrome trim completed the steely look.

The redo—along with a hefty salary increase—was Bradford's way of rewarding Pam for the string of VIP clients she'd brought in over the last two years. The list included corporate gurus, five-star chefs, and fashion icons who had been thrilled at the notion of producing their memoirs through Bradford Publishing, the most reputable publisher in town. The talk was that Pam's charm had lured them in, but insiders knew her offer to promote the client's book was what finalized the deal. From software to chocolate truffles to gold-plated bookmarks, her clients got the best freebies for their book launch. Not to mention media kits and TV interviews.

The metal tips of Pam's three-inch heels clicked against the black-and-white checkered linoleum as she moved to her desk, the trail of Prada perfume lingering in the air behind her. She sunk into a black leather chair. "I guess you guys heard everything Mrs. B. said."

"Hard not to." I sat down, glanced at her collection of cat figurines displayed in a corner bookcase. Trips-without-sex gifts from the older men she'd dated. I was relieved to see she hadn't added any other pieces since January.

She leaned forward and whispered, "If Mrs. B. is right about her husband, I need to find out who the hell is spreading that rumor about me. I have a feeling it's someone from the office."

I kept my voice low. "Who?"

"I heard Em and Lucie talking by the coffee machine yesterday. Em said I dated different men more often than she changed underwear. How would she know? I only confide in you."

I shrugged. "Maybe she overheard you talking on the phone. Sound travels well here."

"Maybe." She paused. "Lucie said Mr. B. ogled me in meetings."

"It doesn't mean anything. Everybody knows he's a big flirt. He ogles all the girls."

She gave a little nod but didn't seem totally convinced.

"Mrs. B. is just fishing," I said. "If you did nothing wrong, why worry about it?"

"You're right. She can't prove a thing. To hell with it." She waved a hand, dismissing the topic. "Thanks again for listening, Megan."

"Isn't that what friends are for?" I smiled. "By the way, Tom told me he bumped into you at Pueblo's."

"You know, he didn't even recognize me," she said, lowering her eyes. "I was so embarrassed. He must have thought I was trying to pick him up or something." She laughed, pushed strands of short white blond hair off her face.

I laughed too. Pam had dated more men in the last year than other thirty-three-year-old women had in a lifetime. Her one stipulation: no married men.

"You'll find someone special one day," I said. "Just wait and see."

"No way. You know the 'white picket fence' fantasy doesn't work for me anymore. I'm all about having a good time with no strings attached. Use them, then lose them. And believe me, I'm enjoying every moment of it." Glossy red lipstick played up her smile.

I should have known better than to go down that road again. A suave investment broker had dated her for almost two years, even promised to marry her. When Pam discovered he was married and had two kids, her naiveté died—and with it her dream.

She reached into her in-basket. "Can you fit a new client into your schedule?"

"Sure." I'd never refused a job from Pam. She'd sent so much work my way that Bradford had become my sole source of income two years later. Even though I worked at home most of the time, she'd arranged for me to have my own office here too. Friendship had its privileges, I supposed.

Pam handed me a book and a CD. "Michael Elliott, a true crime writer. He self-published his first book. It's about his career as an investigative reporter. He needs help with the second one he's drafted. It's on the CD. He's so hot, I was tempted to take on the project myself." She laughed. "He's promoting his first book around town, so try to work around his schedule. Give his project three weeks tops. Focus on clarity and organization of the material, consistency of voice. You know the routine. Bill the company as usual."

Back at my desk, I glanced at *The Inside Track*, the book Pam had given me. There was no photo of the author on the back cover, so I checked the inside flap. There it was.

Pam was right. Michael Elliott was "hot"...and a familiar face from my past. The last time I'd seen him, he was reading Truman Capote's *In Cold Blood* while our English Lit professor lectured the class on Renaissance culture. I had a secret "thing" for this boy with the tousled brown hair and blue eyes, but he didn't even know I existed. The next semester, I heard he'd left McGill University to attend the School of Journalism at Ryerson in Toronto.

I leafed through the pages of his book. It was a compilation of newspaper articles he'd written on criminal activity in major cities across the country over the last decade. Topics ranged from fraudulent marketing schemes to child molesters and included reports on ensuing legal proceedings. I decided to read an investigative piece he'd written on the illicit gun trade in Canada and discovered he'd won a national award for it. My admiration for him suddenly soared. I'd have loved to read more, but I needed to work on his new project.

I popped the CD into my computer and spent the rest of the day skimming through Michael's manuscript. *Drug Trafficking in Canada* focused on a single and obvious topic. I glimpsed passages here and there that referred to organized crime groups, anonymous informants, and police intervention. I had to assume that Michael had done his homework and the information was accurate. There was no time to check it. However, I did notice a less than smooth transition in the flow of the contents. Topics and dates were assembled in a haphazard manner—not in chronological order or theme. That's where I came in. And from where I sat, three weeks would be a tight deadline to meet.

Later that afternoon, Pam stopped by my office on her way out. "Mr. B. just called. He wants me to attend a VIP meeting with him tomorrow morning, but I'm scheduled for publicity photos with Michael Elliott then. Would you mind filling in for me at the shoot? Everyone else is busy. It'll give you a chance to introduce yourself." She looked at me with an expectant look.

"Sure," I said.


The next day, I felt like a schoolgirl and fussed with my hair for half an hour. I couldn't decide what to wear and changed three times before choosing a light blue jacket and skirt.

I was applying my lip liner in the bathroom mirror when Tom

peeked in, looking impressive in a dark suit and tie, briefcase in hand. "Peter's coming by the condo to drop off his company car at lunchtime." He stared at me. "I thought you said you'd be home today."

"Something came up at the last minute."

"Will you be back by noon?"

I turned around to face him. "I don't know. Can't you wait until Peter gets here?"

"No. I have to meet with a client at ten." He checked his watch. "In about an hour. Then I'm taking him out for lunch. On top of that, I've got a blasted headache." He frowned.

"Again?"

"It's okay. I just popped two pills."

"Well...can't you call Peter and set another time?"

"No. I need his car for my trip to Toronto this afternoon. I have to go. A taxi's waiting downstairs." He walked away.

"Wait! Where's your company car?" I followed him down the hallway.

"It's with the mechanic for a tune-up." He opened the front door, then glanced back at me. "Please, Megan, you have to get back here in time for Peter."

"You can't do this to me. I have clients too, you know."

"Sorry. I have no choice." He shut the door behind him.

*Damn it!*

# CHAPTER 2

I walked into Bradford's photography studio and found Michael sitting comfortably in a director's chair. He looked as if he'd just stepped out of bed and all the more charismatic than I remembered. His tanned, chiseled features suggested a preference for rigorous outdoor pursuits, such as mountain climbing or sail boating, rather than writing. Tousled brown hair still framed those blue eyes. He was wearing a dark jacket over light pants and a buttoned-down sports shirt.

I was surprised to see Emily there, chatting with the makeup artist. I wondered why Pam hadn't asked her to stand in at the shoot instead of me but figured she had her own reasons. Ray was checking the lighting. I walked up to Michael and introduced myself.

He stood up and shook my hand with a firm grasp. "Right. You're my ghostwriter. Pam told me about you." He smiled, kept staring at me. "This isn't a come-on line, but I think I know you from somewhere."

I laughed. "You were in my English Lit class at McGill."

"Ah, yes, I remember you now. You used to sit at the back of Professor Becker's class. I kept trying to talk to you, but you kept ignoring me." His smile widened.

Our eyes locked in a split-second of body chemistry, and I felt the blood rushing to my face.

He glanced at my wedding ring. "So you're married now."

"Yes."

"How long?"

"Five years."

Emily edged her way in and put a hand on his arm. "Um…Michael, I think we should get started. Would you like to sit down so Ray can take some pictures?" She glanced at me. "We'll take some of you with Michael in a bit." She waved me away with a nod of her head.

I stood off to the side and watched.

Between shots, Emily found any and every excuse to ease her way over and chat with Michael. She fussed with his shirt collar, asked if he wanted something to drink, made sure his jacket fell just so… Michael smiled politely and kept his cool. My admiration for the man grew each time Emily invaded his private space.

Before I knew it, it was eleven o'clock. Peter was supposed to come by the condo at noon. I was still angry with Tom and hated the way he'd dumped the matter of the company car on me, but I didn't want to leave Peter stranded. I'd have to head for home soon.

I was about to approach Emily when she looked my way. "Okay, Megan, it's your turn. We only need a couple of quick shots."

Her message was subtle but I got it.

As I sat down in a chair next to Michael, he said, "Too bad you never sat this close to me in class." He smiled.

I smiled back and changed the subject. "Do you miss Montreal?"

He nodded. "Especially the downtown area. I grew up in Westmount and—"

Emily cut in. "Did you know the Bradfords lived in Westmount? Their kids went to Selwyn House, an exclusive all-boys private school in the area. Really expensive. Ever heard of the place?" She looked at Michael.

"Yes, I attended Selwyn House," he said.

"Seriously? You were a rich man's kid from Westmount?" Emily's eyes flickered, and I could almost see the dollar signs light up behind them.

Michael shrugged. "I was a spoiled brat. My parents believed the discipline would cure me."

"Well, I have the perfect antidote for that." Emily laughed. "I know some super hot spots in town where we can hang out. I'm sure you'll love them. We can check out a couple of them later." She smiled and looked at him, waiting.

Just then, Ray stepped in to take more pictures. "Sorry to break up the party, but I have a schedule to follow." He frowned at Emily.

Emily glared back at him and moved away. Ten minutes later, she decided Ray had taken enough photos of Michael and me and abruptly ended the shoot. Ray disagreed—he wanted to take more shots. Emily refused. They stood off to one side, wrangling back and forth, the tension between them about to snap.

With no reason to hang around any longer, I said to Michael, "I'd like to meet later to discuss the timeline for your manuscript. Are you free this afternoon?"

"Yes, I am," he said with an easy smile.

"Is three o'clock good for you?" Out of the corner of my eye, I saw Emily approaching.

"Three o'clock is good. Can we meet in my suite at the Elegance Hotel? It's probably a lot quieter than your office." His gaze held mine.

I wasn't crazy about meeting with him at the hotel, but from the earnest look in his eyes, I couldn't refuse. "Okay. What's your room number?"

"788."

"See you later." I ignored Emily's frosty stare and walked out.


Gray hair at the temples, a sagging facial expression, and rimless eyeglasses. Peter Ewans looked as if he'd aged ten years since I'd seen him weeks earlier. As we stood by the front door to my apartment, he handed me the car keys but dropped them. We both made a move to retrieve them. I was faster.

"It's a beige Ford sedan," he said. "I parked it at the back of the condominium in lot 16, like Tom said. The papers are in the glove compartment. The license number is on the key tag. I hope everything is fine." He looked away as if he were trying to come up with something else to say, then quickly asked, "Do you drive to work, Megan?"

"No, I take the bus," I said.

He nodded, then rearranged his glasses over protruding ears and stared at the floor.

Another awkward pause.

"How's Ann doing?" I asked.

He smiled at me. "Ann? Oh, she's fine. Still talking about the brunch we went to—when was it—a month ago?"

"Yes. It was lots of fun." To celebrate Tom's promotion, Peter and Ann had invited us to a fancy brunch at *Le Cartet*. I'd initially met the older couple through Tom at a BOTCOR Christmas party several years earlier, and we subsequently got together once in a while.

"Ann and I, we don't socialize a lot these days, with both of us working and the kids and all. So it was a special treat for us too." He grew quiet and looked down again.

"Maybe we can get together again soon."

He looked up at me with a smile. "Really? I'm sure Ann will be very happy to hear that."

I held his gaze. "Would you like a ride back home or to work?"

His eyes bulged. "In the Ford?"

"No, I meant I'd call a taxi for you."

"Oh...no, thanks. I've arranged for one to pick me up downstairs. It must be here by now." He fumbled with the lock on the door and let himself out without another word.


It was two o'clock and Tom hadn't returned yet from his lunch meeting. I was hoping to see him before he drove off to Toronto, but I had to take the bus and go meet Michael in town.

Shortly before three, I stepped from the sweltering outdoor heat into the air-conditioned Elegance Hotel, one of the jewels in the city's historic Golden Square Mile. Marble tiles paved the lobby and soft music—maybe Chopin—drifted my way from speakers hidden behind parted drapery that revealed the busy street. I had once worked on a magazine article about hotel rates in Montreal and knew that a reporter's salary couldn't begin to cover one week's stay in this hotel. Then again, if you were "a rich man's kid from Westmount," chances are you could easily afford to stay here.

Michael welcomed me into his suite and ushered me along a short hallway into a spacious living room. I squinted at the sunlight flooding in through white vertical blinds suspended from ceiling to floor.

"Here. I'll fix that."

As he drew the blinds halfway, I looked around. Gray wall-to-wall carpet. On my right, two oversized reprints of unknown origin—a flowery design you wouldn't recall even if you'd seen the same one in dozens of hotel rooms. Beneath them, a royal blue sofa. In the center, two magenta armchairs flanking a coffee table. On my immediate left, a credenza topped with a flat-screen TV, an AM/FM radio, a large plant, and water bottles. A corridor beyond that probably led to the bedroom and bathroom. A purple sofa identical to the blue one along the far wall.

Michael gestured toward the magenta armchairs. "Have a seat."

I placed my briefcase on the floor next to the armchair on the left and sat down. I focused on Michael, his slim muscular build more noticeable now under a T-shirt and jeans.

"Want some cold water?" he asked. "I just picked up a pack at the convenience store." He took two bottles from the credenza and handed me one, then sat down opposite me.

"Thanks." I twisted the cap off, took a sip, sensed the coolness trickle down my throat. I hadn't realized how parched I was. Or maybe it was a case of hormones gone wild. "So how did you like the photo shoot?" I asked him, getting back to basics.

Michael smiled. "Ray's great. Emily said they're going to place two photos in *The Gazette* this week with a promo piece about me." He drank some water from his bottle.

I had to know. "Did Ray and Emily stop squabbling after I left?"

"Yes, when I told them I had to leave. Emily escorted me down in the elevator." He paused. "Are you and Emily good friends?"

"No. Why?"

"I practically had to fight her off. It was plain crazy." He chuckled, but the look in his eyes told me he wasn't too happy about it.

*Another strike against Emily.* I made a mental note to tell Pam about her, then put my bottle on the table and moved things along.

I dug out his CD, a pen, and a canary yellow notepad from my briefcase. "I'd like to set up a schedule that'll work for both of us. Maybe we can start with your book-signing events over the next three weeks. If you give me the dates and times, we can set up our meetings around them."

"Sure." He pulled out his iPhone. "I have the info on my calendar."

I wrote down the dates and we discussed potential meeting times. Michael had book-signings and interviews on most days, which only left the evenings free for us to meet.

He shrugged. "Unless it causes a problem at home."

"No, it's fine," I said. "I'd like to review your manuscript in depth tomorrow." I glanced down at Michael's schedule. "We could meet again Friday afternoon to discuss it. Is two o'clock okay?"

"No problem. Here? In my suite?"

*He's still trying to avoid Emily.* "Okay," I said, earning a brief smile from him. "Now, about your manuscript..." I explained the concern I had with the flow of the text.

"You noticed that, did you?" He laughed. "Believe me, it's not my usual way of doing things, but I was in a hurry. Sorry."

"You don't have to apologize."

"Then I'd like to explain."

"Go ahead." I sat back.

"I was covering a couple of illegal drug cases last month. Meeting with street informants and handing over evidence to the police. I got the go-ahead to ride with the SWAT team on drug busts so long as I stayed behind the scenes. Their maneuvers went on longer than I'd planned. Before I knew it, the promo tour for my first book started." He shrugged. "I ran out of time."

I nodded, secretly acknowledging the risk inherent in his work, his courage to follow through in spite of it...and the mellow tone of his voice. I was drawn to him, no doubt about it. I kept thinking how I might have made a play for him myself if I weren't married.

He pointed to the CD, snapping me out of my reverie. "Some details might be sketchy. Just ask me about them. I didn't set up the manuscript the way I wanted either, but you already know that."

"That's why I'm here." I picked up my pen and got back to business.

We worked the rest of the afternoon, grouping similar topics and setting up the contents in chronological order for each topic. We agreed that I'd review a segment at a time and meet with him afterward to discuss any questions I had. I double-checked the meeting times to make certain we had enough free evenings to cover the entire manuscript.

At one point, Michael checked his watch. "Six o'clock already?"

"Oh. Do you have to be somewhere?" I hurried to gather my notes.

"Just dinner. Want to join me?"

"Dinner?" I thought about it. My fridge contained six eggs, two apples, a wedge of cheese, stale bagels, and a jar of mustard.

"If you can't make it, I understand," he said, mistaking my silence for a refusal. "Your husband is probably waiting—"

"No, Tom's away on business. I'll join you."

A blast of hot air greeted us like an open oven door as we stepped outside the Elegance. The heavy downtown traffic only added to the heat and humidity that had lingered in the city for weeks. Luckily, it was a short walk to Santino's—Michael's suggestion for dinner.

I was familiar with the fine Italian restaurant owned and operated by a family of the same name for decades. The red brick façade was unpretentious, adding to its reputation for excellent food and service. Indoors, the foyer housed a huge porcelain fountain with three ceramic angels pouring water from decanters into a basin. *Fontana d'angeli*—Fountain of Angels—was the inscription on the gold plaque adorning it. Wood beams along the ceiling and walls lent an old country ambiance to the place. As we waited to be seated, the aroma of pasta sauce wafted in my direction and stirred my appetite.

The maitre d' walked up to us, the buttons of his black satin vest straining to contain a belly that was a testimony to the success of the place—if not his love of Italian cuisine.

"Hi, Luigi," Michael said to him. "Table for two, please."

"I have the *perfetto* table for you," Luigi gestured, his forefinger and thumb linked to form an "okay" sign. He led Michael and me to a secluded corner at the back of the restaurant, and I realized too late that he'd read more into our relationship than intended.

Maria arrived to take our orders for pasta, then returned to fill our glasses with red wine.

After she'd left, I said to Michael, "I'm curious about something. You self-published your first book, but you're not going the same route with your second book. Why not?"

"I'm lousy at self-promotion." He chuckled. "A friend told me about Pam and Bradford Publishing, so I met with her. From what I've seen so far, I'm glad I took his advice."

I wasn't sure exactly who or what he was referring to, but his fixed gaze gave me butterflies. I glanced down and fidgeted with the cutlery.

"Are you happily married?" he asked, catching me off guard.

"Yes...of course."

"Any kids?"

"Not yet. We're working on it. Have you ever been married?"

"No such luck." A weak smile couldn't hide the shadow flitting over his features.

"That's surprising." I caught myself. "I mean—I would think—"

He shrugged. "Haven't found the right girl yet." He smiled. "Any hobbies? Sports?"

I thought about how tedious my life had become. "Too busy with work. You?"

"I go out for a jog in the morning. Have to keep fit." He patted an abdomen that would be the envy of most men. "You travel much?"

"We've tried to get away, but Tom travels a lot on business." I sipped some wine.

"Even on weekends?"

"Yes. Sometimes he leaves for ten days straight."

"It must get lonely for you."

"I keep busy." I took another sip of wine.

"I get lonely whenever I travel on assignment. I can be surrounded by people and still feel lonely. It's plain crazy, isn't it?" He smiled.

There was sincerity in his expression and voice that I hadn't noticed before. Without realizing it, he'd forced me to face a sad truth deep inside me: that I missed Tom more than ever.

But I'd be damned if I was going to start feeling sorry for myself in front of a stranger. I took a few more sips of wine and searched for a less invasive topic of discussion.

I gazed away and found my answer. Terracotta pots, old-country china plates, and odd pieces of earthenware decorated the wooden beams along the walls. I focused on a row of antique vases. Three porcelain pieces were chipped. Either they were old and valuable, or someone had damaged them on purpose to make them appear that way. "I wonder if those vases are real or fake. What do you think?"

My tactic worked. Michael began to tell me how one of his friends had a knack for finding valuable antiques while browsing in flea markets. I made sure we stuck to other topics that were just as neutral throughout the rest of our dinner.


Later that evening, I opened the door to my apartment and was surprised to find Tom sitting in the living room. "Tom, you're still here. What happened?" I shut the door and noticed his luggage in the hallway.

"I had an accident," he said. "A wheel spun off Peter's car. I crashed into a couple of parked cars downtown. Good thing I wasn't going fast."

"Oh, my God! Are you okay?" I rushed up to him, my gaze flitting over his sports shirt and jeans. No sign of broken bones or cuts. I sat down next to him.

He rubbed the back of his neck. "I have a headache and a bit of whiplash. I'll be fine." He frowned. "It's eight o'clock. I tried reaching you at the office. Where were you?"

"With a new client." We'd agreed from the start that we'd never discuss our boring jobs or clients with each other, so it wasn't as if I had to tell him about Michael and how he'd driven me back home in a fancy sports car. "Did you tell Peter about the accident? And BOTCOR?"

He nodded. "Peter went nuts. The poor guy almost had a nervous breakdown when I told him. BOTCOR put me on a first-class flight to Toronto tomorrow morning and gave me a travel bonus. They're probably pissing in their pants, hoping I won't sue them."

"I thought they ensured regular maintenance checks on their cars."

"They do. The auto shop has high standards, but mistakes can happen anywhere." He shrugged. "It's Peter I'm worried about. He's already got enough issues with management."

"What do you mean?"

"You remember what he said at the brunch? How it was the third time they'd passed him over for a promotion and then handed it to me—a newbie?"

"Yes, but he joked about it and said he was too old for the job anyway."

"It's a different story at work. He told me he's lost everyone's respect there and blames management. Sometimes he gets real angry about it." He shook his head.

"Maybe he shouldn't have left his old job as a chemist."

"Don't get me wrong. He's a hard worker. That's why I kept him on my sales team."

It might not have been the best time to re-visit the subject, but I gave it a shot anyway. "I'm looking forward to getting away for a weekend. Not counting the Christmas parties at Bradford and BOTCOR, we rarely go out."

"What about your best buddy? You go out with her."

"Pam? I meant we—as in you and me. It gets so lonely here without you, Tom."

"I already told you I'm working on it." He stood up, massaged the back of his neck. "Sorry. Didn't mean to snap. It's this damn headache. I'm going to bed. I have an early flight."

"How long will you be gone?"

"A couple of days." He kissed me, then walked out of the room.


I worked from home on Thursday and tried to get a hold of Pam, but Lucie told me she was out of the office with clients and wouldn't be available until tomorrow. I scheduled a meeting with her then.

Friday noon, I arrived at work. As I passed Emily's office, I saw her lift the papier-mâché rabbit on her bookcase and put a small shiny item under it. I assumed it was the key to her desk but didn't give it another thought.

I knocked on Pam's door. "Lunch is served." I held up a brown paper bag. "Two cream cheese and smoked salmon bagels. Two coffee lattes. A bag of chocolate almonds to share."

"Good stuff!" Pam got up from her desk. "I've been in meetings with clients all morning and I'm starving. Let's eat at the table."

I dug the contents out of the bag and placed them on the glass tabletop, then pulled out one of the chrome chairs. "It's been weeks since we got together for lunch."

"I know," she said, sitting down. "I've been so busy lately." She glanced at her watch. "And my next meeting is in half an hour. Thanks for picking these up." She unwrapped her bagel. "Lucie said you wanted to meet to talk about Michael Elliott."

"Actually, it's more about Emily." I briefed her on the photo shoot and Michael's comments about fighting her off.

"Em's a bit of a flirt, but I figured if you were there, she'd behave." She shrugged, then took a bite of her bagel.

"What? You expected me to babysit her? She was all over Michael anyway. And from what he told me, Emily harassed him in the elevator too."

She chewed her food. "In that case, I'll talk to her and—"

"Talk? It's beyond that point. Can you imagine what would happen if Mr. or Mrs. B. heard about this? If anything, it would reflect badly on *you*." I bit into my bagel.

She stared at me, swallowed hard, seemed to be weighing my words. "You're right. They'll think that I can't control my staff. Maybe it's time I fire her."

"I don't know what you're waiting for."

Emily walked in. "Pam, here are the documents you wanted for the Demetri account." She stood there, holding the papers, her eyes boring into me with a look that told me she'd overheard part—if not all—of our conversation.

Pam waved a hand. "Leave them on my desk, Em. Thanks."

Emily looked at her. "So how did your VIP meeting go yesterday?"

"Fine," Pam said, turning her attention back to her bagel.

"Just *fine*? That's all?"

"I don't have time to talk about it," Pam said, her mouth full.

Emily's lips tightened. "Mrs. B. left messages for you. Lucie tried to reach you but—"

"I know," Pam said, annoyance rising in her voice.

"Seriously, you don't have to bite my head off," Emily shouted. She flung the documents she was still holding across Pam's desk, toppling an empty coffee cup, then stormed out.

I whispered to Pam, "Anger-management issues. You can use that excuse to fire her."

"Oh, I have lots more reasons to fire her," she whispered back. "I'll take care of it."

"What about the calls from Mrs. B?"

"I'll take care of that too."


I went to my scheduled meeting with Michael at the Elegance that afternoon.

"A reporter from *The Gazette* just phoned me for an interview," he said as we stood in his suite. "He's on his way up. Had I known earlier, I'd have called you."

"Oh...that's okay." I wondered why he'd bothered to let me in at all, then figured it was the courteous thing to do rather than converse with me in the hotel corridor.

"Can you come back in half an hour?" he asked.

"Sure. I'll leave these here for now." I dug into my briefcase for the CD and manuscript. I found a free spot among the crumpled papers on the coffee table and placed the items there. It beat lugging them back and forth. "See you later."

The heat and humidity that hung over the city was wearing me down. Lucky for me, it was only a block down Sherbrooke Street to Bradford Publishing.

I swung into my office and dropped my briefcase at the foot of the desk, then sat down to check my messages. Three were from clients; the fourth was from Tom. He'd called from Toronto and I knew why. He'd made good on his promise to spend a weekend together. Someone had phoned me at home earlier to confirm the booking. I searched my briefcase for the canary yellow sheet I'd written the information on but couldn't find it. I opened up my agenda and wrote down what I remembered from the call, then phoned Tom back.

"My client wants me to stick around a few more days," he said, letting out a deep breath. "I can't wait to spend a weekend away from the city for a change."

"Me too," I said, smiling into the phone. I glanced down at the page where I'd jotted the information. "Louise from the Pineview resort called to confirm our August 10 weekend. Dinner and Jacuzzi for two. Sounds wonderful."

"Pineview?" He paused. "Damn it. Our people in admin screwed up again. I'm working on a marketing project with Peter and the team at Granite Ridge that weekend."

"Oh. I thought you'd planned something special for the two of us."

"I'm sorry, Megan. Next time. I promise."

"It's always the next time," I muttered, then regretted my words, knowing that his hard work was for our mutual benefit. "I have the Pineview number if you want to call them."

"No, I'll have the admin people fix their mistake. Have to go now."

I glanced down at my agenda. "Wait. One more thing. A man from the life insurance company called. He didn't say what it was about."

"Yeah, he called me before. Tried to up-sell me on a pricier policy. I'm glad I'm not in the insurance business." He chuckled. "Okay, gotta go. Bye, Megan."

No weekend alone with Tom. That's all I could think of after I'd hung up.

I dug out the chocolate-covered almonds remaining from my lunch with Pam. They helped to calm me, but I still needed to vent. I opened up my e-mail. Time for a cleanup of old files. Pressing the delete button over and over did wonders for venting my frustration, not to mention tidying up my files. After I'd finished, I felt better and called back the clients who'd left messages. Two wanted billing information; the third wasn't there, so I left a message.

I dug into my briefcase and retrieved three letters that I'd picked up from the lobby mailbox on my way out the condo earlier. Mrs. Speck had stood next to me then, making idle chitchat, her eyes peering through thick black-rimmed glasses at the letters in my hand. I'd heard she chatted up the letter carrier every day while he sorted the letters, bills, and small packages. He'd hurry to get the job done, but it was all he could do to stop Mrs. Speck from looking over his shoulder. Small wonder.

I shredded the first two envelopes. Junk mail. Given that our bill payments were deducted through Tom's bank account, it amazed me how advertisers still managed to get a hold of our home address. The last envelope was addressed to me. The return address read: Sunny Watering Hole, Bistro Hot Spot, Montreal, Québec. Funny, I'd never heard of the place. I opened it up. Inside was a photo of Tom and Pam. The scene looked familiar. Of course. It was a shot of them sitting at Pueblo's—probably the same day I'd seen them there because Pam was wearing the same outfit. I could tell the photo had been taken through a car window because it wasn't rolled down all the way.

A search online turned up nothing on Sunny Watering Hole. No surprise there. I assumed one of Tom's friends had sent me the photo as a prank. Probably Greg, the new marketing recruit. Tom told me one of the guys from work had sprayed Greg with woman's perfume at Coby's last week on his fortieth birthday party. It had taken three phone calls to convince Greg's pregnant wife, Ashley, that he hadn't been with another woman. I'd felt sorry for his wife. If I'd been in the same situation, I'd have lost it too.

The photo was old news and not worth calling Tom about. He'd get a good laugh out of it on his return.

When I went back to Michael's hotel suite, I found the door slightly ajar. I heard voices and figured the reporter was still there, so I didn't knock. I leaned over and peeked inside.

A woman was standing in the living room, her back to me. Dark brown hair fell to her shoulders in curls. A short skirt showed off a trim waist and long legs. "I come all the way here and you say you're too busy to meet me for coffee?"

"I am. Look around." He gestured toward the room.

She turned and took a few steps toward the left, disappearing from my line of sight. "So much paper... Which reminds me. I saw your publicity photo in the newspaper this morning, the one with that pretty redhead from the publishing company—Megan whatever-her-name-is. Are you holding out on me?" she asked in a soft voice, as if she were promising a child he wouldn't be punished if he owned up to bad behavior. "Well?"

"You mentioned you had something for me?" Michael said.

She walked back to him. "I do." She reached into her shoulder bag and handed him a tiny pendant on a gold chain. "You forgot this in my hotel room the other night. I know how important it is to you."

He accepted it from her without a word.

"I have to run but we need to talk, Michael. See you at dinner tonight. Maybe I can convince you to accept your grandmother's settlement." She reached up to kiss him on the lips.

That was my cue. I stepped back, slowly counted to five, then knocked at the door.

Michael swung it open. "Hi, Megan. Good timing." He introduced me to Jane Barlow.

If Jane was surprised at seeing me in the flesh, she didn't show it. Her blue-gray eyes studied me for a moment before she offered some vague excuse about rushing off.

As Michael and I settled in the magenta armchairs around the coffee table, he said, "Jane works as a paralegal. She's in town to see a client." He paused. "We first met a year ago in a Montreal court when we sat in on a drug possession case. We met again in a Toronto court when I was working on a drug case there two months ago. We dated for a while afterward."

I wondered why he felt obliged to explain his personal history with Jane. As if I cared. "Uh-huh."

"There's nothing serious between us."

His gaze brought back the butterflies. I gathered my thoughts and reached for the manuscript on the table. I was astonished to see my note with the Pineview information on top of the pile. "How did this get here?" I held up the canary yellow paper.

"Oh...that. I lifted your printout to make room for the reporter's stuff, and it fell out from the bottom. I thought it might be important."

"It's not." I crumpled it and placed it beside the other discarded papers on the table.

That evening, I watched the late night news on TV and caught a clip of Montreal's International Fireworks Competition. Up until three years ago, Tom and I used to go see some of those events live. Then our work got in the way and we hardly spent time together, let alone went out. All this to say that I saw Tom all of three times over the next two weeks.

The first occasion was dinner Monday evening after he'd returned from Toronto. I surprised him with a home-cooked meal—a rare occurrence in our kitchen. I'd called my mother to get the recipe for her lasagna, and it had turned out pretty good. She would have been proud.

We had just finished dinner, when Tom's cell phone rang. After a brief conversation, he hung up and announced, "I'm going to Coby's. Have to meet with a new client."

"I thought we were going to spend a quiet evening together," I said.

He shrugged. "I couldn't say no to the guy. If the deal works out, it means a pay bonus for me." He suddenly grimaced in pain, rubbed his temples with both hands. "You got any aspirin? I finished my bottle."

I stood up. "You keep getting these headaches. Maybe you should see the doctor."

"I'm okay. I went for a physical in the spring. It's just stress." He followed me to the master bathroom where I plucked the bottle of pills from the cabinet and handed it to him. He swallowed two pills with a gulp of water. He smiled at me, then kissed me on the lips. "Dinner was incredible. Don't wait up."

I didn't.

I saw Tom a second time that week. I was working at home and he'd arrived from New York, only to pack a clean set of clothes before rushing out to take a plane to Windsor.

Then I spent a few hours with him when I helped him pack for a seven-day trip to Toronto. That trip would take him through to Friday afternoon, August 10, which was the start of his working weekend with Peter and the team. Yet another trip in what I imagined would be an endless schedule of the same.

Ironically, I spent more time with Michael during those same two weeks than with my own husband. Book-signings and interviews with the media filled most of the crime writer's days, so all our get-togethers predictably turned into dinner meetings. Michael was okay with this arrangement since he preferred to discuss his work with me in person rather than on the phone or through e-mail. I was okay with it because it meant I wouldn't have to eat dinner alone.

Every third evening, I'd meet Michael at Santino's. We discussed the material I'd reviewed since our last meeting. Whether I needed clarification of facts or whether he had comments regarding my interpretation of them, our conversation focused on work. But by the time we ordered coffee, our discussion had spread to a range of other topics, from favorite movies to least favorite politicians, interspersed with hilarious experiences from our youth and his backpacking trips to Europe.

I noticed he rarely mentioned his family except to say that his parents were retired and lived out of town. I never talked much about my family either, except to mention Tom's weird car accident and my Mom's penchant for playing bingo. More and more, I looked forward to Michael's easygoing rapport and to our discussions during dinner—the stuff of which I hadn't experienced with Tom in years. I wished it could go on like this forever, but Michael was heading back to Toronto soon, and I doubted I'd ever see him again. Reality soon rushed in with a reminder of my upcoming work schedule at Bradford and its state of dull predictability.

We were sitting in Michael's suite that last Friday, August 10—

my deadline for his project. I used his laptop for a final save of the file and sent a copy by e-mail to Kayla at Bradford minutes before closing. She confirmed seconds later that she'd received it.

I leaned my head against the back of the armchair. "We made it."

"I never doubted it," he said, smiling. "I'm flying back to Toronto tomorrow. I thought we could celebrate our success over dinner... unless you have other plans."

"No plans. Tom's gone for the weekend. Another business trip."

He nodded, familiar with my mantra by now. "How about Santino's for old time's sake?"

The thought of having dinner with Michael one last time gave me pangs of nostalgia. I'd only known him for a few weeks, but it felt like a lifetime. With Tom out of town for the most part, evening meals with Michael had grown into as comfortable a routine as one would expect from two people trying to get into each other's head every other day. Tonight I'd have to say goodbye to him. I hated endings, especially when they had to do with friendships. That I'd picked my friends carefully all my life and had so few close ones could explain my reluctance to part with them.

We were enjoying our pasta dishes—lasagna for Michael and ravioli for me—when his cell phone rang. He dug it out and looked at the display. "Emily. She keeps calling me. At the hotel too. She probably has me on speed dial." He chuckled, slipped the cell phone back into his pocket.

I hadn't heard a word from Pam after I'd told her about Emily's behavior at the photo shoot. Whatever she'd said to Emily later clearly hadn't stopped her from hounding Michael. Why should I care anyway? His love life was none of my business.

In fact, Michael would no longer be a part of my life after tonight. Only brief memories would remain: our animated discussions, the way he laughed when I told him about a funny incident that happened to me when I was a kid, his steady gaze that gave me butterflies...

By the time Maria served coffee, the verbal exchange between us had dwindled to a few words. Michael kept his gaze fixed on the table. I couldn't tell if he was eager to leave or sad that he was.

On my part, mixed emotions had taken over. I couldn't think of anything to say without sounding trite.

Michael drove me home afterward. We didn't speak, and I was thankful that the low hum of the air-conditioner filled the silence. When we came to a stop at the front of my condo, he surprised me when he turned off the engine and stepped out. He walked around to the passenger side and opened the door for me—not his usual routine whenever he'd dropped me off.

He offered his hand. I took it and got out of the car. We stood facing each other for a long moment. The expression on his face was as pained as the way I felt.

"I hate saying goodbye." He wrapped his arms around me and held me tight. "I'm going to miss you, Megan." His lips brushed against my cheek.

My legs felt weak and butterflies flew erratically in my stomach. I swallowed hard and muttered, "Yes...I'll miss you too."

He pulled back and smiled. "Thanks for everything."

As he moved away, I saw Mrs. Speck in the window of her second-floor apartment. She had opened the curtains and was standing there, bony arms crossed. Even in the moonlight, I could see her black-rimmed glasses and her gray hair pulled back in a tight bun. I pretended not to notice her.

I waved goodbye to Michael one last time and watched him drive off, sadness adding weight to the humid night air. I was losing a friend, if not an ideal dinner companion. Yet I felt a deeper loss—one similar to the pain I'd felt when I was sixteen and my first boyfriend dumped me. I thought the world would come to an end then.

*Get over it,* I scolded myself. *The world won't come to an end. Besides, you can't be in love with two men at the same time—one of whom you're not even married to.*

Okay. So Michael was gone. Difficult as it was, I'd have to accept it and move on.

Little did I know how soon our paths would cross again.

# CHAPTER 3

I slept in till noon on Saturday. With Tom gone for the weekend, I had lots of time to tackle the house chores.

The phone rang.

It was my mother. "So? Am I a *nonna*-in-waiting this month?" she asked, her words laced with a hint of Italian dialect she'd retained since her youth.

"No, Mom. You didn't make the Granny list. I'm not pregnant."

"It can't be," she said. "You're from Irish-Italian ancestry. Practically blue blood. Look at my seven brothers and sisters and my four in-laws. They have thirty-three children altogether. Their children are already having children."

A rare tumor had dashed my mother's hopes of having more children after I was born. I suspected she was eager to have my babies fill that void—maybe just as eager as I was to give birth to them. "It's not a race, Mom."

"I know, but the timing is perfect, so don't wait too long," she said, as if I were holding the eggs back from the sperm on purpose.

"You can't possibly imagine how often I blame myself for not getting pregnant. I don't need another guilt trip."

A deep sigh at the other end, then silence.

Damn it, I'd hurt her feelings. "I have to go now," I said, softly. "I have work to do."

"That's the problem. You and Tom work too much. You need to take a few days off. Go on a trip. Your father and I used to take trips every year when he was alive."

"I have a job, Mom. I can't just leave whenever I want."

"Nothing should stand in the way of a happy marriage, Megan. Family values. That's what my parents brought with them when they crossed the ocean. That's what I'm teaching you now."

I gave it another try. "I'm in the middle of housework," I said. "I'll call you later. Okay, Mom?"

"Okay, but not too late. I'm going to bingo with my friends tonight."

I'd just hauled out the vacuum when the doorbell rang. I ignored it. I figured it was a pesky salesperson. But after the fourth ring, my patience ran out. I slammed the button on the intercom in the hallway and shouted, "Yes?"

"Madame Thomas Scott?" A male voice echoed in the foyer downstairs.

Who would use such an unusual version of my name? "Who is this?"

"I am Detective Lieutenant Moreau of the Sûreté du Québec." I perceived a heavy French-Canadian accent this time. "I would like to see you about a grave personal matter."

*A grave personal matter?*

A lump suddenly materialized in the pit of my stomach. I buzzed him in and opened the door to my apartment. My heart pounded as two men in plainclothes soon stepped out of the elevator, each wearing a badge on a chain around his neck. As they neared, I recognized the insignia as that of the Québec Provincial Police force, or QPP, as the English-speaking population knew it.

"*Bonjour,* Madame Scott. I am Detective Lieutenant Jean Moreau. This is Detective Sergeant Claude Duchaine. May we come in?"

"Of course." I caught the scent of cigarette smoke on Moreau's clothes as he breezed past me into the living room. A tweed jacket, a lilac shirt, and a tie that looked as if it had been used to wipe off paintbrushes gave the impression he'd selected his clothes in the dark. While strands of mousy-brown hair made a futile attempt to cover the top of his head, a thick mustache filled the narrow space between thin lips and a pointy nose. Sporting a black attaché case, he could have passed for a fifty-year-old salesman peddling insurance door-to-door.

Duchaine stood at least four inches taller and that much wider than Moreau. A buttoned jacket strained to contain his beefy physique. His brown hair was cropped short, tinged blond on top, and balanced out a square jaw. I placed him at about thirty-five.

"Please sit down," I said, indicating one of two black leather sofas.

"*Non, merci,* Madame Scott," Moreau answered for both of them, his dark eyes peering at me from under eyebrows as bushy as his mustache. "But perhaps you would like to sit down."

I looked at their faces, grim with purpose. A sudden weakness hit my knees and I sunk into the sofa.

"We regret to inform you..." Moreau paused. "Your husband, Thomas Scott, is dead."

My heart beat out of control. "No! It can't be. It must be a mistake."

"It is not a mistake, Madame."

"Do you have proof?"

Moreau retrieved a black notebook from his jacket and flipped it open. "Thirty-four years of age, slim, dark brown hair, tattoo of two roses on the lower back—"

I raised a hand. "Stop...please." He had just confirmed that the love of my life was gone.

My eyes began to sting and I started to cry. I grabbed a few tissues from a box on the table and sobbed until I thought my heart would break. All the while, the two police officers stood waiting.

I took a deep breath and tried to calm down. This wasn't the time to fall apart. I needed answers. "I'm sorry," I said, choking on the words as I wiped away the tears.

"There is no need to apologize," Moreau said. "Is there anything we can do for you?"

I nodded. "Can you tell me how Tom died?"

Moreau shook his head.

"Was he in a car accident?"

"No."

The fact that Tom might have died from a stroke crossed my mind. He was a Type A personality and his excessive workload wouldn't have helped any. I'd also read that younger men weren't as impervious to strokes as doctors had once thought. "Did he have a stroke?"

Moreau shook his head again.

"Was he attacked?"

Again, silence.

I waved my hands in the air. "For God's sake, Detective, you must have some idea of the cause of death."

"We expect an autopsy report in several days. I am not a medical expert, Madame Scott."

I bit my tongue and refrained from telling him exactly what I thought he was. Instead I came up with more questions. "Where did he die? Who found him?"

"A business associate thought something was wrong when your husband did not meet him before a scheduled game of golf this morning."

"What business associate? Do you have a name?"

He motioned to Duchaine. *"Votre calepin, sergent."*

The sergeant produced his own black notebook. "His name is Peter Ewans." Duchaine's heavy French accent implied he had the same heritage as Moreau.

"Peter...yes," I said. "He was working with Tom this weekend."

Moreau studied me. "Madame Scott, did you ever suspect your husband was having an affair?"

His question threw me. "An affair? Of course not. We're trying to have a baby."

He kept his eyes on me. "The body of a young woman was found next to your husband."

"What?" I said.

He glanced at his notebook. "Pamela Strober."

I couldn't believe my ears. "Pam?"

"You know this woman?"

"Yes. She's—she was—my boss at Bradford Publishing."

"Did you know that your husband was spending the weekend with her at a Pineview cottage?"

"It's impossible. She doesn't date married men." That excuse now sounded so pathetic. As I did, I imagined. "Pineview?" The name only now sunk in. "Tom didn't go to Pineview."

Moreau said a few words in French to Duchaine who nodded and took notes.

My knowledge of the language wasn't perfect, but I did manage to grasp *le mobile du meurtre*—the motive for the murder. "You think my husband was murdered?"

Moreau raised an eyebrow. Maybe he was surprised that I understood French. "Anything is possible." He studied me. "Where were you last night, Madame Scott?"

# CHAPTER 4

"I'm sorry, Detectives," I said to Moreau and Duchaine. "I want my lawyer present before I answer any more questions." I stood up.

"Very well." Moreau put his notebook away and so did Duchaine. "Until our investigation is complete, we are withholding information about this case from the media. Consequently, we ask that you keep our conversation confidential."

"Of course," I said, then surprised myself by saying, "I want to see my husband."

Moreau frowned. "But Madame Scott, it is not necessary. His identity has been confirmed."

"I have a right to see him, don't I?"

He nodded. "As you wish. When would be convenient for you?"

"Now."

The tall steel and glass building on Parthenais Street housed the QPP headquarters. It also housed the morgue—the destination for people who died under "unnatural circumstances" such as murders, suicides, and work-related deaths. The stench of the place alone was enough to kill you, so the corpses had an advantage in this respect. No kidding. Combine the odors of bleach, urine, fish, rotten cheese, and formaldehyde with stainless steel trolleys and refrigerator drawers, and you have the morgue.

I was led to the viewing area, but nothing could have prepared me for it. A gasp caught in my throat. It was Tom, all right, but he looked nothing like the handsome husband I once knew and loved. My eyes focused on the corpse of a young man with pasty white skin, blue lips, and agony etched all over his face. There was no indication of a knife or bullet wound or any other signs of trauma that might point to a physical confrontation—at least not on the part of the exposed torso that I could see.

Sadness washed over me and sank deep inside until it hurt.

*What were you thinking, Tom?*

*Why would you risk our marriage, our future?*

*How could you betray me?*

He'd left me too soon. Too soon to share our most intimate loves and fears. Too soon to build a future and have children. Too soon to work things out between us.

Then again, what was there to work out? Nothing. Not a damn thing until Pam had walked into our lives.

Pam. My so-called friend. My blood boiled at the thought of that woman and how she'd taken the best part of my life away from me forever. I felt empty, betrayed. Anger replaced grief and surged inside me. All I kept thinking was how I wished Pam would still be alive so I could kill her myself.

I clenched my teeth in anger. A guttural sound emitted from my throat.

"Mrs. Scott?"

I turned to see the morgue attendant peering at me through rimless glasses.

"We have several personal items belonging to your husband," he said in a quiet voice. "Would you like to take them home with you?"

I couldn't speak, so I nodded yes.

After I signed the release form, he gave me a plastic sleeve containing Tom's keychain and leather wallet. The keychain was a letter T in sterling silver. I'd had Tom's initials engraved on the wallet and given him both items as Christmas gifts last year. In return, he'd given me a pair of diamond stud earrings that I'd worn every day since. The attendant assured me that Tom's overnight bag and its contents would be sent to me after forensics was done with them.

In keeping with protocol, Moreau arranged for a police cruiser to drive me back home. I didn't object. Everything had happened so fast and seemed so surreal—as if I'd just viewed a movie in fast-paced clips. I couldn't trust my emotions or my senses. I only knew it wasn't wise to walk out of here alone in my current state of mind.

Back home, I drifted into the bedroom and opened the door to the walk-in closet. Two hangers lay on the floor. Tom's sweaters were in disarray on the shelves. These signs gave the false impression he'd rushed off on a business trip and would soon return. I picked up the wooden hangers—Tom never used wire hangers—and folded his sweaters. I ran my fingers along his shirts and suits, adjusting a jacket that hung lopsided and a tie that threatened to slip to the floor. I arranged his shoes, making sure each pair was aligned in each cubicle.

I was about to leave when I noticed his briefcase tucked in a corner behind a rack of pants. How odd. It had always accompanied him on trips. Then again, he wouldn't have had much use for it at Pineview—not with Pam there. I gave the closet a final check, as if the orderliness of this aspect of Tom's world would somehow prepare him for the next one, then I shut the door behind me.

The floor leading to the kitchen stretched ahead. It seemed to take forever to get there. My eyes fell on the table and chairs and the pile of dirty dishes in the sink. Nothing seemed familiar.

I pulled out a chair and sat down. The nerves in my body began to unravel, but the tears wouldn't come. I no longer felt the pain of having lost the greatest love of my life. It felt more like a twinge in my heart, as if a close friend had just announced he was leaving on a trip for a long time and I knew I'd never see him again.

Reality struck and hatred surged through me in the next moment. Tom had betrayed me. He had cheated on me with a close friend, to top it off. A close friend who said she didn't date married men. I laughed out loud. How ironic. The man I'd loved for the past five years, I now hated with an equal dose of intensity. It goes to show how you never really know someone—even if you think you do.

I ran through the events of recent weeks, trying to evoke the warning signs I might have missed, anything that could make the pieces fit. Nothing came to mind that hinted of an affair between Tom and Pam. Nothing except their chance meeting at Pueblo's...

No matter. Pam was with him at Pineview. She hadn't just popped in Saturday morning to have a cup of coffee with him either. Tom had done a stupid thing and, by some weird twist of fate, he'd paid the ultimate price for it. And so had Pam.

My mind went on a tangent. I grappled with the possibility they were murdered. The notion was terrible enough to fathom, but the fact that the police might consider me a suspect petrified me even more. That's what Moreau had implied, hadn't he? That I had a motive. Good thing I'd had the common sense to cut short his interrogation.

I needed to talk to someone I trusted. I picked up the phone and hit the first speed button. After three rings, my mother answered. I asked if she'd be home this afternoon. She said yes. I said I was going over. Moreau be damned.

It was a ten-minute taxi ride to my mother's two-room condominium. Several years after my father had passed away, she'd sold their small suburban home and moved downtown to be closer to me and have easier access to the shopping areas. Her pension income wasn't enough to cover the mortgage payments, so I'd been helping her by giving her a few hundred dollars every month. I didn't tell Tom because I respected her desire to appear self-sufficient.

My mother led me into the kitchen, our usual chatting place whenever I visited her. "You look a little pale," she said. "Why don't you sit down and eat something?" She motioned toward the serving plate of grapes, Brie cheese, and slices of fresh Italian bread she'd placed on the table. It could have served four. "If you want me to, I could cook you some pasta instead."

"No, no, this is fine." I sat down across from her. "Mom, I'm afraid I have bad news." I knew how much she respected Tom, so I tried to be gentle when I broke the news about him.

Her eyes welled up. "Oh, my God, not my precious Tom!" She shook her head, disturbing a cloud of white hair that had once been dark brown. "Oh, no. Not Tom."

Her reaction didn't surprise me. Tom had been the standard by which she'd judged all previous suitors in my life—not that there had been many. Only Tom warranted the right to be her son-in-law. She'd shown her approval by throwing a lavish wedding reception that two hundred family members had attended.

She took a tissue from the counter and wiped her eyes, then moved to the chair next to mine. "How did it happen, Megan?" she asked, placing a hand on mine.

Her caring touch moved me, but I'd promised myself earlier I'd be brave for her sake. "The police don't know yet," I said, fighting back the tears. "They asked me not to talk about the case with anyone, so keep it between us, okay?"

"But the family needs to know. We have to hold a wake, make funeral arrangements—"

"In due time, Mom. There's something else you need to know."

Her grief changed to shock when I told her about Pam. "He was sleeping with another woman?" she whispered, as if saying it any louder would be bring down God's wrath upon us.

"More than that. She was a close friend. Can you imagine? I still can't wrap my head around it." The emotional barrier I'd struggled so hard to maintain until now broke down. "Oh, Mom, I loved him so much," I said, shaking, the tears rushing forth. "We wanted babies."

"I know, I know." She stood up, grabbed a couple more tissues, and handed me one.

I dabbed at my eyes. "I trusted him. He lied to me. How could I have been so blind?"

"These things happen. Sometimes the truth is right in front of us and we don't see it—or don't want to see it. It might seem difficult now, but you'll find a way to go on."

The sadness in her eyes told me she understood my pain. My father had died from cancer six years earlier, but the loss was still as fresh in her mind today as it was in mine. As far as Tom was concerned, I figured I was way ahead of the game: I'd cut my losses the moment the police had told me about Pam.

My mother gestured toward the plates on the table again. "We can't let this food go to waste," she said, sitting down. "Now eat. You need your strength."

I'd slipped into the role of the pampered daughter once again—a privilege that had no age limits when it came to my mother. I wasn't hungry, but if only to please her, I plucked a cluster of grapes and put it in my plate. "What about you? Aren't you eating?"

"The doctor said I have to cut down on bread and sweets and watch my cholesterol." She placed a hand on a tummy that had expanded into her waistline over the years. "Ah, what the heck do they know anyway?" She leaned forward, took a slice of bread from the plate, and spread butter over it.

We had coffee and almond biscotti in the living room. I sat in my father's burgundy wing chair and ran my hands along the smooth teak armrests. My mother polished the armrests twice a year with lemon oil, even though the chair didn't get much use any more. She'd refused to give it away after my father had died. "Family values," she'd said as an excuse to hang onto it, believing that deep in her heart, it kept her close to him.

I indulged in a moment of self-pity, knowing that I'd never feel that way about Tom. Lesson learned. I'd have my head examined before I'd ever trust another man again.

The solace I'd found at my mother's vanished when I returned home. I wandered into the bedroom and stared at the unmade bed. It wasn't right to sleep in the same sheets I'd shared with a man who had married me for better or for worse and had chosen to give me worse. Even if I'd found out about his affair with Pam after his death, it didn't lessen the pain and rejection any.

I tore the sheets off the bed, stripped off the pillowcases, and ditched the whole lot in a garbage bag. The sheets I'd stored in the linen closet met the same fate except for a set I'd received as a gift from my mother that I hadn't used yet.

I fingered my wedding ring—a gold band dotted with tiny diamond chips. I slipped it off and dropped it into my jewelry box. I removed my diamond earrings and put them in the box too. "There.

Now it's over for good, you two-timing cheat."

I thought about Pam and remembered the digital photos. I raced to the computer in my office. Within seconds, I'd deleted every photo of her taken at Bradford's Christmas party, at staff birthday events, at dinners we shared... Satisfied, I headed back to the bedroom.

A cacophony of ringing phones echoed down the hallway. The one in my home office rang with a normal ring tone, and the one in the kitchen had a rolling ring tone. The office was closer. I rushed back there and grabbed the receiver, thinking it might be Moreau.

"Hello, Megan. This is Peter Ewans."

He'd surprised me. "Oh...Peter, how are you?" My words almost denied the fact Tom was dead.

"I don't know if you've heard yet...about Tom."

"Yes. The police were here earlier."

"Ann and I...we'd like to offer our condolences."

"Thank you."

"Tom's death was such a shock to us. We can't imagine what you're going through. I want you to know, for my part, I've lost a dear friend."

*A dear friend?* Strange choice of words. If only I could think straight. I had so many questions. "The police told me you found Tom."

"Yes. I went looking for him when he didn't meet me before our tee-off. I tried his cottage first, but the door was locked. I looked through the front window and saw him facedown on the floor, not moving."

"Were there any signs of a struggle?"

"I saw broken cups and plates on the floor near the kitchen table. I guess Tom and Pam were having breakfast when—" He stopped.

"It's okay. I know all about Pam."

He let out a sigh. "I'm so sorry, Megan. Tom told me things weren't going too well between you two lately."

"What?"

"He said you were in the process of getting a divorce."

"A divorce?" I laughed at the absurdity of it. "He lied."

Peter went on as if he hadn't heard me. "We all brought our wives to Pineview. It was a company outing. I expected to see Tom there alone. I didn't know he was bringing Pam."

I lost it. "There was no talk of divorce! Do you hear me, Peter? You knew Tom was having an affair, and you covered up for him."

"No, that's not true. He told me about the divorce...threatened to fire me and anyone else if we told you about Pam...said he didn't want to hurt you." Another deep sigh. "Megan, I'm fifty-two years old. It's not easy to get another job. I have a home, family, my children's education to think about. I couldn't afford to lose everything. Not at this stage of my life."

So I wasn't the only one who'd suffered an injustice. I calmed down and took a deep breath, then focused on my unanswered questions. "What happened after you found Tom?"

"I ran over to tell Louise, the manager. She called the police." Peter paused. "You asked me earlier about signs of a struggle. Do the police suspect foul play?"

"I don't know. They're waiting for the autopsy results."

"I can tell you this much: it wasn't a pretty sight. Tom and Pam were sprawled out on their stomachs not far from the door."

"So they *could* have been attacked."

"I don't think so. I didn't see any blood. Just scratch marks on the floor."

"Scratch marks?"

"As if they were trying to crawl their way out. They were foaming at the mouth and—"

I shut him out. That gross image and the one of Tom's pallid body on the steel slab at the morgue flashed before my eyes. A nauseous feeling swept over me. I hung up and made it to the bathroom just in time. After two purges, my stomach settled. I washed my face, brushed my teeth, then went back to the bedroom and opened a window. Cool, dry air had replaced the humid heat of the past month. I gulped in a deep breath. The scent of lilacs, soothing and refreshing, drifted up from the lawn. Beads of water from a light rainfall glistened on the grass and on the yellow and purple pansies lining the path to the condo. I took in another breath of fresh air, left the window open a bit, and sat down on the bed.

I had to make sense of it all before I lost my sanity for good.

I concentrated on Peter's words, this time with more objectivity. If he'd seen no traces of blood and no disorder in the cottage, except for the dishes that Tom or Pam might have knocked to the floor by accident, maybe they hadn't been murdered after all. Maybe something else had caused their deaths.

Or maybe it was just wishful thinking on my part.

# CHAPTER 5

Nothing disturbs me more than hearing the phone ring early in the morning. So when the ringing broke the silence in my apartment on Monday morning, I thought, "Oh God, now what?" The display on the phone in my kitchen read UNKNOWN CALLER. My heart beat like mad until I heard a familiar voice.

"Megan, did I wake you?" Michael asked at the other end.

Instant relief. "No, I was up." The sound of traffic echoed in the background. I thought he was standing near an open window in his hotel suite, then I remembered the windows at the Elegance Hotel weren't the sort you can open. "Where are you?"

"Outside my hotel. I'm on my cell. I called the office, but they said you weren't going in today. Are you okay?"

The reality of Tom's death rushed back to me. I blurted out the news.

"I'm coming over," he said.

"You don't have to—" But he'd already hung up.

*Come to think of it, wasn't he supposed to be in Toronto?* I'd find out soon enough.

I checked my watch. Ten past nine. On any normal workday, I'd have been working on a project, meeting with a client, or confirming appointments for upcoming projects. But this day was far from normal.

I assumed that everyone at Bradford Publishing had heard about Pam's death by now. I took it for granted the police were already there and in the process of interrogating the staff. I imagined the shockwave running through the place, the chaos in the work routine, the phones ringing off the hook with calls from Pam's clients...

Worst of all, I imagined the office gossip circulating about "Pam's affair with Megan's husband."

I decided to call the office anyway—if only as a matter of duty. No use putting off the inevitable. I hit the speed button on the phone before I changed my mind.

Kayla answered after the first ring. "Oh, Megan, how are you? I was just about to call you."

It sounded as if she'd been standing by the receptionist's desk and had jumped on the phone after the first ring. Someone next to her echoed my name. As the sound of chatter in the background fell to a murmur, I visualized Kayla silencing the staff with an outstretched hand.

"Everyone's been so worried about you," Kayla went on. "Our sincere condolences on the loss of your husband."

"Thank you." I noticed the exclusion of Pam's name. Whether Kayla was trying to be considerate or discreet, I didn't know. Maybe both. "I have to print out a hard copy for a client and will probably drop in later. I'm taking the rest of the week off."

"Of course. Take all the time you need. Um...could you hang on a sec?" She put me on hold. I had nothing more to say to her and contemplated hanging up, but she returned moments later. "Okay. I'm alone in my office now. This place is a zoo. Police investigators are here questioning everyone. The staff is clinging to me like I have inside information or something. I even caught Emily snooping in Pam's desk again. She must have a duplicate key."

I said nothing. I had enough problems without worrying about what kind of mischief Emily was getting herself into this time.

Kayla went on. "No one here knows what happened. Only that Tom and Pam died at Pineview on the weekend. Do you know anything more?"

I had to give it to Kayla. She always went straight to the point. "No. The police are waiting for the autopsy results." Just then, the buzzer rang. I made up some excuse to Kayla and ended the call.

I hit the button to allow Michael into the building, opened my apartment door, and waited. I tried to be brave, but when I saw him step out of the elevator and rush down the hallway toward me, I burst into tears.

He wrapped his arms around me. His leather jacket made a scrunching noise as he held me closer. I felt comforted and safe in his embrace. Then I remembered the way his lips had brushed against my cheek Friday night. I grew uneasy and slowly pulled away from him.

With concern in his eyes, he said, "I'm sorry for your loss, Megan. If you want to talk about it, I'm a good listener."

I knew him well enough to see that his offer was sincere. I'd clearly misconstrued his embrace as one with romantic overtones and felt embarrassed about it. I led him inside.

After we settled in the living room, I gave Michael a recap of Moreau's visit and my trip to the morgue. "I can't believe Tom lied to me—even about Pineview."

"He wanted to make damn sure you didn't show up there to spoil his plans."

"I should have insisted on going with him," I said, my mother's words of advice coming to the fore. "If I'd been there with him, he might still be alive today." An image of Tom and Pam crawling on the floor and foaming at the mouth popped into my head. I blinked, wishing I could wipe away that scene for good.

"Did you think his life was in danger?"

I shrugged. "No."

"So why would you have gone with him?"

He had a point but yet I insisted. "It makes no difference. I should have—"

"The police don't know the cause of death. It could have been accidental. Right?"

"Maybe, but I could have prevented—"

"Stop blaming yourself." Michael's voice was firm. "Things happen for a reason. Look at it this way. If Tom had brought you along, chances are they would have found your body on the floor next to his."

His logic helped me to focus on the facts. It all came together at once and triggered a memory. "Moreau asked me where I was Friday night."

"What did you tell him?"

"Nothing."

"Why not?"

"I was afraid."

"Of what?"

"That he would get the wrong idea if I told him I was with you."

Michael shrugged. "It was only dinner."

*So that's all it was for him? Dinner?*

Okay, I could live with that. I'd obviously mistaken his easygoing rapport with me as something else. "Of course, it was only dinner," I said, "but eight times in the past three weeks might raise a red flag to someone else."

"It was business," he said. "We discussed my work."

"Moreau might interpret it as much more."

"That's plain crazy."

"Not at all. When he was here, he asked Duchaine to take note of a possible motive for murder."

"That's a stretch."

"Maybe, but I didn't want to give him a reason to follow through on it."

He shook his head. "It's a long shot. First, he has to prove Tom was murdered. Second, using our relationship as a motive doesn't cut it. You have nothing to worry about."

I weighed his arguments and opted for caution. "I'd feel better if I knew my rights. Know any good lawyers?"

Michael nodded. "Dan Cummings. He's a top-notch criminal lawyer and a good buddy of mine. He works out of Montreal and Toronto."

There was something about Toronto. "Weren't you supposed to be on a plane back home Saturday morning? For radio interviews?"

"I did them by phone instead. I just couldn't pass up a lead I picked up on a story here. It turned out to be important, so I delayed my flight home. I'm glad I did." His eyes rested on mine.

I didn't know how to interpret his reply. Did he mean he was glad he stayed in town to follow a lead? Or was he glad to be here to console me? I promised myself to stop reading more into Michael than was actually there. "Why did you call me this morning?"

"No particular reason." He shrugged, gave me a brief smile. "Have you notified your family yet?"

"Yes. My mother."

"And Tom's family?"

"His adoptive parents died years ago in a plane crash to South America. He has no other relatives that I know of."

"Life's a bitch sometimes," Michael said. "I was very close to my grandmother in Toronto. She died about a month ago. It happened right after that court case there I told you about."

"I'm sorry. How did she die?"

"A nineteen-year-old. DUI. He was driving his father's car and struck her one night when she was out walking the family dog. I'm still dealing with the repercussions...financial and otherwise." A tiny muscle pulsated along his jaw.

I assumed the settlement I'd overheard Jane mention in his suite had to do with his grandmother's death. Maybe Jane counseled— and comforted him—during that time.

He shrugged. "You can't fight destiny, but time sure is a great healer."

"I'll need more than time on my side if the police start questioning me again."

"I can speed things up. I'll call Dan right now." He pulled out his cell. "He's not easy to reach. I might have to leave a message. Do you have a cell number?"

"No." My cell phone contract had expired. I spent most of my time at the office or at home anyway. Each had access to a regular phone line. "You can give him my home number."

Michael placed the call and waited. "He's not answering." He left his cell and my home phone number with a message. He dug into his jacket again and pulled out his wallet. "Here's Dan's business card." He held it out to me.

"Thanks." I tucked it into the front pocket of my jeans. "How about some coffee? I only have instant, but it's Colombian."

"Sounds good."

He took a seat at the kitchen table while I filled the kettle with water.

"Waiting for news from the police is driving me nuts," I said.

"I know how you feel. It's as if your life's on hold." He paused. "I'll be flying back to Toronto on Tuesday. I have a couple of book-signings scheduled and enough material to start working on my next book."

Emotions surged inside me, ready to explode like a can of soda pop someone had shaken but not opened. "That's great," I said, forcing a smile. My eyes began to sting and I turned away. I blamed Tom's death for making me sensitive to any upheaval that came along. I took two mugs from the cupboard and placed them on the counter, then took two spoons out of the drawer, taking my time while I tried to compose myself.

"Don't worry," Michael said. "I won't leave town without making sure you have legal representation. If Dan's too busy to take on your case, I'll find another lawyer for you."

I kept my back to him. "Oh, you don't have to do that. I'll ask around for—"

Michael's cell phone rang. He answered it. "Hey, Dan. How are you doing, old buddy?" His voice brimmed with enthusiasm. Dan's reply made him laugh. "Too long... Yes, I know. We'll catch up soon." The conversation took on a serious note as Michael explained the nature of his call. "In an hour?" He looked at me.

I nodded yes.

"Okay. Thanks, buddy. See you later." He hung up. "Talk about timing. Dan's in town. He's staying at the Regency Hotel."

No sooner had the words left his mouth than the doorbell rang. I rushed down the hallway and pressed the intercom button.

"*Bonjour,* Madame Scott. This is Detective Moreau. May I come up?"

I buzzed Moreau in, then opened the door. "He probably has the autopsy results," I said to Michael as he reached my side. A sudden wave of nausea hit me. "I think I'm going to be sick."

"Take a few deep breaths. You'll be okay." He wrapped an arm around my shoulders and gave me a brief hug.

Moments later, I was introducing Michael, in beige khakis and rolled-up shirt sleeves, to Moreau, the embodiment of the public servant in a white shirt, dark blue jacket, and an attaché case. A Kodak moment.

I shared a sofa with Michael. Moreau unbuttoned his jacket and sat opposite us, his attaché case close by. He gave his mustache a rapid stroke. Was it my imagination or was he somewhat on edge? Maybe his uneasiness had to do with the contents of the folder he was opening up.

"Madame Scott, what I am about to tell you is confidential." His eyes flitted from me to Michael and stayed on him.

"It's okay," I said. "Michael is a good friend. Anything you have to say to me is okay to say in front of him."

I caught the glint in Moreau's eyes. It didn't take a genius to see he was speculating about the nature of my relationship with Michael and the myriad of possibilities that could affect his future line of questioning. *"Très bien."* He fingered a document. "The autopsy is not completed, but we have received an initial examination from the forensic pathologist." He frowned. "It states your husband and Pam Strober died unnatural deaths."

"What do you mean by *unnatural*?" I asked.

He glanced back at the report. "It was a substance consistent with a fatal poison."

"Poison?" I repeated.

Michael leaned forward. "What kind of poison?"

"Potassium cyanide," Moreau said.

"How is that possible?" I asked.

A deeper crease gathered between the detective's eyebrows. "We do not know if the victims ingested, inhaled, or touched the poison. It does not appear to have been given by force, but our pathologist cannot confirm this." He returned the file to his attaché case.

A sinking sensation swept over me. "Are you saying they could have committed suicide?"

Moreau nodded. "It is a possibility."

"So is murder," Michael said.

"*Naturellement,* Monsieur Elliott."

"Do you have any suspects?" Michael asked him.

The detective eyed him with sudden interest. "If it is determined to be murder, everyone is a suspect." His gaze swung to me, then back to Michael.

Anger rose inside me, but Michael remained silent and calm. I took my cue from him and remained quiet too, assuming it might be in our best interests to do so.

Moreau addressed Michael. "As I mentioned to Madame Scott the other day, the police will continue to withhold information from the public. I must insist that you keep our discussion confidential as well."

"No problem," Michael said.

The detective pulled out his notebook. "Madame Scott, if you please, I have more questions."

He was persistent but I was prepared. "Sorry, detective. Not without my lawyer. Here's his business card." I handed it to him.

He peered at it, then slipped it into his attaché case.

I remembered one more urgent matter. "Detective, I'd like to make funeral arrangements for my husband."

"The pathologist has not yet completed his work, but I will contact him regarding the formalities." He picked up his attaché case and stood up. "Good day, Madame Scott, Monsieur Elliott."

After Moreau left, I stormed back into the living room. "Did you see the way he gawked at us? And that insinuation? He might as well have come right out and accused us of murder." I waved my hands in the air.

Michael frowned. "I can see it now: the vindictive wife and her obliging friend."

"I'm serious."

"So am I."

I plopped down next to him on the sofa. "Every time Moreau shows up here, the situation goes from bad to worse."

"Once Dan comes on board, he'll put a stop to this crap."

"What if he refuses to take me on as a client?"

He shrugged. "I don't see why."

*Fingers crossed on that one.* My mind took off on a tangent. "Potassium cyanide. I don't know much about it. Do you?"

"It's one of the most lethal poisons around. Death can occur within minutes from the tiniest amount. It's extremely painful."

"What are the symptoms?"

"Dizziness, stomach pain, among others."

"We have a few minutes. Let's check the Internet."

I led Michael down the hallway and into my office.

"You're quite the collector," he said, gesturing toward my two bookcases crammed with literature I'd gathered over the years. "Hemingway, Milton, Shakespeare."

"Mostly from my university days. I used to have lots of free time to read for pleasure then. Now it's called work."

"Tell me about it."

I sat at my computer and clicked on the first website that came up on a Google search. The site explained how potassium cyanide worked. "It says that less than one hundredth of an ounce is a lethal dose if the substance comes in contact with a liquid. " I scrolled down. Shocking photos of poisoned lab mice surfaced. I exited the site.

Another site listed the effects on the body from cyanide ingestion. Michael leaned over my shoulder and read them off the screen. "Initial symptoms are confusion, dizziness, headache, difficulty breathing, vomiting, abdominal pain—"

"There's more." I guided the cursor down the list. "Coma, seizures, cardiac arrest—"

"Talk about cold-blooded murder. This is gruesome stuff. What sick, demented person would use cyanide to kill someone?"

"I can't possibly imagine. No one deserves to die like that." I checked my watch. "You can keep on searching if you want. I need to change my clothes before we go see Dan." I got up.

"Okay." He slid into my chair.

"Oh, I almost forgot." I grabbed a CD on my desk. "I need this for a client."

I headed for the bedroom and slipped the CD into my purse, then made a beeline to the bathroom. I studied my face in the mirror. My complexion was pale. Dark auburn hair only accentuated the fact. As a rule, I didn't wear much makeup in the summer. I'd apply some sunscreen, then sit outdoors on weekends and get my fifteen minutes of sunshine, but I hadn't had the time to do much of anything these days except work. So I compromised. A few strokes of powder bronzer on my face and a touch of lipstick did the trick.

From the walk-in closet, I pulled out a beige cotton jacket, a white crew-neck top, and a pair of clean jeans. It spelled casual, yet conservative, and portrayed a figure other than the grieving widow people might expect from a woman who'd just lost her husband.

But I didn't care. I'd have lots of time to mourn later if I felt like it. Right now, my freedom was at risk. Whether I was prepared to accept it or not, my future depended on one man alone: Dan Cummings.

# CHAPTER 6

A cool breeze scattered red and yellow maple leaves across the lawn—a sign that autumn was on its way earlier than usual, with a snowy winter close behind. Just the thought of it chilled my Mediterranean blood.

I half-listened to Michael as we walked down the path from my condo, though I did catch the gist of his chat: something about how living and working inside four walls for too long drove him nuts, how spending time outdoors was good for his health, blah-blah-blah. I suspected he was making small talk as a way to quell my nerves before our meeting with Dan. I was worried that his "buddy" wouldn't take me on as a client.

Two blocks down, we hailed a taxi. We rode eastward along Sherbrooke Street, home to heritage buildings, art galleries, and upscale shops. The drive was a memory lane of sorts for me—one that I enjoyed whenever I took the bus to and from work. Each time I passed the Montreal Museum of Fine Arts, I recalled my first visit there. I was only eight and too young to appreciate it. I'd returned a dozen times since then.

Michael's voice dispersed my thoughts. "I met Dan four years ago in a Toronto court. He has this amazing ability to retain volumes of legal jargon. I envied him for it. Things leveled out when he told me how much he envied my knack for digging up leads and getting into trouble." He chuckled.

I smiled but didn't feel much like talking.

Up ahead was Crescent Street, or "party central," as locals called it.

Along this street and bordering ones were French cafés, Irish pubs, and restaurants that offered the finest in culinary eateries spanning the gamut from American to Russian. In my younger days, I'd often meet friends for dinner in the area and follow up with coffee at Pueblo's. The image of Tom and Pam sitting at that same café now tarnished those memories forever. Too bad I hadn't seen through their "impromptu" encounter. Then again, why would I mistrust a loving husband who gave me no reason to doubt him and a close friend who made dating single men her lifelong ambition?

"We're here," Michael said as the taxi came to a stop at the curb.

The Regency Hotel stood twenty stories high on Mountain Street and shared its prestigious downtown location with a bustling trade district. The interior décor was a far cry from the old-style opulence of the Elegance. In the lobby, ceiling pot lights cast a warm glow on dark wood tables, brown leather sofas, and porcelain tile. Gold wallpaper with a tiny repetitive motif of the letter "R" adorned the walls. Tinted glass panels replaced the standard elevator walls and gave one the feeling of being airborne between floors.

Dan welcomed us into his tenth floor suite. "Hey there, buddy," he said, exchanging a hearty embrace and pats on the back with Michael. He extended a hand in my direction. "My condolences on your recent loss, Megan."

"Thank you." I caught a whiff of his cologne. The blend of woodsy spices told me there was a warmer aspect to this man than the strategic thinking intrinsic to his profession.

I glanced around. Pot lights, cushy sofas, and a glossy table with four black Parson chairs. The same stylish vibes as the lobby. I noticed a digital recorder, a black pen, and a notepad on the table. I assumed Dan didn't like to rely on his memory alone when he interviewed clients. On second thought, I'd never hired a lawyer before, so maybe they all took the same safeguards against memory loss, if only to preserve the integrity of their information.

"Haven't heard from you in a while," Dan was saying to Michael. "What no good have you been up to?"

"Remember that book I was working on?"

"The one about the court cases you covered?"

Michael nodded. "I published it."

Dan smiled. "That's great news. Congrats, buddy." Another pat on the back.

"Thanks. I'm on a book tour now...hitting the major cities..."

While the men conversed, I compared them. Dan stood about four inches taller than Michael and had the kind of build that might have secured him a football scholarship in earlier days. Now salt-and-pepper hair and a fleshy waistline added years to his age. His leather shoes made a statement about the style of attire that people in his profession could afford, while Michael's jeans and running shoes embodied the dress code for blasé writers. The dissimilarities between these two friends extended to the way they spoke. Dan often dropped words in a sentence, as if he were in a hurry. Michael's tone was calm, his choice of words intentional.

After Michael gave Dan a brief recap of how we'd been working on his manuscript together the last few weeks, Dan invited us to sit at the table. "The recorder is for my personal use only." He switched it on and cited the date, location, and names of the parties present, then glanced at me. "Megan, let's begin with the police investigation into Tom's death." He picked up his pen. "What have they told you so far?"

I gave him a re-cap of Moreau's two visits and the results of the preliminary autopsy.

"So you didn't know anything about Tom's trip to Pineview?" Dan asked.

"Not until Moreau told me." I mentioned Louise's original phone call and Tom's claim that the booking was a mistake. "I was stunned to find out Tom had gone to Pineview and not Granite Ridge as he'd told me. But I don't think Moreau believed me."

"Why would you say that?" Dan asked.

"Moreau didn't say as much, but I know he thinks they were murdered. In his eyes, I'm the most likely suspect. That's why I'm here. I want you to represent me."

To my surprise, Michael added, "And me."

Dan looked at him. "Why you?"

"Moreau was sizing us up. If it turns out to be murder—"

"It was murder," I said. "Tom wouldn't have killed himself. He had too much to live for."

Michael gave Dan a discerning look. "I can picture Moreau coming after us for a speedy arrest."

"Then he isn't doing his job," Dan said. "I'll consider your involvement after I hear all the facts." He switched his gaze to me. "Where were you on Friday, August 10th, the day and evening prior to your husband's death?"

"I was working with Michael in his suite at the Elegance Hotel," I said.

Dan scribbled a note. "What time did you leave?"

"About seven-thirty."

"What did you do the rest of the night?"

"I had dinner with Michael at Santino's."

"And then what?"

"He dropped me off at home."

"What time was it?"

"About nine."

"What did you do afterward?"

"I went to bed."

Dan turned to Michael. "Do you have a receipt from Santino's?"

"Yes," Michael said. "I used my credit card. Left the waitress a good tip."

Dan nodded. "Then she'd probably remember you both. What did you do after you dropped Megan off?"

"I went for a drive."

"Where?"

"What difference does it make?"

"If the subject ever comes up in a police interview, you'll need to prove your alibi."

Michael shrugged. "I drove out of town."

"Why?" Dan asked him.

"To meet with an informant."

"Did you happen to speak with this person on the phone?"

Michael grinned. "Are you kidding?"

"Required for trace purposes. Provides proof of your

whereabouts."

"No phone calls. A mutual acquaintance set up the meeting."

"Where did you meet?"

"Can't say."

"Can't or won't."

"Both."

"You have to give me something to work with, buddy." Dan reached for his hankie and patted his face.

Michael had told me how Dan suffered from overactive glands and used a hankie to wipe perspiration from his face whenever he was tense. I supposed this was one of those times.

"I won't jeopardize my informant's life," Michael said.

"I can appreciate that, but nothing beats a solid alibi," Dan said, tucking away his hankie. "Moreau will launch his investigation by seeking out motives. From what you've told me, he's already pointed a finger in your direction." He looked at us. If he interpreted my association with Michael as anything but friendship, he didn't show it.

"Okay, okay." Michael raised his hands, palms up. "I was in Sainte-Adèle, up in the Laurentians."

"You rented a car?" Dan asked him.

"Yes, a Mustang Coupe."

"From where?"

"Avis on Metcalfe Street."

"When?

"About a week ago."

"Did you return it?"

"Not yet."

"Where is it?"

"In my hotel parking."

Dan jotted more notes. "Aside from your informant, did you speak with anyone else in Sainte-Adèle?"

"I stopped to get a coffee at a roadside diner on the way up," Michael said.

"Did you keep the receipt?"

"No, I paid in cash. I don't like to use plastic in strange places."

"Any other stops?"

"I fueled up before returning to Montreal."

"Where?"

"At an independent gas station outside of town. And before you ask me, yes, I paid in cash. No, I don't have a receipt because the point-of-sale machine wasn't working." Michael paused. "If it helps, the cashier at the counter was an older guy with a white beard."

Dan took more notes. "What time did you get back to Montreal?"

"Just before midnight."

"Any witnesses see you return Friday night?"

"A clerk at the front desk said hello to me. I doubt he'll remember me, though. There were lots of people hanging out in the lobby. Some kind of party going on in one of the halls."

"What about you, Megan?" Dan asked. "Any witnesses see you come back home?"

"Mrs. Eloise Speck. A neighbor who lives on the second floor." I was grateful for the old woman's intrusive habits for a change. "I think she saw Michael drop me off Friday night."

"All right." Dan turned off the recorder. While he scanned his notes, he flipped his pen back and forth in rapid succession. I took it as a sign of nervousness or deliberation, or both.

I prayed that he'd take us on as clients. If he didn't, I'd have a hard time finding another lawyer I could trust half as much as Michael trusted Dan.

Dan pulled out his hankie. A pat of his brow and a tuck back into his pocket rounded out the process. He looked at us. "I can see where this situation might be heading. Unless either one of you is concerned with a potential conflict of interest, I'll represent you both."

"No problem." Michael smiled. "Thanks, buddy."

"Yes, thank you," I said.

"I can't make any promises. Maybe we can freeze this investigation in its tracks before any charges are laid against you." Pen and notepad in hand, Dan heaved himself out of the chair. "I have to make a phone call. Help yourselves to some coffee when it's ready." He flipped the switch on a coffee machine sitting on a side table, then crossed the living room floor and disappeared around a corner.

Michael stood up and stretched his arms. "So far, so good—despite my screw-ups with the receipts."

"Don't be so hard on yourself." I walked past him to the window and gazed upward at the metal cross atop Mount Royal Park, the highest site in the center of the city. At one hundred feet high, it graced the downtown skyline and was a popular tourist attraction. Ever since 1643 when its original wood version was mounted, locals have acknowledged it as a symbol of hope. *Hope.* How apropos.

Michael came up to me, peered sideways into my face. "You're angry with me because I didn't get receipts, aren't you?"

"No, I'm not."

"Yes, you are. I can tell by the way your eyes are shooting those tiny daggers at me."

"I'm angry but not at you. What if this whole mess takes a turn for the worse? It's bad enough I'm under suspicion, but how are you going to prove your alibi without receipts?"

"Don't worry. Dan will take care of it. You'll see." He whispered, "So what do you think of my buddy so far?"

"He's methodical. I hope he can get Moreau off our backs before it's too late."

He grinned. "After Dan gets through with him, Moreau won't have a choice. He'll have to write us off...concentrate on catching the real murderer."

I couldn't share his optimism. Life was too short for wishful thinking.

I gazed out the window at the people walking along Sherbrooke Street. We humans were so naive about the danger around us. We could only speculate about how often we might have brushed against its borders as we wandered through the rituals of our lives, not paying attention to strangers who crossed our paths. We only had to look at the news for stories covering the abductions of children and women in broad daylight. More often than not, their lives had come to a dreadful end within hours, maybe even minutes. The image of Tom's pallid body at the morgue suddenly flashed through my mind. I blinked it away.

"Cyanide," I said to Michael. "I keep wondering what kind of monster could have carried out such a horrible death."

"The guy's a lunatic. I'd bet the cops have already pulled a list of potential suspects from their data base."

"Small consolation. It hasn't prevented Moreau from zooming in on us."

He shrugged. "I can't blame him. The perpetrator is often someone within an immediate circle of family or friends. Statistics support that fact."

"Oh, thanks. I feel so much better now." I shivered and wondered if Dan had upped the air conditioning in the suite to compensate for his perspiration problem.

"You're trembling." Michael put a hand on my arm. "Come. Let's have some coffee."


We were sitting at the table and into our second cup when Dan rushed back, tiny beads of sweat lining his forehead. *Not a good sign.*

He sat down and switched on the recorder. "All right. We checked out Pineview. It's near Knowlton, about sixty miles southeast of Montreal. Sainte-Adèle is about fifty miles north of here. The similarity in mileage from here to Pineview or to Granite Ridge is something the police might jump on to refute your alibi, Michael." He pulled out a hankie and dabbed his forehead.

"You're not serious," Michael said. He stared at Dan as if he expected him to follow up with a redeeming statement.

"Did you drive anywhere else?" Dan asked him, tucking the hankie away.

"Short distances in the city. Why?"

Dan frowned. "We need tangible facts to prove both your alibis ASAP."

"How are you going to manage that?" Michael asked him. "I already told you I didn't keep any receipts." A tiny muscle pulsated along his jaw line.

"My team will visit the gas station in Sainte-Adèle," Dan said.

"Interview the cashier you described."

"Some people don't do well with facial recognition."

"Most gas stations have surveillance systems. We'll try to get a copy of the video tape."

"What about the surveillance video at the Elegance?"

"We'll try to get that too. Could help to narrow the time gap in your trip that evening." Dan jotted a note, then looked up at me. "Does your condo have a monitoring system?"

"I think there's a camera in the lobby," I said.

"How about the rear exit?"

"I'm not sure." I mulled over his question. "I didn't leave the condo by the back door after Michael dropped me off, if that's what you mean."

"The police might think so."

"The lack of a surveillance system could work in her favor," Michael pointed out.

"In the absence of a feasible alibi?" Dan nodded so-so. "It's an argument I could use to support the claim that Megan was home the rest of the night. Might create a reasonable doubt in the minds of the jury."

"The jury?" Michael's eyes went wide. "Whatever happened to innocent until proven guilty?"

"Look at this from another perspective." Dan tapped his pen against the table, and I felt as if I were in a classroom again. "An alleged double murder makes headline news and creates public unrest. Pressure from higher-ups forces the police to solve the case ASAP. That's why a flawless defense is of major importance for us. It has to include confirmation of your alibis."

"I'm a realist," Michael said. "I look at the facts. What if you can't prove our alibis?"

Dan shrugged. "We'll do the next best thing."

"What's that?"

"Prove your innocence."

"Like I said before, I thought that was a given."

"Not theoretically." Dan frowned. "We'll have to work the flip side of the coin. Explore other factors. Work at creating doubt about your guilt. Hint at the existence of other suspects. For example, we'll verify the check-in times of the guests and staff at Pineview. People who might have entered Tom's cottage in the hours before and after his arrival. Not all suspects can cover their tracks."

"So you're doing Moreau's legwork for him."

"Not really. He has to go through the same motions."

"For different reasons," Michael said with a smirk.

Dan looked at me. "Can you stay away from Bradford Publishing for a day or so?"

"I took the rest of the week off," I said. "Why?"

"My team will interview the employees at Bradford. They might open up more about Pam if you're not around."

*That's a good one.* I wondered if anyone else at the office had found out about Tom's affair with Pam before I had. Emily? Lucie? Peter had known about it long before Pineview. How did that expression go again? Ah, yes. *The wife is always the last to know.*

Dan went on. "If we go to court, the prosecutor is going to pitch tough questions. We don't want the jury to have any doubts about either of you. Don't want them to wonder why we didn't ask the most obvious question to the most obvious suspects." When he pulled out his hankie, I could have bet my life on what he was going to ask us next. "Was the relationship between you two intimate at the moment of Tom's death?"

A flush warmed my cheeks. "No, it was not," I said with as much resolve as I could muster.

Dan's insinuation didn't faze Michael. "Megan and I had a professional relationship while we worked on my novel," he said, his voice even. "We remain close friends today. End of story." He looked straight at Dan without blinking.

"Credible," Dan said, tucking his hankie away. "Might convince the prosecution. If we ever get to that stage."

Anger replaced my embarrassment. "But it's the truth."

Dan shrugged. "Even so, the police might not buy it. They'll shove your relationship with Michael under a microscope. Try to prove you two had a fling of your own. That's where motive comes in. They'll use your connection to Michael to show you planned to get rid of Tom. We have to prove you're both beyond reproach. In every respect."

"You're right about that," Michael said. "When cops feel pressured to make an arrest, they pick up the most obvious suspects— sometimes based only on a scrap of evidence. One way or another, they manage to get a conviction in court. Stats on the number of guys who spend years in jail and are found innocent later are proof of it. It's plain crazy."

Dan raised his pen in a cautionary gesture. "A word of advice, Michael. Until Moreau completes his investigation, I advise you to remain in town."

"You're not serious," Michael said. "I've got a book tour to wrap up."

"If you leave now, it might provoke undue suspicion."

"If you put it that way, no problem. I'll cancel my flight."

"All right." Dan flipped to a new page in his notepad. "Megan, do you know if anyone ever threatened Tom or wanted to see him dead?"

"If he had any enemies, he didn't mention them to me," I said.

"How did he get along with business associates? Bosses? Fellow employees?"

"Okay, I guess. Except for Peter Ewans, a co-worker. Tom told me Peter was upset when Tom won the senior management promotion over him."

"Peter Ewans. Why is that name familiar?" Michael looked at me. "Wait a sec. Wasn't he the guy who dropped off the company car at your condo? The one that Tom crashed?"

"Yes." I briefed Dan on the incident.

"How did Tom react?" Dan looked up from his notepad.

"He said it was an accident. But Peter had a hard time getting over it. He gave Tom tickets to Place des Arts—two of the best seats in the house."

"Let's backtrack. Did Tom's promotion create any animosity between Peter and him?"

"I don't think so. It wasn't the first time Peter had been passed over for a promotion. He told Tom he felt as if he'd lost respect at work and blamed management, though."

"Peter must have had loads of resentment brewing inside him for years," Michael said. "Loss of advancement, loss of additional income, loss of reputation—"

"People get promoted every day," I said. "Their competitors don't kill them because of it."

"Oh, I don't know about that," Michael said, a wry smile on his lips. "The news is full of stories about ex-employees who got mad as hell because they were laid off. Did they go out and get counseling? No way. They got revenge. They went back to their workplace and shot their bosses and co-workers dead."

Dan tapped his pen, ending our banter. "So Peter confided in Tom. A two-way street? Maybe Tom confided in him too?" He gave me a pointed look.

"If you mean about Pam, the answer is yes." I recounted my phone conversation with Peter. "He covered up for Tom because he was afraid he'd fire him."

"Add that to the list of Peter's resentments," Michael said, raising an eyebrow.

"Enough to kill him?" I shook my head. "I doubt it."

"Resentment runs deep in some people when they're forced to do stuff they don't want to do. Peter could have been waiting for the right opportunity to strike. And he did."

I looked at him. "You're moving too fast. We haven't even begun to make the pieces fit. We don't know for sure who the real target was. It could have been Pam and not Tom."

Michael shrugged. "Maybe both."

"All right," Dan said. "My team will interview Peter and other BOTCOR employees. Megan, do you know if any Bradford employees harbored resentment against Pam?"

Emily came to mind. I didn't know much about her private life, except that she lived with her mother who couldn't afford to live alone. I could empathize with that. It was clear Emily was jealous of Pam and mimicked her, but petty office antics aside, I doubted she'd want to kill her.

"We all got along pretty well," I said.

"What about Pam's family? Friends?" Dan asked.

"I never met her family. I was her...closest friend." I almost choked on the words.

"Any men friends?"

"She dated a lot, but I never met any of them."

"Any enemies?"

"I don't know."

"Any bad blood between her and clients?"

"No, they loved her. Wait. There's Mrs. Bill Bradford, the owner's wife. She gave Pam a rough time at the office one morning." I recapped the incident.

"We'll check into it." Dan's pen skimmed across the page.

There was a knock at the door.

Dan switched off the recorder. "I've taken the liberty of ordering lunch for us." He opened the door to a hotel attendant who wheeled a serving table into the room.

As we enjoyed our club sandwiches and a fresh pot of coffee, the dialogue wove its way to common acquaintances that Michael and Dan knew. I was surprised when a familiar name popped into the conversation.

"Remember the drug possession case we worked on together last month in Montreal?" Dan asked Michael.

"How could I forget?" Michael shook his head. "I'd tailed the guy for weeks. My testimony meant nothing after he was acquitted." He turned to me. "I had leads on this guy the length of my arm. Then I heard he walked because the police had contaminated the evidence."

Dan nodded. "Their defense team was my biggest competition. Remember the paralegal that worked for them?"

Michael's expression froze. "Jane Barlow?"

"The one and only. Sharp as a Samurai sword and twice as lethal. Never missed a detail." Dan smiled. "She approached me for a job a few weeks ago."

"You're kidding." I expected Michael to bring up Jane's visit to his hotel suite but he didn't. Maybe he thought it wasn't worth mentioning since they'd stopped dating.

"I hired her." Dan beamed as if he'd discovered the next best thing to imported leather shoes.

From the dazed look on Michael's face, it was clear Jane hadn't told him she was working for Dan. Michael shrugged, reached for his glass of water.

"I know what you're thinking, buddy. She's only twenty-five, but she's brilliant. Ambitious too. Going to make a fine lawyer one day." Dan stuck a thumb in the air. "We just wrapped up a corporate case here this week. She's staying in a suite down the hall. Phoned her minutes ago. Asked her to get the witness interview process rolling for your case. It helps that she speaks French better than I do." He chuckled.

Michael smiled but said nothing, kept his eyes fixed on the glass of water in front of him. He seemed tongue-tied about Dan hiring her. Or was it because his best buddy had assigned her to our case? Maybe he was wondering if the breakup of their relationship might affect legal interaction between them in the future.

The awkward silence intensified until Dan asked him, "You have a problem with my hiring Jane?"

Michael looked up. "Me? Oh...no. No problem. She's the best."

"Any other questions about our discussion so far?"

"Um...yeah." Michael glanced at me. "Megan and I were talking earlier about the cruelty of death by cyanide poisoning. If you could show we were incapable of such an attack, wouldn't it help clear us?"

"Maybe on moral grounds," Dan said. "No previous record of violence. No criminal record. And so on."

"I know one thing that would swing suspicion away from us," I said.

"What?" Michael turned to me.

"Finding the real murderer."

"It's a long shot."

"Megan's right," Dan said. "It only takes one tiny lead to crack a case." He rose to his feet. "All right. It's a wrap for now. I'll update you both by this evening. Where can we meet?"

For no reason other than the convenience of being in my own

home, I said, "My place." I looked at Michael. "If you don't mind coming over."

"Not a problem," he said, slipping into his leather jacket.

"In the meantime, I'll give you my cell number." Dan jotted it down on the back of two business cards and gave us each one. "Another word of advice. Don't answer questions from the police or the prosecution unless I'm present. Understood?"

"Or reporters," I added.

"Especially reporters," Dan said, then gave Michael a pat on the back. "No offense."

"None taken," Michael said with a grin. "I know too well how those guys operate."

Michael and I rode the elevator down in silence. The satisfied look on his face told me he felt confident about his buddy's legal preparation—albeit with Jane resurfacing in his life. The uncertainty of our predicament didn't seem to bother him one bit. Was I surprised? Not really. I'd garnered that much about him from having worked on his book. Given the nature of his job, he thrived on uncertainty: meeting with informants under the darkness of night; traveling to unfamiliar places to get a scoop on a story; following a gut feeling even if it defied logic...

I couldn't live that way. I needed stability in my life. I believed that humans were creatures of habit. I didn't know who originated that expression, but it described my method of living. The predictability of routine gave me a sense of control. My job was proof of it. I worked in a structured world where I respected appointments with my clients, scheduled every phase of a project down to a T, and set up Plan B in the event of a setback—not that it happened often, if at all. My routine at home followed a pattern too, with specific chores planned and carried out each week so that order prevailed and chaos was non-existent—at least to the extent that I could ensure it.

Sure, Dan's expertise reassured me. With horror stories of legal corruption hitting the news every other day, I was grateful to have an ethical and competent lawyer like him on my side. And from the sound of it, Jane was just as qualified.

But was it enough to protect Michael and me from a detective who seemed hell-bent on incriminating us?

Moreau's suspicions about us kept me on edge and had me contemplating what his next move might be. Not knowing in which direction his game plan was heading did nothing but aggravate my uncertainty about the future.

# CHAPTER 7

Outside the Regency, a blazing sun had pierced through the clouds and chased away the cool summer morning. I kept thinking how the weather was so volatile these days—just like my life since Tom's death. With my freedom at stake, I expected more of the same and wondered if things would ever return to normal.

"The heat wave is back." Michael removed his leather jacket.

My eyes strayed to a newsstand on the sidewalk. "Hold on a sec." I picked up a copy of *The Gazette,* then walked back to him. "I doubt the police spoke to the media yet, but it doesn't hurt to check."

He nodded, surveyed the heavy flow of traffic. "Are you going home or staying downtown?"

"I'll flag a taxi later and head back to the condo. But first I'm going to drop by the office."

He stared at me. "You're kidding, right?"

"I have to use their printer. A client wants a hard copy of the project I drafted for him."

"You realize the hornet's nest you could be walking into? Getting grilled by the staff is the last thing you need right now."

I didn't answer.

"Want me to go with you?"

"Of course not. I can take care of myself."

He studied me for a moment as if he were debating the fact. "I can drive you back home later, but I need a change of clothes. Want to come over to the hotel after you're done?"

"Okay. See you later."

On the ride up the elevator to the office, my stomach began to knot. Maybe Michael was right. My appearance there would make jaws drop and tongues wag. Did I need more stress in my life? Then again, why should I care about their gossip? I owed it to my client to deliver the goods as promised, and that's what I was going to do.

I pushed open the door to Bradford Publishing. Kayla was standing at the front desk, speaking with a receptionist I'd never seen before. A BlackBerry tucked in her skirt waistband reinforced the respect her five-foot-nine frame already commanded. They both looked up as I walked in.

"Hi, Megan." Kayla walked up to me but stopped short of giving me a hug. It wasn't her style.

"Hi." I pulled the CD out of my purse. "Here's the project I told you about."

"We'll take care of it for you." She took the CD and handed it to the receptionist. "Get me a printout of this, please." She waited until the girl had walked away, then gave a nod toward her. "I hired a temp for the week."

I assumed she meant Lucie was away. "It's so quiet. Anyone else on vacation too?"

"Oh, no one's on vacation. After the police left this morning, I gave the staff the rest of the day off. Direct orders from Bradford himself. They can't function properly under these circumstances anyway." Her gaze softened. "Is there anything I can do for you, Megan?"

"I have Bradford clients—"

"I'll follow up with them to re-schedule." She took a step closer and whispered, "Emily's still in her office. She's applying for Pam's job and working on her cover letter to Bradford."

"What?" I couldn't hide my surprise.

"If dressing like Pam is a major requirement, then she fits the bill." She kept her voice low. "I'd have fired her months ago. She spends way too much frigging time in the darkroom—in more ways than one, if you know what I mean."

Just then, Emily strutted down the corridor toward us on black high heels identical to a pair Pam had bought at Browns Shoes last month. She couldn't possibly afford designer strap sandals on her salary, so I assumed she'd dug them out of Pam's office closet. Bits of mascara smudged the rims of her eyes and streaks of pale skin showed through where tears had washed away the makeup. That girl was going to be at a loss without her mentor around to crack the whip whenever she spoke out of line or applied her lipstick wrong.

She walked up to me. "So sorry for your loss, Megan." She put her arms around me in a limp and hasty hug as if she were going through a forced ritual. "Do you have any news?"

"Not until the autopsy results come in."

"I meant news from the police. Do they have any leads on the killer?"

"They haven't called it a murder investigation as far as I know."

"What else could it be?" Her eyes flashed in anger. "Seriously."

I didn't answer.

"So what are you doing here?"

"I came by to drop off—"

"Seriously, don't you have more important things to do, like take care of Michael Elliott?" She glared at me.

"What are you talking about? I handed in his project on Friday."

"That's not what I meant." She rolled her eyes. "He never returned my calls. Do you happen to know why?"

"No. Why don't you call and ask him?"

"Very funny," she said with a smirk. "You guys sure spent a lot of time together, huh?"

I didn't like where she was going with this, so I played dumb. "For a book project? I think three weeks was rushing it. I could have used another week or two."

"I'll bet you could have." She spit out the words. "Who knows how much more friendly you and Michael could have become if—."

Kayla jumped in. "Cut it out, Emily. This isn't the time or place to—"

"This doesn't concern you," Emily snapped at her. She looked back at me, her eyes narrowing. "It's the first chance I get to date a respectable guy like Michael and guess what? You've been screwing him right under our noses!"

The blood rose to my face. I had the sudden impulse to whack her on the head with the newspaper I was holding and knock some sense into her. Instead I said, *"Seriously,* Emily, I just lost my husband. I have more important things to deal with these days than your delusions." I looked down at her shoes. "And have some respect for the dead." My comment left Emily gazing at her feet. I exchanged a quick goodbye with Kayla and walked out.

Michael was right. Coming here was a mistake. I thought about Emily and the hostility she'd just displayed toward me. She'd always envied the close relationship I'd had with Pam. She'd probably seen it as a block to a similar friendship she'd hoped to cultivate with her mentor, but it hadn't happened and it wasn't my fault. Her snide remarks about my friendship with Michael had originated from the same jealous place in her heart.

Another thought crossed my mind, one that could put me in a lot of trouble if Emily had acted on it: that she'd shared her fantasies about Michael and me with the police this morning.

# CHAPTER 8

I met up with Michael in the lobby of the Elegance. He'd stopped to buy twelve small bottles of water and was holding a six-pack in each hand.

On our ride up the elevator, he asked how my visit to Bradford had gone. I said "fine" and left it at that. I'd decided to keep my chat with Emily under wraps and save myself further embarrassment.

I was surprised to find the coffee table in Michael's suite the way we'd left it Friday evening: strewn with crumpled notes and pages of his manuscript that hadn't made it to the final version that afternoon.

He followed my gaze to the table. "Sorry for the mess. I didn't have time to clean up." He set the bottles down on the floor while he hung his leather jacket in the hallway closet. "The hotel staff won't touch my crumbled papers unless I put them in a wastebasket, but there isn't one in this entire suite. I left them three notes but no luck. You could say we have a communications problem."

I didn't say so, but I hoped his extended presence in town would serve a more useful purpose than writing notes to the cleaning staff. I was counting on his ingenuity to provide a foolproof alibi for us and wipe out any conjecture in Moreau's mind that we were guilty of murder.

Michael set the water bottles on the credenza next to the TV. "I'll get a change of clothes, then be right back." He rounded the corner and disappeared.

I sat in my usual chair by the coffee table, opened up the

newspaper I'd bought earlier, and skimmed through the headlines. There were no write-ups linked to Tom or Pam—not even a two-liner on the Pineview deaths that might have excluded the names of the victims. It told me Moreau had kept his word about barring the media from his investigation after all. Or maybe he had no leads in the case, which could account for the absence of an article. Anyone else might argue that his investigation was far-reaching and therefore not yet completed, but I was inclined to think he'd made no headway whatsoever. Why face public criticism and announce it?

I was just as certain that Moreau hadn't dropped Michael and me from his scope of inquiry. Even with the prospect of Dan on board, my instincts told me the trend of ill-fated events was far from over. The ambiguity surrounding Tom's death amplified this feeling inside me, as did the realization that Moreau, with no other suspects in hand, might intensify his efforts to pin us with murder.

My apprehension lingered after Michael and I arrived at my condo half an hour later and crossed paths with Mrs. Speck. As she stepped out of the elevator, her eyes darted from Michael to me, then back again, like a hawk checking out its prey. I slammed my hand against the Close Doors button to cut short her inspection.

Upstairs, I found a basket of red and white carnations outside my apartment door. The card read: "Deepest condolences from Bradford Publishing and staff." The gesture of compassion had been timely and considerate—Kayla's style of doing things. I carried the flowers inside and placed them in a corner of the living room.

While Michael opened up his laptop in the kitchen and caught up on his e-mail, I settled down in my office to retrieve phone messages.

Kayla was the first caller. I assumed she'd phoned to see if I'd received the flowers, but then I was surprised when she left a message telling me to call her back ASAP. Tom's boss and Louise from Pineview were the next callers. They expressed their sympathies. I didn't feel like talking, so I didn't call any of them back. Only one call mattered to me, and I wouldn't rest until I got it: Dan's.

I walked back to the kitchen where Michael was hunched over

his laptop, tapping away. "I wanted to go through Tom's personal papers...legal files," I said to him, raising a thumb toward the hallway. "Would you mind if I take care of...?"

"No problem," he said with an easy smile. "I'm busy writing. Don't worry about me."

I retreated to my bedroom behind closed doors. I sat on the bed and forced myself to approach Tom's passing in a logical manner, the same way I'd helped my mother take care of things when my father had passed. I had to search for Tom's last will and testament, plan the funeral and church services, pack up his clothes for drop-off at a Salvation Army outlet...

I wandered into the walk-in closet. Tom kept a small fireproof filing cabinet there, in a corner behind his shirts. Neither of us believed in storing legal documents or other such papers in a bank safety deposit box.

I tried to open the drawer but it was locked. I had no idea where Tom kept the key.

On a whim, I bent down and pushed aside his pants on the rack. I reached into the corner and pulled out his briefcase. I tried to open it but it was locked too. I retrieved a penknife that Tom kept in his side table in the bedroom and forced open the lock.

Inside the briefcase were a couple of BOTCOR marketing pamphlets, Tom's appointment book, and his cell phone. It was probably the same phone he'd used when he didn't want me to know where he was calling from, the one that came up as UNKNOWN CALLER on the display screen on the home phone.

I flipped it open and checked the messages. There was only one. It was from Bradford Publishing. I recognized the phone number. It was Pam's extension. I took a deep breath, then pressed the key to listen to the message.

*"Hi, Tom. It's Pam. Looking forward to spending another hot weekend with you. Can't wait to see you this afternoon."*

I shivered. It was as if Pam's ghost had returned to haunt me. I snapped the phone shut and flung it into the briefcase.

I studied the two narrow pockets along the inside of the briefcase. They could hold a small item. I stuck my fingers inside the first.

Nothing. Inside the second pocket, I felt something metal. A key! I inserted it into the lock of Tom's filing cabinet. It worked!

I pulled open the drawer and found a copy of our apartment lease, our fire insurance policy, and our last will and testament in which we'd named each other as beneficiary and executor. I also found a copy of Tom's life insurance policy for one hundred thousand dollars that he'd bought shortly before we were married. My name was on the first page as sole beneficiary. I didn't believe in having life insurance, so I hadn't taken out a policy for myself, much to Tom's chagrin.

There was nothing else in the cabinet but a few monthly statements issued on the joint bank account I held with Tom—the one we'd set up for the purchase of our new home three years earlier. I'd just started my freelance business then and my income wasn't consistent. I gave Tom whatever I could afford, and automatic deductions were transferred from his personal account to our joint one every month. Tom dealt with a different bank and I had access to it online, but I'd been so busy that I hadn't checked it in years. It was a comfort to know that I could dip into the joint funds should an emergency arise.

I looked at the closing balance on the most recent statement. My jaw dropped.

The July statement read $128.16.

*What the hell?*

The other three statements revealed similar low balances at the end of each month. A deposit of a thousand dollars was posted every month—half of it mine—but cash withdrawals had drained most of the funds every month. All our hard-earned money was gone!

It didn't make sense. There had to be another joint account somewhere with forty thousand dollars in it. Maybe Tom had opened another account without my knowledge. Then again, why would he do that?

I practically tripped in my hurry to get to my purse and dig out the bankcard. I raced to my office, closed the door, and accessed the bank site from my computer. I couldn't get through. My card had probably been deactivated because I hadn't used it in so long.

I picked up the phone and called the bank. After the usual ID verification ritual, the service representative confirmed the only joint account on record was the one I knew about. As far as finding out if Tom conducted other business in his name only, the rep explained I'd have to go to the bank in person with Tom's last will and suitable ID to prove I was the official executor of his estate. I also needed to bring the required legal documents, namely a Certificate of Death from the provincial authorities or a copy of the coroner's report. I confirmed I would.

I drifted back to the closet and returned the bankcard to my purse. I put the papers back in the cabinet and shut the drawer but left the key in the lock for easy access.

I had to get myself organized. There was no time to waste.

I slipped back into my office. From my computer, I accessed the government website, clicked under the heading, "What to do in the event of death," and downloaded the appropriate forms. I made a list of the people and companies I'd have to contact regarding Tom's passing: the bank, insurance company, funeral home, accountant, notary, BOTCOR for Tom's employee pension fund...

I was getting hungry. I dug out a bag of chocolate-covered almonds from my desk drawer and was disappointed to find that only three remained. I ate them, then prepared letters to each name on my list. As soon as I'd receive the legal proof of death, I'd send the letters out.

I went back to my bedroom and revisited the closet. Tom's briefcase was still open. I realized I hadn't completed my search and now reached for his appointment book. Maybe something in it would tell me more about his personal banking.

I sat on the floor and fanned through the pages. Notations indicated meetings on a daily basis. Out of curiosity, I skipped to Friday, August 10, to see what kind of schedule he'd kept on his last day. He'd penned in two meetings and a note: *P.S. Bradford 4:00 p.m.*

I leafed a few pages back and stopped at an entry under July 23: *P.S. Pueblo's.* It was the same day I'd spotted Tom sitting with Pam at Pueblo's. The initials P.S. stood for Pam Strober! The following day in July, another entry: *P.S. Hôtel La Rivière,* a fancy hotel where dark chocolates are offered as a turndown treat before slipping under the covers. My stomach churned at the thought of them in bed together, yet I continued to scan the entries, urging myself on with a drive inherent only in those who believe that pain builds character.

I found an entry on July 26: *P.S. Toronto.* Lucie had told me Pam was away on business that day. Tom was in Toronto then too.

Armed with a new perspective, I flipped through the pages to see if Tom's inscription of P.S. appeared prior to the period I'd covered.

Other initials surfaced but they weren't Pam's. The cities noted beside them had often been on Tom's marketing itinerary: Toronto, Windsor, Boston, New York. Maybe the names of business associates or potential clients?

I turned to the back of the book and found a directory of names, addresses, and phone numbers. I scanned the pages. Most of the names were female.

I flipped back to the first day of January and worked my way forward. Every set of initials matched a woman's name in the directory. I recognized the company names next to some of them— no doubt business contacts. Dozens of other female listings just had names. *Who were these women?*

An uneasy feeling filled my gut. There had to be an explanation.

I glanced away and noticed a shoebox tucked under the cubicle that stored Tom's shoes. It was a tight squeeze, but I yanked it out and opened it. Hundreds of receipts were stuffed into it. The first one was from Coby's for $200.00, the next from Hôtel La Rivière for $400.00, another for $350.00 from a fancy restaurant downtown... Piles were from nightclubs, fancy restaurants, and upscale women's clothing stores in towns Tom had visited on business.

*He'd spent all our money on other women!*

My heart filled with anger, then sank as the dream of having my own house vanished. I stuffed the box back under the cubicle, not sure what purpose the receipts might serve in the future, if any. I flung Tom's appointment book into his briefcase, slammed it shut, and shoved it back in the corner.

*He'd had sex with other women, then had the nerve to come home and sleep with me! He'd put my health, if not my life, at risk!*

I tiptoed back to my office and quietly closed the door. I struggled with embarrassment for a few moments, then called my doctor and made an appointment to get tested for HIV/AIDS and other STIs.

I hurried back to my bedroom, holding back the tears until I'd closed the door. Then I broke down and cried. I muffled my sobs with a pillow so Michael couldn't hear me.

The next thing I heard was the clattering of plates in the kitchen. I glanced at my watch. Six o'clock. Where had the time gone?

I slipped into the bathroom and splashed cold water on my face. I waited until the most of the redness had disappeared, then headed for the kitchen.

I found Michael rummaging through my cutlery drawer. I hadn't given it much thought, but all of a sudden the presence of another man in the house so soon after Tom's death made me uncomfortable.

Another man. It was something my mother would say. I scolded myself for thinking of my relationship with Michael along silly, romantic lines.

He smiled at me. "Hi there. I was about to go get you." He set a fork next to our dinner plates on the table. "Pull up a chair."

I sat down and stared at the meal he'd prepared. With the expertise of a gourmet chef, he'd brought renewed vigor back to the tired omelet. Bits of parsley and basil decorated the edges. Melted mozzarella cheese formed a soft cloud in the center. Slices of tomato added color. "It looks good, but I don't have much of an appetite."

"Indulge me. Try it." He sat down next to me and dug into his plate.

I took a bite, then another, until I'd eaten it all. "That was so good. Where did you learn to make an omelet like that?"

"In Paris. I was on assignment there a couple of years ago. I roomed with a friend of a friend who happened to be a chef named Picasso." He went on about the roommate he rarely saw who worked evenings and slept during the day. "We'd leave each other notes. His were in French, which was bad enough, but his handwriting was worse." He chuckled.

I laughed too, thankful that he kept the discussion going without reference to the murder investigation or to the redness around my eyes.

I made a move to get up. "How about some coffee?"

"I got it." He went over to the counter and turned on the coffee machine.

I smiled to myself. I could get used to this.

With coffee cups in hand, we headed to the living room to watch the local news. I was hoping for a new development in the murder case. Any little detail, no matter how insignificant, would give me a sliver of hope. In a way, I was relieved when nothing came up. The upside was that we'd bought more time. More time to prove our alibis. More time to find the killer. More time to get Moreau off our backs.

I held the remote and hopped from station to station. My reasons for not parking it on a specific station ran the gamut of excuses available to viewers: boring, already viewed, in progress, lousy actors, theme too old, theme too young, whatever. I knew too well the program choices weren't the problem. It was the anxiety of waiting for Dan's phone call that was throwing my attention span off track.

Irritated from the futile exercise of channel hopping, I handed Michael the remote. "Here. Maybe you'll get lucky."

He went through a similar routine but soon caved in and dashed out to the corner strip mall to rent a video, seeing that I didn't have access to video on demand. He returned with a huge bag of popcorn, a packet of chocolate almonds, and an old video, *The Addams Family*. "I thought we could use a few laughs," he said, popping the disc into the slot.

He was right. Even though I'd seen the movie years before, it was hard not to laugh at the hilarious antics of the ghoulish family whose medieval abode looked out over a graveyard. It gave me a chance to escape from a reality that had weighed me down for days.

So I had no explanation for my outburst half an hour into the movie. "Tom slept with other women!" I threw my arms up in frustration and knocked over the popcorn bowl, scattering pieces all over the carpet.

Michael grabbed the remote and pressed the pause button. "How do you know this?"

"I found his appointment book. It has the names of women he met on business trips." I choked back the tears, got down on my knees, and began to pick up the popcorn. "I found a box of receipts. The money we saved to buy a house is gone. He spent it all. Damn him!"

"Megan, don't do this." He joined me on the floor.

"He'd slept with Pam and that was revolting, but I couldn't let it go at that. Oh, no. I had to go and dig up a truth that was a hundred times more repulsive."

"Megan, please—"

"I'm an intelligent woman, right? So tell me, Michael, how the hell did I miss the signs? Why couldn't I see he was cheating on me?" I tossed popcorn into the bowl.

"He was your husband. Why would you look for signs? You trusted him."

"He destroyed that trust. When I think of all the lies he told me. We were trying to have a baby." The tears began to flow.

Michael placed a hand on my shoulder. "I'm really sorry, Megan."

"I was so naïve. Damn! Damn! Damn!" I thumped my fists against my thighs.

"Stop it." Michael grabbed me by the wrists. "You're not to blame. You understand me?" His eyes locked on mine.

I felt the intensity of his gaze and froze. I'd seen that yearning in Tom's eyes before. There was no mistaking it.

Michael whispered my name and pulled me closer.

My thoughts scattered as he pressed his lips to mine. I couldn't deny the thrill of his kiss. My heart began to pound against my chest. A tingling spread throughout my body, and I kissed him back—harder.

Something clicked in my brain and I came to my senses. *What kind of wife was I?* My husband had just died. Hell, I hadn't even buried him yet.

I felt as if I'd broken one of the Ten Commandments. I wasn't sure which one. Adultery? No, my husband was dead. It didn't apply.

Regardless, I felt shame—as if I'd sinned. Maybe even a mortal sin—the worst kind. I blamed my strict Catholic upbringing for laying yet another guilt trip on me.

I pulled out of Michael's embrace and struggled to regain my composure. "What are we doing? This isn't right."

"I'm sorry," he said. "It's my fault."

"It's nobody's fault." I turned away and pretended to look for popcorn under the sofa while I searched for an excuse to explain what had just happened. "We're under a lot of stress. Yes, that's it. The police think we're murder suspects. Furthermore, we haven't a clue what Moreau is planning for us. We could end up in jail if Dan can't prove our alibis. What's worse than living with that kind of anxiety? Tell me. Just tell me." I was rambling, venting, avoiding the real issue: why was my heart still fluttering?

"Don't worry." Michael's tone was calm. "Dan will come up with a solid defense for us. You can bet on it." He dropped the last bit of popcorn into the bowl.

The phone rang. I made a dash for it.

It was Dan. "Is Michael there with you?"

"Yes."

"Stay put. I'm coming over."

# CHAPTER 9

Dan's demeanor Monday evening increased my apprehension. The worry lines stretching across his forehead made me wonder if the odds stacked against us were worse than I thought.

As for Jane, I barely recognized her. Gone were the soft curls and short skirt she'd worn in Michael's suite. Her hair hung straight down to her shoulders. A band pulled it away from her face to reveal high cheekbones and accent blue-gray eyes. She wore a navy jacket, a matching skirt that stopped right above the knee, a white shirt, and a pearl necklace. The look was austere, but I supposed it was all about depicting reliability and a sense of business ethics. The only thing that betrayed her woodenness was the scent of her perfume. A blend of lavender and vanilla, it alluded to a lighter, more carefree side of her personality and was more in line with her age group. Rather, *our* age group.

Dan introduced Jane to us. She smiled at Michael and shook his hand, but neither one mentioned having recently seen the other. Then she shook my hand. Her grasp was strong but not too tight. I played along for Michael's sake and made no mention of our initial meeting at the Elegance either.

As we settled around my kitchen table, Dan said, "My team did one heck of a job collecting valid data from prospective witnesses. I wasn't as lucky." He shrugged. "I met with Moreau at the station. Didn't get much there."

No surprise. Since the police weren't obliged to share evidence with a defense lawyer unless they lay charges and the case goes to trial, it was a catch-22 of sorts. The bottom line: Dan would have had more luck looking for a mite in a truckload of mattresses than trying to pick the detective's brain for any facts about his investigation. If he had no leads, Moreau wouldn't reveal his inability to solve the murders. On the other hand, if proving our guilt had become his sole preoccupation, he wouldn't share that with Dan either.

"Unfortunately, I had to pull team members off your case to work on other projects originally scheduled for this week," Dan went on.

"So where does that leave us?" Michael stared at him across the table.

"I'll be handling your case myself. Staying in Montreal longer than planned. Jane and I will continue gathering info on your behalf."

*Oh-oh.* If the statements they'd obtained from witnesses had influenced his decision to extend his stay, it meant things weren't looking too promising for us.

Dan retrieved some folders from his briefcase, then looked at Jane. "By the way, good job in the field today."

"That's what I'm here for." She opened her notebook and pulled out a pen. She sat next to Michael, her back straight up against the chair. Her expression showed no emotion as she watched Dan place six manila folders on the table. I wondered how many years of practice it had taken her to get that poker face down pat.

"I hope you have good news for us." Michael eyed his buddy with the usual spark of optimism.

"Some good. Some not so good." Dan opened the first file. "All right. Our expert's report on potassium cyanide. Not dangerous when dry. When it comes into contact with acidic water—even moist skin—it releases a deadly gas. Less than a fraction of an ounce can kill you. Sometimes a bitter almond smell is detected, but not always. Safe to assume that Tom and Pam collapsed and died almost immediately."

Peter Ewans' description of the scene was still vivid in my mind. I blanked it out. "So they had no chance whatsoever of getting out of the cottage alive."

"That's right," Dan said.

"Where did the police find the cyanide?" Michael asked.

"They're withholding that information," Dan said.

"What about the time of death?"

"They're withholding that too."

"Any fingerprints?"

Dan shrugged. "Don't know. Want my unofficial theory?"

"Go ahead."

"Aside from Tom's and Pam's, there must have been dozens of fingerprints in the cottage. The police are working through the eliminations. Not much to go on so far. Odds are the suspect wore gloves and a mask as safeguards when handling the cyanide."

"Peter mentioned seeing broken china on the floor," I said. "Maybe Tom and Pam ingested the cyanide in their coffee or food."

"Possible. Final autopsy results will reveal more." Dan put the file aside and opened up the second one. "Witness reports. Louise Kirk, manager at Pineview. She confirmed the cleaning staff left the cottage at four o'clock Friday afternoon. Tom and Pam arrived at seven that evening. A BOTCOR employee saw Tom and Pam drop off their luggage at the cottage and go directly to a party held in another cottage. They stayed there until midnight."

I was sitting next to Dan and across from Jane. From time to time, I jotted details on a canary yellow notepad and felt her eyes on me. She tried not to be obvious about it but didn't succeed. She was sizing me up—perhaps curious about my marriage to a cheating husband, no doubt curious about my connection to Michael. I could tell she was still interested in him by the way her gaze drifted in his direction whenever he spoke and every so often when he didn't. That she'd chosen to sit next to him at the kitchen table was a sure giveaway.

Michael gave no indication he'd taken their relationship to a new level since their meeting at the hotel weeks ago. It would explain the pass he'd made at me minutes earlier. I blanked it out. I didn't want to go there. Why complicate my life?

Dan fingered a report. "The management at Pineview." He looked at Jane. "You want to do the honors?" He held it out to her.

"Thanks, Dan, but I don't need it." Jane switched her gaze to me. "Stewart Kirk and his wife, Louise, own and manage the resort.

They have access to the facilities 24/7. They purchased Pineview ten years ago and never had trouble with the law. Mr. Kirk's two brothers handle the front desk in the evening and have *carte blanche* to the property as well. All four have solid alibis, as do the rest of the staff."

"What about the security policy at Pineview?" Michael asked.

"Lax," she said, turning slightly toward him. "It basically runs on an honor system."

"Surveillance cameras?"

"None."

"How many cottages does Pineview have?" I asked Jane.

"Fifteen," she said.

"How many were occupied by BOTCOR staff?"

"Ten," she said without hesitation, which convinced me she'd read the findings more than once or had a photographic memory. "Why do you ask?"

"People who go to a resort can get laid back when they're hanging out with a group of friends," I said. "If BOTCOR employees occupied most of the cottages, maybe Tom or Pam felt safe and left their door unlocked. Anyone could have gained access to their cottage while they were out."

"You mean to plant the cyanide," Jane said.

*Was she doing it on purpose to make me spell it out?* "Well, yes," I said.

"Easy access," Dan said, scribbling a note. "It's a doubt we can raise in our defense." He lifted another report from the file. "A list of the cleaning staff at Pineview. Most are semi-retired workers. Each had access to the cottages."

"Did any of them see anything suspicious?" Michael asked him.

"No," Jane cut in, surprising me. "I interviewed all five of them. They had solid alibis. I did the usual background checks on them. Those came up clean too."

"Who else had access to the cottages?" I asked.

"Each guest had a key to their own cottage, of course," Jane said, blinking hard, as if I'd asked a silly question.

I ignored her and began to draw circles on my notepad. Doodling helped me to think.

Dan opened up the next file. "My team couldn't get a copy of the Elegance video tapes. The police have one, but they don't want to share." His lips tightened. "Megan, we have a witness report from Mrs. Speck at the condo. She confirmed your return home at about nine Friday evening."

*That interfering witch finally came through for me.*

"Michael, the desk clerk at the Elegance saw you in the lobby when you returned to the hotel around midnight." Dan paused. "Oh, one more thing. Sales receipts at Santino's substantiate you both had dinner there until eight forty-five."

Jane had been looking at Dan while he was speaking. The muscles around her eyes tightened at the mention of my having had dinner with Michael.

"About a potential problem we raised earlier," Dan was saying. "We confirmed there's no surveillance camera at the rear exit of your condo, Megan. The police might question your whereabouts after Michael dropped you off."

Exasperation crept in. "What does it take to prove I was asleep in my bed?" I said.

"Maybe a video tape," Michael said, smiling at me.

I smiled back. "Right." I sensed that Jane was staring at me again, but I pretended not to notice. Instead I wrote a note to myself on the yellow notepad. I'd go and see the superintendent about installing an additional video camera at the rear of the building.

Dan lifted another report in the file. "On to Sainte-Adèle. We tracked down the clerk at the gas station." He looked up at Michael. "He didn't remember you."

"What about their video tape?" Michael asked, repeating what had now become the catchphrase of the evening.

Dan shook his head. "The surveillance system was malfunctioning. No tape is available."

"That's plain crazy," Michael said, his eyes wide in disbelief.

Jane turned to face him. "It's true, Michael. I also spoke with the owner of a *dépanneur* located nearby. I was hoping his store had a surveillance system in place, but it didn't. I wish I had more positive news for you. Sorry." She reached out and put her hand on his.

He gave her a brief smile. "Not a problem. You did the best you could."

"You drove to Sainte-Adèle *and* Pineview today?" I asked Jane, shattering the moment between them.

She slid her hand off Michael's. "Yes, I did." She gave me a half-smile, as if one side of her mouth felt I deserved it while the other felt it wasn't worth the effort. "I was visiting friends up north Sunday night. Dan paged me this morning and asked if I'd check out the gas station in Sainte-Adèle. It was minutes away, so I said yes. Since Dan was busy in town, I offered to drive to Pineview to do the interviews there too."

*What team spirit! Extra Brownie points for you!*

Her smart-ass attitude was beginning to annoy me far more than her diligence. I needed a release. I clasped the edge of my padded chair with both hands and dug my thumbs in, imagining I was digging them into Jane's eyes.

"My team confirmed the mileage on your rental car, Michael," Dan said. "It's what we'd discussed. The equivalent of a two-way trip to Sainte-Adèle, plus a few extra miles driving around Montreal."

"Or the distance driving to and from Pineview—give or take a few miles," Michael said, the irony apparent in his voice.

"Don't even go there," I said, wary of any evidence that had the potential to backfire. "Moreau could use it against us. Right, Dan?"

"He might." Dan pulled out his hankie. Wipe, fold, tuck.

Michael leaned forward. "I don't like where this is going, buddy. Isn't the onus on the cops to prove we went to Pineview in the first place?"

Dan nodded. "From the prosecution's perspective, whoever planted the cyanide at Pineview needed controlled conditions. Plus a clear path and no witnesses. If Tom and Pam had reached the cottage before you did and stayed there the rest of—"

"We already know that didn't happen."

"All the more reason the prosecution could argue you had the opportunity to sneak in and plant the cyanide, say, between ten and eleven that night."

"That's plain crazy," Michael said, raising a hand in the air. "Like Megan said, anyone could have walked in if the door wasn't locked."

"Other suspects might surface in the interim. Regardless, we have to be prepared to defend our position from every angle. Raise doubts about the evidence the prosecution presents in court. If it ever comes to that."

Michael shook his head, said nothing.

Did he feel as if he were being singled out as a suspect? If so, I had to show him he wasn't alone. "But Dan, Tom told me he was going to Granite Ridge. I had no reason to believe he'd gone to Pineview. Neither did Michael."

"The prosecution might refute your claim," Dan said. "Show how your conversation with Louise substantiated the fact you knew Tom was going to Pineview. Even if he lied about it afterward."

"Peter can vouch for me," I said. "He covered up for Tom. Maybe he could provide us with an alibi of sorts."

Dan nodded his head from side to side. "It's dubious. The prosecution could create a doubt about Peter's credibility as a witness based on his cover-up for Tom. It would cancel out the truthful answers."

"Great. That's all we need." Michael ran a hand through his hair. "A case against us based on lies."

The frustration in his voice was justified. The likelihood we could be facing murder charges was unthinkable, yet possible, if we couldn't prove our alibis.

Dan moved on to the next file. "The BOTCOR employees. Solid alibis."

"Peter Ewans too?" Michael asked him.

"I'll check." He flipped through the file, pulled out a report, and gave it a quick scan. "Peter and his wife arrived at the BOTCOR party at the same time as Tom, Pam, and other guests. They all stayed there until late that night."

"It doesn't mean anything," Michael said. "Peter could have slipped out to plant the cyanide while everyone else was distracted at the party. No one would have noticed."

"Possibly," Dan said. "However, witness comments contradict the impression you have of Peter. It's in here somewhere." He leafed through the file until he found it. "A BOTCOR employee said Peter became ill right after he discovered the bodies. Paramedics had to give him a tranquilizer on site."

"It's a natural reaction to a traumatic event," Jane said.

"Or a case of nerves," I said.

"Definitely a guilty conscience," Michael said. "A likely suspect."

Dan shrugged. "Circumstances might suggest it. However, studies show that Peter's temperament doesn't fit the stereotype of a cold-blooded killer."

"Why not? From what I learned in investigative journalism, the quiet ones are the ones you have to watch out for."

Dan tapped his pen. "We can speculate all we want. It's what Moreau thinks that counts. Let's move on." His gaze zigzagged along another page. "We interviewed the auto mechanic who repairs and does maintenance on the leased BOTCOR vehicles."

"So you do have suspicions about Peter after all," Michael said, a glimmer of hope returning in his eyes.

"It's a precautionary move on our part." Dan studied the report. "The Ford was in excellent condition. The last tune-up was a month ago. The mechanic claims it's odd that a wheel could have fallen off the vehicle like that."

"Unless the mechanic didn't do it." Michael raised an eyebrow.

My mind grasped a horrific possibility. "Hold on. Maybe Peter was jealous of Tom's success, but I doubt he'd kill him. It was an accident."

"How can you be so sure?" Michael asked me. "Here's another one for you. How well do you know Peter?"

"I know he's a good family man. Somewhat insecure and nervous. Why?"

He grew pensive. "Think back to the day he delivered the Ford to your place. Did he say or do anything out of the ordinary?"

"He dropped the car keys when he handed them to me, but like I said, he's a nervous type of guy." I thought about it. "Wait. There was something else. When I asked if he wanted a ride back home, he was surprised. He thought I was referring to the Ford. When I said I meant a taxi, he seemed relieved."

"It's sounding more and more suspicious to me," Michael said.

"Let's not jump to conclusions," Dan said. "Peter's reaction might have been based on company policy. An outside party not authorized to drive a company car, for example." He glanced back at the report. "More notes. When my team mentioned the loose tire incident to him, he went white. Looked like he was going to pass out."

His words were lost on Michael. "It could have been an act."

"Maybe he has a health problem we don't know of," I said, doodling triangles on my yellow notepad.

"I don't buy it," Michael said. "I'd bet his plan to get rid of Tom failed the first time. He waited for the next suitable occasion— Pineview. Motive and opportunity."

"Possibly," Dan said. "But why risk killing Pam?"

"Why not? Megan could have been sitting in the Ford with Tom the day the tire flew off. Peter would have killed them both."

His comment triggered another memory and I voiced it. "Peter said something else when he called me Saturday morning. He passed along his condolences but thought Tom would be going to Pineview alone." I paused. "Tom told him we were getting a divorce."

"Just more lies." Michael waved a hand in the air. "Peter's suffering from a double dose of guilt. It happens to the best of murderers. He's still a prime suspect to me."

"Pure speculation at this point," Dan said. "We haven't completed his background check yet. Have to determine a link to cyanide, and so on."

Peter's work background surfaced to mind. I knew that what I was about to reveal would defeat my argument in support of him, but I had to be truthful. "Peter worked as a chemical engineer before he joined BOTCOR."

"Aha!" Michael clapped his hands together. "The trump card."

Jane jumped in. "Dan, do you want me to check Peter out for you? I'd be happy to." She seemed so eager to please that I wondered if I'd misjudged her earlier.

"As a witness," Dan said. "Verify his former contacts in the chemicals industry. Get a character reference from the personnel department at BOTCOR. Ask about potential problems with staff, addictions of any sort. That kind of thing. Speak with his wife, neighbors, friends."

Jane's pen slid across the page to keep up with his instructions.

I moved on to doodling squares and waited until they'd finished their conversation. At one point, Dan moved the folders around and the photo of a cottage slipped out. I assumed it was the one where Tom and Pam had stayed. He picked it up quickly and put it back. Maybe he thought it would upset me if I saw it.

"Dan, was that a picture of the Pineview cottage?" I asked him.

"Yes," he said.

"Can I see it?"

He fished it out and handed it to me.

I studied the photo. Three wooden steps led up to a narrow veranda at the front of the single-story cottage. A narrow window bordered the left side of the door. Eyelet curtains allowed a partial view of the inside. What I found most surprising were the four glass panels on the door. "There's a simple lock on the front door. It would have been easy to break a glass panel and open the door from the outside." I passed the photo to Michael. "I'm surprised Peter didn't try to break in."

"I'm not," Michael said. "If he planted the cyanide, he'd have made damn sure not to walk in and give them mouth-to-mouth."

"I agree," Jane said. "With Peter's experience as a chemical engineer, he'd have known the dangers of exposure to cyanide. He wouldn't have risked it."

"The proof keeps piling up," Michael said, grinning. He handed Dan the photo.

Our discussion triggered yet another memory—one that required immediate action on my part. "Excuse me. I'll be right back." I went to the bedroom and retrieved Tom's appointment book from the closet, then returned to the kitchen. "This belonged to Tom," I said to Dan, offering it to him. "It could help our investigation. The names in the directory at the back might produce a lead to the real killer."

Michael looked at me with admiration. "It takes a lot of courage to do what you just did."

"Not if it's our passport out of hell," I said.

Jane leaned forward. "What exactly did you find in there, Megan?"

"The names of women my husband slept with," I said, keeping my voice even.

"Oh." She sat back.

I thought I saw a flicker of compassion in her eyes, but it faded away as she turned her attention to Dan.

Dan scanned the pages of the directory and stopped once in a while to peruse the names. "If we make inquiries into the names listed here, we might have to present testimony stemming from them. Kitschy details could surface in a court of law." He glanced at me. "Cause you potential embarrassment."

"Do whatever you have to do," I said. "Maybe we'll get lucky and flush out the killer."

"New witness information might help your defense, but proving that other suspects are guilty is beyond the scope of our responsibilities," he reminded me, then handed the book to Jane. "Start the interview process. Contact as many people as you can." He reached for the next file and opened it up. "My team spoke with Mrs. Tricia Bradford, wife of fifty-five-year-old Bill Bradford. Reputable family on both sides. Old money—millions—on her side. Mrs. Bradford is busy with charities, social committees, lawn parties. Influential in high-society circles. Rumor has it she's a silent partner in Bradford Publishing."

"What about her alibi?" Michael asked Dan.

"Confirmed. She left to visit her mother in Hampstead on Friday morning. Stayed there a few days."

"So what?" Michael said. "Money talks. If the boss's wife wanted Pam out of the way, she could hire a hit man and cover her tracks like a pro."

Dan shrugged. "Why take the chance? Assuming she's found guilty of murder, that's twenty-five years in jail. Hefty price to pay for revenge. Not to mention she could forfeit the right to her husband's estate. Huge stakes."

"You amaze me, buddy," Michael said. "I thought the contents of wills were off limits."

"People talk." Dan gave him a discerning look.

"So Mrs. Bradford is still in the running as a suspect."

"Possibly, but it's not up to me to prove it." Dan flipped open the last file. "All right. Witnesses at Bradford confirm Pam left the office at four that Friday."

It validated the notation I'd seen in Tom's appointment book, yet something nagged at me. "If it took them three hours to get to Pineview, they must have stopped along the way."

"Probably for a bite to eat," Michael said.

"Possibly." Dan lifted a few reports from the file and fanned them out in his hand. "The staff interviews. I left this bunch for last. The interview with Emily Saunders was exceptional."

"Good or bad?" I asked, trying to quell the uneasy feeling stirring inside me.

He plucked a report and placed it on the top of the pile. "Bad. Her comments would damage our defense. No doubt about it." He kept his gaze on the report.

After my run-in with Emily at Bradford, my instincts were on high alert. "What did she say?"

Dan let out a deep breath. "That you and Michael were lovers."

# CHAPTER 10

This time I was certain I saw Jane flinch. Not only flinch but shift in her chair.

She caught me looking at her and pretended to cross her legs.

I pretended not to notice. I was battling my own demons.

*Michael and I were lovers.* At least, that's what Emily had said.

The memory of Michael's kiss flashed through my mind. Butterflies fluttered inside me. I struggled to hide my feelings.

Michael spoke up. "Emily asked me out a few times. I said no. She's pissed off and taking it out on me through Megan."

"Anger is a normal reaction on her part," Jane said in a soft voice. "She felt rejected."

I found my voice. "It's more than that. Emily has anger-management issues."

"All right." Dan's brow puckered, as if what he was going to say would cause us more concern. "Emily worked at the office Sunday afternoon. After closing hours Friday, a call had bounced from Megan's office to the front desk. Emily checked the message."

"I was out of the office last week, so my phone was on call forward," I said. "Who was the caller?"

He glanced back at the report. "Unknown. A technical device was used to disguise the voice. The message said: stop sleeping with Michael Elliott or else."

"What?" I felt a slight blush.

Michael's jaw tensed. "That's a blatant lie, if not a threat."

Dan nodded. "Emily said the police took it as a threat too."

It was my turn to cry foul. "She told the police about the call? I can't believe she'd promote another lie about Michael and me."

"What do you mean, *another lie*?" Michael stared at me.

I summed up my chat with Emily at the office. "I think she blames me for Pam's death and is spreading rumors to get back at me."

"Makes two of us," Michael said.

"Rumors are harmless schoolgirl antics," Jane said.

"It goes beyond harmless." Dan laid aside his pen. "Michael, the police now have grounds to suspect you had a motive for killing Tom. Your secret love affair with Megan."

"That's plain crazy." Michael leaned forward. "How can the cops rely on a ridiculous message from an unknown caller?"

"They can check company phone records to verify the legitimacy of the call," Dan pointed out.

"It's a long shot. Emily could have asked a friend to call the office from an unlisted number or a cell phone. I think she concocted the whole thing."

Granted, Emily's accusation about me might have stemmed from a dark place in her heart, and yet... "Emily can be dramatic at times, but I can't believe she'd lie to the police when it involves a murder investigation."

"You have a point," Dan said. "She could be charged with obstruction of justice."

"Dan, maybe I should have a girl-to-girl talk with Emily," Jane said, leaning forward. "I'm sure I can clear up this little misunderstanding."

"Not a good idea, Jane." Dan shook his head. "We need to play down the anonymous call. If we draw attention to it, Moreau might use it as a springboard. His investigation could take off in a number of predictable directions. Most of them based on motive."

Jane squared her shoulders. "The anonymous call can be construed as hearsay."

"Doesn't matter," Dan said.

"Why not?"

"The implication is there." A sharp glance from Dan ended the debate.

"I'll bet Moreau already latched onto it," Michael said. "He'll chase anything if it leads back to our doorstep."

Dan patted his brow with a hankie, then put it back in his pocket. His expression remained somber as he addressed Michael and me. "All right. A word of advice before we wrap things up. You're both at the top of the suspect list as far as Moreau is concerned. Don't give him good reason to pursue you." He gathered his files in a pile.

"What do you mean?" Michael asked.

"He won't stop until he finds reasonable and probable grounds."

"And that's supposed to scare me? Let him bring it on." Michael raised his hands in the air. "If he thinks he's going to dig up dirt to incriminate me, he's in for a huge disappointment." He stuck out his jaw in defiance.

"That's goes for me too," I said, trying to sound as bold.

Yet part of me wondered how we'd ever break free from a chain of events that was headed for disaster.

# CHAPTER 11

I heard a commotion outdoors Tuesday morning and peeked through the horizontal blinds in the living room. Camera crews had set up their equipment in front of the condo. Reporters were competing for prime locations near the entrance. I assumed information about the murders had leaked out to the media somehow. I was glad I'd drawn the blinds the evening before. It eliminated any chance that a roving camera lens would now zoom in and invade my privacy.

On the back of this latest development, another horrid thought ran through my mind: every detail of my life was about to be placed under a microscope for the entire world to see.

I walked past my office and noticed the flashing red light on the phone. I wasn't surprised. I'd switched off the ringer on both phones last night to get some sleep. Now I switched them back on and checked my messages.

The two calls were from reporters. It was a miracle they'd managed to get my phone number—it wasn't listed. Maybe someone at Bradford had given it to them. Emily, I thought unkindly. From their voice messages, it was clear they were eager to get me in front of their cameras. Fat chance. I planned to remain indoors, safe and sheltered.

Then I remembered I had an appointment with my gynecologist this morning. I had no choice. I had to leave the shelter of my condo and find a way to dodge the media coverage.

On that note, I was somewhat curious about the extent of the coverage. Maybe one of the local channels had given the murders prime airtime this morning. I checked my watch. Eight o'clock. I hurried back to the living room, plopped down on the sofa, and clicked on the TV.

I'd missed the first seconds of the broadcast but caught a glimpse of a female reporter pursuing Moreau up the front stairs of the police station. The person holding the camera had a hard time keeping it steady and most of the shots focused on Moreau's briefcase or his back. Just before they reached the front doors, the reporter asked Moreau if he had any leads in the case. He turned and said "No comment" into the microphone before he vanished inside.

What followed was a clip of a BOTCOR marketing executive whom I recognized from a company Christmas party. His name wasn't familiar, but the silver-haired man in a gray suit attested that Tom's contribution to the firm had resulted in "a substantial financial boost to the bottom line during his short career span."

How crass! It was all about the money for those leeches—right up to the end.

I sat up when I recognized the front of my condo building in the next clip. A camera zoomed in on the entrance where another female reporter stood talking with... Oh, no. Mrs. Speck! She was being interviewed in the foyer downstairs. I turned up the volume.

"I seldom saw Mr. Scott," Mrs. Speck was saying, tugging at a black shawl that looked as if she'd dug it out of storage from the 1800s. "No siree, it didn't surprise me they'd separated." Her lips shut tight to form a thin crooked line.

"What makes you think they were separated?" the reporter asked her.

Mrs. Speck stuck out her pointy chin. "I happened to see Mr. Scott leave the building with a suitcase that Friday afternoon."

"I understand Mr. Scott traveled a lot on business," the reporter went on. "He must have packed a suitcase many times before. What was so different this time?"

"He didn't return," Mrs. Speck said. "He usually returns on Sunday night. I said to myself, this is not a good sign, no siree." She adjusted her glasses. "On the weekend, I noticed several strange men coming and going from Mrs. Scott's home at all hours of the day and night."

"Strange men?" the reporter prompted her.

"I'm a law-abiding citizen, so I won't go into the details in public, but I was appalled at the notion that—may the Lord forgive me—a woman of ill repute might be living under the same roof as me."

My jaw dropped. "That bitch!"

The reporter pulled the microphone away and concluded her coverage.

I aimed the remote at the TV and turned it off, wishing it were that easy to turn Mrs. Speck off too. She'd just launched my "ill repute" as this morning's official topic of gossip.

It was reassuring to know I wasn't Mrs. Speck's only victim. A newly married couple on the third floor had told me how they'd often caught her eavesdropping at their door. She'd pretended to be dropping off a magazine that had been left at her door by mistake. Other occupants got wise to her habits after she'd start up a conversation with them about the magazines they subscribed to—information she'd acquired from peeking over the letter carrier's shoulder as he sorted the mail in the lobby.

It made me wonder how often she'd eavesdropped at my door or—.

The phone rang and I jumped. I cursed the media out loud for putting me on edge. I rushed to the office and checked the display on the phone. It was Bradford Publishing. I answered it.

"Hi, Megan," Kayla's voice came through the other end. "Did I get you at a bad time?"

"Not at all. I received your flowers. Thank you."

"Oh...well, it's the least we could do for you." She sounded a bit flustered. "Megan, I hate to be the bearer of more bad news at a time like this, but Mr. B. has requested that we refrain from giving you any more contract work until this...situation is resolved."

"Situation?"

"He's concerned about the bad publicity surrounding Pam's and Tom's death and their connection to you."

"What? That's horrible! How can he even justify—"

"I'm sorry, Megan. I hope it all blows over soon."

Great. Tom had squandered thousands of dollars from our joint savings account. The rent had to be paid by the end of the month, let alone the bills. I had a bit of savings left but no viable source of revenue. *How the hell would I survive?*

Kayla went on. "If you want to send me an invoice for your work to date, I'll make sure a check is sent out to you ASAP."

I mumbled my thanks and had barely hung up when the phone rang again.

UNKNOWN CALLER.

I picked it up, intending to hang up as soon as the marketer began his pitch.

Annoyance turned to relief at the sound of Michael's voice. "Hope I didn't wake you," he said, sounding cheery.

"No, but the reporters did. They're parked outside the condo." I gave him a recap of the interview with Mrs. Speck. "That wicked witch of the east! She painted me as a prostitute and said every word of it on live TV, to top it off."

He laughed. "Strange men visiting you? Dan will get a kick out of it. As for Moreau, I don't know."

"I'm sure he'll be flattered."

He laughed again. "I'm out jogging and was thinking of going over to see you. Are you up for a visit?"

"I don't think it's a good idea."

"Right. The media." Michael paused. "Can you hold on? Jane's on the other line." After a few seconds, he returned. "Sorry, Megan."

"Any news about the case?"

"No. Jane just wanted to come over to the hotel."

"Oh."

"I told her I was out, that I'd be busy the rest of the day. Speaking of which, how about meeting me for lunch at Santino's?"

"I can't. The reporters will hound me as soon as I step outside."

"Throw on a pair of sunglasses. Wear different clothing. They won't recognize you. And use the rear exit."

I thought about it. I hadn't bought groceries in days. I had a doctor's appointment at eleven o'clock anyway. Escape seemed like a good option—especially the incognito part.

"Okay. See you at noon."

I walked toward the kitchen and caught a whiff of the rich Colombian brew completing its pre-programmed drip. Nothing smells better than fresh brewed coffee, except maybe a pastry shop that sells fresh baked goods and fresh brewed coffee. I suddenly craved a cup.

But first things first.

I put an eye to the peephole of my front door to make sure the corridor was empty. It was. I opened the door wide enough to stick my arm out and retrieve my rolled-up copy of *The Gazette*. It was a mystery how the delivery person got into the building to begin with, but I was thankful for any small favor that happened into my life these days.

I poured coffee into a huge mug and popped two slices of whole grain bread into the toaster, then sat down at the kitchen table. I removed the elastic band around the newspaper and opened it up. The headline on the front page read: "Mysterious Cyanide Murders at Pineview Resort."

My heart skipped a beat. I wondered if Moreau was responsible for releasing the story to the media. If so, why hadn't he warned us ahead of time?

Maybe he had a new lead or solid evidence on hand—something that would drive the investigation in the right direction.

I read the first of two articles. It portrayed me as a "grief-stricken, young widow." Given that I hadn't spoken with any reporters so far, I marveled at their ingenuity in coming up with that description. I supposed it was my good fortune that they offered a sympathetic approach as far as my emotional state was concerned. A photo of me taken at a Bradford Publishing event last year had found its way into the piece. Someone had given it to the press without my knowledge or permission. Again, I assumed it was Emily and hated myself for doing so, but who else could it be? With Ray working in the lab, it would be easy to get any photo she wanted.

The second article described Tom as "an up-and-coming marketing executive with a national corporation" and Pam as "a vivacious publicity manager with a bright future in the publishing industry." Pictures of Pam with clients were splattered across the page in media hype style. The photograph of a cottage at Pineview was also included, though not the one Tom had stayed in. Like the other article, this one stated the police had no concrete leads and continued to ask the public's support in solving the murders.

I wanted to scream. Moreau had zilch. The write-ups contained information, but any seasoned investigative reporter could obtain that sort of data from a phone call or personal interview. The only significant detail—that Tom and Pam had been murdered with cyanide—had definitely come from the police and no one else. I cut out the articles to show Michael.

While I munched on a toast topped with almond butter, I flipped through the rest of the paper. A short article about a drug arrest in Sainte-Adèle caught my eye. There was no byline, so I didn't know who had written the piece.

I scanned other articles and picked up three spelling errors and revised two sentences in my mind. The ability to pick out typos and revise muddled text had its advantages. It took my focus off the murders. It also extended to another aspect—one that engaged my muscles: it made me crave tidiness and cleanliness around me.

My eyes roamed over the cluttered counter, a sink full of dishes, and a floor that hadn't been washed in weeks. It was time for a crackdown. I cleared away the dishes and washed the kitchen floor. I moved on to the bathroom and scrubbed it until it sparkled. Satisfied that these activities had appeased my yen for restoring order, I headed for the bedroom to pick out something to wear to Santino's.

The phone rang. I detoured into the office.

"Have you seen today's news?" my mother asked at the other end of the line. She subscribed to a handful of local papers and considered herself an expert in public affairs, or more precisely, the affairs of people in the public eye. Her interests spanned from fundraising events to government policy for seniors—anything that kept a conversation going with friends and relatives. I wanted to believe I'd inherited her penchant for seeking out information but not her need to chat.

"I read the articles in *The Gazette*," I said in response to her question, praying she wasn't referring to the TV coverage. "I'm sorry I couldn't tell you sooner about the cyanide."

She sighed. "It felt like déjà vu."

"What do you mean?"

"For twenty years your father worked for that horrible plastics company. And every day he was exposed to a mix of chemicals. Cyanide was one of them."

"I don't remember the doctors mentioning that."

"They didn't. Your father told me. Remember how the hospital didn't want to get involved in my lawsuit against the plastics company?"

"Yes."

"Well, that was the reason. Anyway, it was all for the better. I didn't need more grief." She let out another sigh. "Megan, I promised I would respect your privacy, but I have to ask you. One tabloid said Tom was a member of a doomsday cult that commits suicide with cyanide."

"Mom, you can't accept everything you read as fact," I said. "Tom loved life too much to kill himself. We both know that."

"So who could have done such a hateful thing?"

"I don't know."

Silence hung on the line. I put myself in her place and tried to imagine what might be going through her mind. She'd often heard me complain about Tom's frequent trips, but he'd shone so brightly in her eyes, she'd chosen to ignore my whining for the most part. But now his death had changed everything. Did she wonder whether or not I'd found out about his affair and sought revenge against him? Would she think such dreadful thoughts about her own daughter? Would any mother?

Her voice shattered my reverie. "I can take care of the arrangements for the wake, if you want. We can have it at my place."

"Only if you're up to it," I said.

"I'm fine. At my age, I have to make every minute count."

I thought about her remark but let it go. People in my mother's age group often spoke as if they were going to die at any moment. She lingered a bit longer on the line, chatting, maybe sensing I hadn't told her everything, maybe hoping I'd use her as a sounding board the way I often did before.

Instead I held back.

I didn't want to cause her unnecessary grief, so I didn't tell her the man I'd married—the same man she'd thought would make such a fine husband and great father—had cheated on me with more than one woman and might have infected me with a life-threatening disease.

Nor did I tell her the police might conduct a search of my home any day now because they considered Michael—a man whom I'd met weeks ago—as my lover, and that we were potential suspects in a double murder.

I especially didn't want to tell her the murders had drawn not only the attention of the media but also the curiosity of one particular police detective who was prepared to pursue Michael and me to hell and back if required.

No, some things you just don't tell your mother.

After we said our goodbyes, I headed back to the bathroom. I was about to step into the shower when the phone rang again. I rushed over to answer it, but there was silence at the other end of the line.

I checked the display. It was a long-distance number that wasn't familiar to me. I assumed it was a representative from one of those telemarketing companies that called umpteen times a week. They used a computer-generated listing that dialed multiple phone numbers at once and left you hanging if someone else answered before you did. So I hung up.

At ten-thirty, I made my getaway through the rear exit of the condo—right into a hornet's nest of reporters.

# CHAPTER 12

A dozen reporters were lurking in the parking lot behind my condo.

I remembered Michael's words of advice and strolled along, not making eye contact with anyone. He was right. No one recognized the "grief-stricken, young widow" clad in a baseball cap, jean shorts, a white T-shirt, and sunglasses. The ponytail had been a last-minute decision—my attempt at shaving off years to foil the reporters' plans. It had worked.

The wide branches of the maple trees lining the street offered no respite from the heat and mugginess that had returned to the city and would linger for another spell. Good thing it was only a fifteen-minute walk to the medical clinic on Sherbrooke Street.

I checked in, then sat down in the small waiting room. My turn came up half an hour later. The gynecologist examined me and took the usual samples required for STI testing. He confirmed I'd have the results in several weeks. He took a blood sample for HIV testing and said I'd have those results in minutes. I prayed all the while. The results came back negative, and my anxiety level dropped until he said I'd have to return in three months for more HIV testing as a precautionary measure.

The outdoor air hung heavy with humidity. Before I'd walked the three blocks to the underground subway station, my T-shirt had absorbed the dampness and was beginning to cling to my skin. I welcomed the coolness of *Le Metro*, but it was too short a train ride downtown to the McGill station for a complete cooling down period.

A gust of hot air greeted me as I resurfaced at the street level. The sun seared the pavement and sent up tides of heat that blurred my vision of objects in the distance and made breathing a chore. The two commercial blocks east to Santino's stretched out before me like two miles. The pedestrians in front of me had slowed down to a crawl. Cars, trucks, and buses inched along too, bumper to bumper, like one gigantic funeral procession.

I fought to take in each breath from surroundings so thick and dirty with gas emissions that I could almost taste the greasy stench. My eyes burned and my throat ached with dryness. More than ever, I wished I'd brought along a bottle of water.

I accelerated my pace, but three students who'd stopped to chat in the middle of the sidewalk, a young man walking a dog, and two women toting shopping bags hampered my efforts. I picked up speed and whizzed past those who wandered along in no apparent hurry and avoided others who were on a collision course toward me. When I stumbled into a vendor's rack of clothes, I realized I'd been running all the while.

Parched on the inside and clammy on the outside, I reached Santino's and pushed open the glass door with the last bit of energy I could muster. I removed my sunglasses and spotted Michael sitting at our usual table at the far end of the restaurant. He waved at me and I waved back.

I tore past the water fountain in the entrance, its three porcelain angels in various states of undress.

I dashed past Luigi, the manager, without saying hello and hoped he would forgive my rudeness.

I squeezed by a waitress carrying a tray laden with serving dishes and almost caused her to topple it.

I came up to our table and noticed an icy carafe in the middle of it. I reached for the fluid that would save my life. I filled a glass and gulped down half of it before I realized it was white wine.

"A little hot out there, eh?" Michael grinned.

"Tell me…about it." I plopped into a chair and tried to catch my breath.

"Did reporters chase you all the way here?"

I shook my head. "I waltzed right by them through the parking lot." I took a deep breath. "They'll have to go chase a more worthwhile story."

"No way," Michael said, a twinkle in his eye. "A good reporter sticks with a story until all their questions are answered."

"If they can catch me."

I looked away to see Luigi approaching our table. In broken English, he said to me, "I see picture in the paper. Sorry for your husband loss, Madam." He handed us the menus and told us lunch was on the house.

I waited until Luigi had left with our orders, then whispered to Michael, "He recognized me."

"Why not?" Michael shrugged. "We've had dinner here lots of times. The guy knows our faces as well as his own."

"I meant from my picture in the newspaper. Didn't you read *The Gazette* this morning?" When he answered no, I pulled out the articles I'd tucked in my purse earlier and handed them to him. "Check out the headlines. I think Moreau released the information to the press."

Michael scanned the articles. "So what if he did?"

"He could have warned us ahead of time."

"He doesn't have to let us in on anything." He handed the articles back to me.

"Why not?"

He shrugged. "That's just the way it is. He's the prosecution."

I tucked the clippings away. "I'm surprised Dan hasn't contacted us yet."

"He's probably busy interviewing witnesses."

"Why do I feel as if we're going in circles with this interviewing process?"

"I know what you mean. Last night I kept thinking about the old guy at the gas station in Sainte-Adèle."

"What about him?"

"I think I can jog his memory if I go see him in person."

"Why bother? Jane showed him a photo of you and nothing

clicked."

"Yeah. A picture of me in a dress jacket taken at a book-signing." He shook his head. "It's different when you see someone in person."

"I know where this is going, but I'll ask anyway. What do you have in mind?"

Michael grinned. "Want to drive up to Sainte-Adèle with me? It'll do us good to get away for a while."

I thought about it. Leaving town for a few hours seemed like a good idea. A change of scenery wouldn't hurt either, but... "Do you think it's wise? Dan said we—"

He waved a hand. "He won't miss us. If he needs to reach us, he has my cell number."

"What if Jane calls you?"

"Jane?"

"Aren't you two...close?"

"No. I told you there's nothing between us."

"Not in her mind. I've seen the way she looks at you."

"It's her problem, not mine. Besides, I'd consider it a conflict of interest now that she's working for Dan."

"Did you tell her?"

He nodded. "After we left your place last night, she hinted at coming up to my suite. I made it very clear to her then."

"How did she react?"

"She told me it would be our little secret. We didn't have to tell Dan about it. Like the time Dan and I were working on the drug possession case in Montreal a month ago."

I stared at him. "You were dating her when she was on the opposing legal team?"

He glanced away. "Yes, and I promised myself I'd never lie to my buddy again."

*So that's why Jane didn't say anything in front of Dan either.*

Michael went on. "After I finished my run this morning, I came back to the hotel. Minutes later, Jane knocked at my door. I saw her through the peephole but didn't answer."

"You think that's going to discourage her?"

"Hey, whose side are you on anyway?" He grinned.

"I'm just stating the obvious. She's determined. Maybe after this case is over—"

"Two months with Jane was enough time to find out it wouldn't work."

"Two months? You must have had *something* in common."

"Only one thing. We were fascinated with lawyers who managed to trump the system and keep their guilty clients out of jail. We'd stay up all night rehashing drug possession cases, arguing how we could have changed the verdicts, which cases I should include in my book... What I couldn't handle were her crazy mood swings."

"So she's moody. Who isn't?"

"It's different with Jane. She doesn't discuss personal things. She keeps her emotions bottled up. When things don't go her way, she gets...controlling."

"Controlling?"

"The day you met her at the hotel, she was returning a gold chain I'd left in her suite the night we broke up. But I didn't forget it there. She hid it and used it as a pretense to see me." He shook his head. "Thanks to Dan, she's back in my life again."

"Not in the same way, though."

"True." He smiled and leaned forward. "So how do you feel about driving up to Sainte-Adèle with me this afternoon?"

I had to wash my hair, but I couldn't tell him that without sounding girly. "Tomorrow morning would be better."

"No problem." His smile faded as his eyes darted to something or someone behind me, but he didn't have time to warn me.

# CHAPTER 13

The rich cedar and sweet citrus blend of Pam's perfume gave me a jolt. My heart started to beat against my chest, even though logic told me it wasn't possible—she was dead. I sensed movement beside me as the scent of Prada intensified, invading my space.

Emily removed her sunglasses and peered down at me. "Hi, Megan." Her eyes were sunken and bloodshot from either a good cry or too much booze. Probably both, judging from the smell of alcohol emanating from her.

"Hi," I said, wondering if she'd followed me here.

She smiled at Michael. "I thought you were going back to Toronto on the weekend."

"Something came up." His tone was flat.

"Oh. Is that why you haven't returned my calls since the photo shoot? Seriously, Michael." She kept smiling but her eyes sent out a different message.

"I told you," he said. "I was busy."

Emily smirked. "Yeah, too busy to talk to me but not too busy to have lunch with Megan." She spoke as if I weren't there.

"Megan just lost her husband," Michael said.

"Well, I suffered a loss too." Emily's eyes welled up. "Pam was like a big sister to me. We had lots of stuff in common. Things that we shared deep inside us. Not visible to anyone else." She threw me a side-glance.

Anger rose inside me. "I know exactly what you mean, Emily. I guess it's hard to see the truth when you've been blinded by deception for so long."

"Deception?" She frowned, clueless.

"Don't you have to get back to work, Emily? Spread more lies about anonymous phone calls and—?"

"They weren't lies," she said, raising her voice.

Our waitress stopped by. "One more at your table?"

"No," I said louder than I'd intended.

The waitress nodded and scurried away.

"I heard Bradford gave you the axe." Emily sneered at me.

"It's temporary," I said in response to Michael's questioning look.

"Don't be so sure," she said. "There are lots of changes in the works at Bradford."

I was certain she was referring to her potential takeover of Pam's job. I pretended I didn't know anything about it.

"I'll leave you two alone. I'm sure you have lots to talk about." She turned to leave, then stopped. "Oh...Michael, if you ever come to your senses again, call me. You have my cell number. I'm all about giving certain people a second chance."

I watched her move toward the take-out counter, pay for her order, and walk out the door. I looked at Michael. "What a bitch! How on earth did she know we were here?"

He shrugged. "Probably a coincidence. She certainly can't take no for an answer." He reached for his glass of wine and took a few gulps.

I did the same, but I still needed to vent. "She's jealous of our friendship. No wonder we're in so much trouble with Moreau."

Michael leaned forward. "I owe you an explanation."

"Me? For what?"

"For the way Emily acted just now."

"That's easy. She's obsessed with you and she hates my guts."

"Maybe, but she did leave me messages. I never called her back. It was rude not to, but I had more important things on my mind."

"Of course you did. Your second novel, the story leads you were following—"

"That's not what I meant." His voice was soft. His eyes rested on mine and brought back the butterflies. I didn't know how to respond.

The waitress arrived and set our plates down on the table. "We prepared this dish according to Luigi's special instructions. The pasta is made fresh daily right here in our own kitchen—not from a package." She sounded as if she'd been rehearsing for a TV commercial. "Enjoy your meal."

Her intrusion was well timed. It took the pressure off a conversation I knew was headed in the wrong direction. I dug into my chicken pasta salad and changed the topic to a safer one.

While we ate, I had the sensation of being watched. I wondered if Emily had decided to return for another round of mudslinging, but a glance around the restaurant told me she hadn't. Drawing on logic, I convinced myself it was an illusion brought on by the stress of recent events and concern about future ones. I was nervous about not having a regular paycheck, let alone not having access to Tom's insurance money until the legalities were sorted out. Add Moreau's suspicions about me and...well, it would drive anyone nuts.

I thought I'd talked myself out of it, but minutes later I still couldn't shake off the feeling. "Michael, this is going to sound weird, but I feel as if someone is watching me."

"You're right." He nodded with his chin. "I think the people at the table behind you are talking about you."

I turned around. Five senior patrons seated at a nearby table proved my faculties were intact, though not accurate, when a woman among them waved at me. I recognized her as one of my mother's friends and waved back.

She stood up and walked over. Blue eyes sparkled beneath a puff of white bangs as she smiled at me. "You're Megan, aren't you, dear? Connie's daughter?"

"Yes, I am," I said.

"I'm Alice. Your mother's friend. We go to bingo every Wednesday at the Seniors Club. Do you remember me, dear?"

"Yes. I met you at my mother's apartment once."

"That's right." Her expression grew somber. "I was so shocked to read about your husband in the paper this morning. I called your mother to make sure it was her son-in-law. I'm so sorry for your loss."

"Thank you."

"When I saw you sitting here, I couldn't believe my eyes. I told my friends about you. Anyway, dear, they send along their condolences too." She gave a tilt of her head.

Behind me, two women and two men nodded and waved at me. I waved back.

"We wanted to tell you that you're in our daily prayers," Alice said. "We hope the police catch whoever did this."

"I'm counting on it," I said.

"Take care, dear." She smiled at me and stole a glance at Michael before joining her friends.

"The fact she called my mother to check out the story gives me the creeps," I whispered to Michael.

"Why? She came over to talk to you. It's a good sign."

"How?"

"It means you have public sympathy on your side."

"You think it could help our defense?" I asked, keeping my voice quiet.

"It can't hurt." He leaned forward. "Why are we whispering?"

"I don't want anyone to hear what we're talking about, so can you please keep your voice down?"

"Sure." His eyes darted past me again. "Don't look now, but your fan club is leaving."

I turned around anyway. Alice was leading her friends out the front door. With their departure, I relaxed somewhat.

Yet after coffee had been served, the feeling of being watched lingered on. I brushed it off as a materialization of my guilty feelings about Tom's death this time. I made a mental note to contact Dr. Madison, my shrink, after the murder investigation blew over. I'd visited her in the spring to find out if stress had been a factor in my inability to conceive. She'd determined I was obsessing about it too much—the same conclusion my family doctor had drawn. Small wonder.

After lunch, Michael and I said our goodbyes, and I headed for the subway. The idea I'd have to fend off reporters discouraged me from heading back home. What was the rush anyway? I had no deadlines to meet or bosses to answer to. I was free to do as I pleased for a change. I decided to go shopping—albeit, window-shopping.

*Montréal.* The French aspect, along with the vast choices of stores, restaurants, nightlife, international sports and art events were only some of the reasons this welcoming City of Festivals drew millions of tourists every year. This year was no exception. The sidewalks stirred with camera-toting pedestrians as diverse in multicultural backgrounds as the city's growing cosmopolitan makeup. Attired in shorts to saris, they peered at the displays in store windows along Sainte-Catherine Street, the primary commercial artery of downtown Montreal.

I hadn't shopped in ages—not the shop-till-you-drop kind of shopping. Between work projects, I'd occasionally treat myself to an hour or so of serious spending. But even a whole day wouldn't have been enough. My favorite spots were the complexes, among them les Cours Mont-Royal, le Centre Eaton, and Place Montreal Trust with its indoor waterspout of almost one hundred feet high. I'd visit the fountain often when I was attending university. Waterfalls have a calming effect on me, and this one especially soothed my frayed nerves before final exams.

I continued my trek now along Sainte-Catherine Street. The towering skyline, the upbeat pulse of the city core—I took it all in as a first-time sightseer would. I'd have continued walking above ground, but the humidity was beginning to wear me down again.

The Christ Church Cathedral loomed ahead. Its imposing neo-Gothic architecture was a sharp contrast to the glass veneer of surrounding office towers. Built under this historic site was Les Promenades Cathédrale—a modern shopping center and the ideal place to escape from the muggy heat. I hadn't attended church since I'd graduated from high school, but the fact the mall was built under a sacred structure suddenly appealed to me. I felt protected. I had to maneuver crowds of people to get there. Only this time I fell into pace with those who walked ahead of me.

Inside the mall, I eagerly checked out the end-of-season sales. Montreal had a certain fashion sense—*sens du style*—not seen in other urban areas, and frequent sales were part of the experience customers enjoyed. Despite the fact I was on a tight budget, I tried on shoes at Aldo and skirts, tops, and pants at the Le Château, Tristan, and Liz Claiborne. As fate would have it, nothing fit. Sometimes it's the event of shopping that matters, not the purchases.

My luck changed when I walked into the Linen Chest. I found a comfy set of Egyptian cotton sheets on sale. Though the cost was beyond what I'd usually paid for sheets, this set had an 800-thread count. I thought about it for all of two seconds, then pulled out my credit card. If I had to sleep alone from now on, it might as well be in luxury.

Now that I'd tasted the power of a good purchase, I was tempted to extend my shopping spree. The underground mall was interconnected to thousands of other retail outlets through a twenty-mile Underground Pedestrian Network. Mega opportunities for bargains.

I'd just purchased a bag of chocolate-covered almonds when Michael suddenly popped into my mind. What if he had news and was trying to reach me? How could anyone reach me? I had no cell phone. I decided to head back home. There would be other days and other ways to spend my money.

*Or Tom's money?*

I was still waiting for the legalities to be sorted out. It could be days, maybe weeks, before I'd have access to Tom's bank accounts and the proceeds from his insurance policy. I prayed it would be sooner rather than later. Although Kayla's promise of a speedy check was reassuring, Bradford Publishing delivered their payments on a sixty-day cycle. I could make cold calls and try to get new clients, but the publicity about the murders might make them think twice about dealing with me. I could sell my wedding ring and diamond earrings—the only expensive jewelry I owned...

An overwhelming feeling suddenly washed over me. I needed to get out of the underground mall. I needed fresh air.

When I surfaced at the street level, the humidity hit me harder than before. So much for spending time in a cool underground mall.

But something else had returned—the same eerie feeling I'd had earlier.

Someone was watching me.

I went into a cold sweat. I dug into my purse for my sunglasses and put them on. The dark amber shades provided a sense of security, yet I couldn't shake off the sensation I was being watched. I stopped in front of a store window and pretended to check out the clothes display while I studied the reflection of people passing behind me. A man in a suit. A young woman holding a child by the hand. That McGill University was located close by explained the stream of students wearing the institution's trademark T-shirts or sporting a knapsack with the McGill insignia on it. More suits went by. More knapsacks. Nothing out of the ordinary.

I concluded there was only one reason for my frame of mind: I was on the verge of paranoia. I headed for the nearest subway station back home.

While I was waiting for a pedestrian traffic light to change to green, a young man in a red T-shirt, baggy shorts, and a backpack walked up to my right. The volume on his iPod was so loud that I could hear the music blasting from it. I glanced up at him and wondered what percentage of his hearing he'd lost up to now. He met my gaze with a smile. I turned away. It was clear he'd mistaken me for a much younger woman.

More people gathered behind me, adding their personal choice of fragrances to the less aromatic ones emanating from the street traffic. A man's spicy after-shave. A flowery perfume. Someone else had forgotten to use underarm deodorant or needed to use a stronger brand on hot, muggy days.

I glanced up at the traffic light.

A powerful push propelled me off my feet!

I plunged forward and hit the pavement.

Brakes screeched. Dust hit my face, filled my lungs.

A firm grip on my arm yanked me up.

I struggled to my feet and caught my breath. I looked up into the terrified eyes of the iPod guy.

"Are you okay?" he asked, releasing his tight grip on me.

"I...I think so." I glanced around and got my bearings. Crowds of people were crossing the intersection from both sides of the street, but aside from my rescuer, any witnesses of my near-fatal experience had moved on. "Thanks for pulling me out of there." I gestured toward the street and winced as a sharp pain ran along my left shoulder. I looked down to see a bloody gash on my upper arm.

"Ah, it was nothing." He blushed and tugged on his T-shirt. White letters spelled out McGill University.

"Did you see who pushed me?" I asked.

"Huh? I thought you slipped or something." He looked down at the curb. "Hey!" He bent over to retrieve my sunglasses and handed them to me. "These yours?"

"Yes. Thanks." I dropped them into the shopping bag I was still clutching by some miracle, then adjusted my purse over my right shoulder and extended my hand. "Thanks again."

He stepped back, waved his hands. "It's no big deal, lady. Gotta go. Late for class." He disappeared into the crowd.

I'd scared him off. Small wonder. Why would he shake hands with a stranger—an older woman at that? I attributed it to a "Mrs. Robinson" moment of sorts and put my sunglasses back on.


I returned to my apartment, still debating whether or not I was losing my mind. Had I slipped off the sidewalk because of my own carelessness as the iPod guy had claimed, or had someone pushed me into the traffic on purpose?

I'd heard of similar "accidents" occurring in *Le Metro*. Whether a pedestrian had been pushed or had jumped in front of a speeding train of their own free will, the result was always the same: it had happened so fast that no one had seen anything. Subway authorities would evacuate the station and shut down the system along that segment of the line while the police investigated the incident and maintenance crews cleaned up the mess. Commuters who knew better had adopted the habit of standing along the back of the platform to avoid being pushed in front of a subway car as it sped into the station.

The outcome of my experience paled in comparison, thanks to the iPod guy's swift reaction. I weighed the possibility he might have shoved me into the street but dismissed it. It would have proved too tricky to maneuver a push from where he was standing beside me. I was convinced the thrust had come from behind.

I stepped into the shower and let the cool water from the jet stream massage my aching shoulder and bruised arm—confirmation of my flying leap off the curb. I switched the shower setting to a pulsating spray and slowly turned around. The stream hit the middle of my back, and I sensed a soreness there that I hadn't noticed before. I needed no additional proof. Someone had shoved me from behind. And hard at that.

I reached for the soap on the ledge. Its cranberry aroma reminded me of the scented candles my parents used to light at Christmas when I was a kid. My mother would spend days preparing food and shining the cutlery for guests. Plates of veal cutlets, stuffed squid, breaded smelts, lasagna, and bottles of Chianti were spread out on a dining room table that seated eight but was stretched to twelve for such occasions. A smaller table for my young cousins and me was set up close at hand. For dessert, my mother served homemade Tiramisu, almond biscotti, date and nut cake, cappuccino, Irish Whiskey Pie, and Irish coffee. The last two items were offered to please the other half of the family, my mother would say. Yet it was no secret how much my father's relatives anticipated a taste of "Little Italy" every Christmas. The best part of dinner was my Uncle Joe's recounting of humorous tales we never grew tired of hearing, over and over each year. The celebration extended into the late night hours for the older folks, but I'd sneak away with my cousins and fall asleep, exhausted yet content, on top of the overcoats the guests had piled on my parents' bed.

That same warm, fuzzy sense of belonging and security surged back now, providing a respite from the craziness that had pursued me since the weekend. I smiled for no particular reason but the memory of those family occasions that had formed an intrinsic part of my upbringing. Family values, as my mother would say.

The feel-good mood lingered as I stepped out of the shower and put on a thick terry robe and slippers. Mmm...what could be better?

Chocolate almonds, of course. I was about to dig into my purse for the tiny supply I'd bought downtown earlier when I remembered the larger package of almonds Michael had brought back from the video store. It lay on the living room table. I tore it open and chewed on a couple of plump almonds while I prepared a cup of warm milk—the perfect combination soother for frayed nerves. Then I called Michael and told him about the incident.

It was a big mistake.

The panic in his voice canceled my efforts at staying calm. "What? Why didn't you call me sooner?"

I wiped my sweaty palms along my terry robe and tried to keep my voice steady. "I'm fine. Just a few scratches."

"Killing Tom wasn't enough. Now the killer wants you out of the way too."

I opted for another theory. "Maybe it was a random thing—like some psycho shoving a person in front of a car. It does happen, you know."

"My gut tells me otherwise."

I was afraid of that.

He let out a deep breath. "It's too damn dangerous for you to leave the house alone."

"For heaven's sake, Michael! Do you expect me to live in a cage the rest of my life?"

"No, but—"

"I'm a big girl. I can take care of myself, you know."

"Really? Is that why people keep dropping dead all around you? Is that why someone shoves you into the traffic?"

There was a long, uncomfortable pause.

"I'm sorry," he said. "I was out of line. It's just that I—"

"Don't say it."

"Say what?"

"That you're worried about me."

More silence. "Did you call the police?"

"What for?"

"To ask for protection."

"Why bother?"

"It's your right."

"Fat chance! Moreau would say I was turning myself into a victim to avoid being labeled a murder suspect."

Another pause. "You realize your attacker could have followed you from Santino's. Damn it! I shouldn't have asked you to meet me there." From the anxiety in his voice, I visualized the muscles pulsating along his jawline.

"Listen to me, Michael. I made that decision. Now I have to live with it."

"I should have driven you back home, made sure you were—"

"I already told you. I don't need a babysitter."

"You have to understand something. Until they find this guy, you're a sitting target."

He was right. Working as a ghostwriter had given me anonymity and a sense of security I'd taken for granted. Now the double murders and the ensuing publicity they'd generated had exposed me, if not my attempts at clearing my name.

I gave Michael's comment more thought. "As bad as it might seem, there's a positive side to what happened."

"Yeah? Like what?"

"I flushed out Tom's murderer."

"And you almost got killed in the process."

"Don't you see? It doesn't matter what I do or where I go."

"What are you saying?"

"Nothing's going to change the fact that someone wants me out of the way, and I don't know who or why."

# CHAPTER 14

I opened my door to Michael at eight o'clock Wednesday morning. Dark glasses. A white T-shirt that showed off the deep tan he'd soaked up from jogging outdoors every day. Charcoal cargo shorts. The butterflies in my stomach took flight again.

"Good thing you wore shorts," he said, smiling. "It's hot out there. Are you ready to go?"

"Come in for a sec." I waved him in and closed the door behind him. "What if Dan or Moreau tries to reach us? I don't want them to think we did something stupid like skip town." My tone was harder than I'd intended.

He removed his sunglasses. "No problem. I called Dan later last night and told him we were going to Sainte-Adèle this morning. I explained it might be the only chance I had to prove my alibi."

"*Our* alibi."

"Right." His gaze held mine. "I told him about your stalker too."

"You didn't."

"He's your lawyer. He should know these things."

"That's not what I meant. I'd have called him myself, but I wasn't in the mood to talk about it last night. It gave me the creeps just thinking about what happened yesterday."

I was too embarrassed to tell him that I'd slept with the lights on all night, that I'd cradled a kitchen chair under the front door handle as an extra safeguard, and that I'd slept with a carving knife under my pillow—all for the sake of keeping my sanity intact.

Michael went on. "I asked Dan if he knew why Moreau had

released the story to the media yesterday."

"What did he say?"

"That it was possible Moreau had consulted a shrink for an opinion. The shrink had probably said Tom and Pam hadn't taken the cyanide voluntarily. They'd tried to save themselves. So Moreau labeled their deaths as murders and fed the story to the media."

"Why ask a shrink? Any idiot could have reached the same conclusion from analyzing the scene."

"For a cop, there's no better backing than an expert's statement, whether it's right or wrong. Plain crazy, isn't it?" He paused. "I haven't told you the real reason I wanted to go to Sainte-Adèle."

"So tell me."

"On one condition." He grinned.

"What?"

"The information-sharing will fall under our ongoing confidentiality agreement if you promise to help me with my next book."

"But I don't work for Bradford anymore."

"Who said anything about Bradford?"

"Oh...okay, I promise."

"I have a lead. It has to do with an illegal drug ring in the Laurentians. That's the other reason I wanted to catch up with the old guy at the gas station again."

"What do you mean?"

"He's my informant. His name is Willie."

"Oh. And why are you asking me to go along again?"

"My French is bad but his English is worse. I need an interpreter. Someone I can trust." He paused. "There's more. Willie's harmless, but the scumbags who stop there for gas aren't. What Willie overheard could have fatal consequences for him if his sources find out he's an informer. I doubt the gangs have the place under surveillance, but if we showed up there as a couple, it wouldn't invite suspicion. Are you still okay to do this?"

I gave it some thought. I'd ghostwritten articles for former government officials who'd blown the whistle on high-level scandals and fraud. I'd worked on memoirs about child abuse and rape. None had come close to Michael's chilling encounters with street-wise informers who rarely showed their faces in the light of day.

"If it means you can prove your alibi, I'll go with you." I picked up my purse from the coffee table. "About Willie, what if he told Jane he didn't remember you because he didn't want to blow his cover?"

"Exactly why I want to see him in person."

I dug the house keys out of my purse. "And what if he took the video tape from the store and hid it to protect you, then lied about a glitch in the system?" I led Michael out the door and locked it behind us.

"Right again. Let's go find out."

We took the elevator down and walked out the rear exit of the condo building into the parking lot. Sated by Moreau's recent handout, the reporters had abandoned their surveillance of the premises and were nowhere in sight.

Regardless, I didn't let my guard down because a more challenging presence could surface at any moment: the killer. My eyes swept across the lot. Except for an older couple getting into their car, no one else was around.

Michael's cell phone rang. He took the call. "Hi, Jane... Tonight? No, I can't. I'm busy. I don't know. Okay. Bye." He hung up and mumbled, "Some people never know when to quit."

"Problem?" I asked.

"Nothing I can't handle." He smiled at me.

It was going to be another scorcher of a day. The sun had already heated up Michael's Mustang Coupe. Even after he'd opened the doors to air out the car, the black leather seats remained hot to the touch. He reached for two sports magazines in the back seat and handed me one. I got the message and placed it under my bare thighs.

The northwestward itinerary from Montreal to the Laurentians followed Highways 15 and 117 for the most part, making the drive less complicated. The scenery was easy on the eyes too, what with fifty miles of tall trees and wide open spaces dotted with farms and villages that time seemed to have forgotten. I might have been doing Michael a favor, but I actually looked forward to the relaxing forty-five-minute drive to Sainte-Adèle. Anything to take my mind off Moreau and my money problems.

Michael turned on the radio. An old Bruce Springsteen tune came on. "I found this cool station in Montreal," he said. "It plays music from the 60s and 70s. Thanks to my father, I grew up listening to rock bands like Led Zeppelin and Pink Floyd. I got hooked on the stuff." He chuckled. "I listen to it whenever I'm writing. It inspires me."

"My parents were low-key," I said. "The Beatles, Bee Gees, Stevie Wonder—"

"I could change the station if you—"

"No, it's okay. It covers the spectrum."

Michael nodded, kept his eyes on the road ahead. "When I lived in Montreal, I'd come up to Sainte-Adèle in the winter with a bunch of guys. We did some skiing, checked out the restaurants and bars, the girls." He smiled.

"Tom and I went there twice the first year we were married."

"Really?" He glanced at me as if he were surprised I'd divulged a detail about my married life. Or maybe he was surprised I'd ever left the confines of Montreal—city girl that I was.

"It was in September. We wanted to see the leaves change to their fall colors. All those reds, yellows, and oranges spread over the mountains. It takes your breath away."

"Yes, but it hides the ugliness underneath." He clenched his jaw.

"What do you mean?"

"Rumor has it a secret lab manufactures drugs in the area. That's over and above other activities linked to criminal groups working there."

"It's hard to imagine that kind of thing going on here. It's so scenic and touristy."

"All the better. Who'd suspect it, right?"

"I'm assuming Willie does."

He nodded. "The guy's practically invisible to them."

"How?"

"The dealers brag about their exploits in front of him. They think he's too scared to talk. In fact, Willie said he had something important to tell me about a drug dealer in this area. That's why it's critical I see him today."

"I read a newspaper article about a recent drug arrest here. Did you write that piece?"

He gave me a brief smile. "There are lots more where that came from."

We approached the outskirts of Sainte-Adèle, then took the next exit off the highway and drove five miles further to Saint-Gustave. Typical of small towns located in the Québec countryside, it had century-old homes with cone-shaped roofs, a church with a silver spire, a bank, a school, and a Ma and Pa store with hand-written signs displayed in the window. Many of the houses had narrow porches painted white. The vinyl siding was blue, pink, or red. The structures were built close to one another, as if to denote a community spirit based on sharing and support. Picturesque maybe, but I couldn't see myself living in such a restricted setting.

The main street of Saint-Gustave spanned only three miles. It came to an abrupt end at a patch of grass and tall trees just before the town limits. If I hadn't turned my head to the right, I'd have missed the gas station and adjoining *dépanneur*, or convenience store.

"We're here," Michael said. He pulled into the parking area and turned off the engine. He retrieved his camera from the glove compartment. After he'd taken two photos of the premises, we went inside.

A young man in a striped shirt stood behind the counter, flipping through a newspaper. He looked up at us as we approached. *"Puis-je vous aider?"*

*"Oui, bonjour,"* Michael said with a smile, then nudged me with a side-glance.

*"Nous essayons de contacter un vieux monsieur qui travaillait ici la semaine dernière,"* I said, asking about the old gentleman who worked here last week. *"Il s'appelle Willie."*

The clerk's eyes went wide and he shook his head. *"Willie ne travaille plus ici."*

"He said Willie doesn't work here any more," I said, translating for Michael.

"Ask him where he lives," Michael said to me.

"I cannot tell this," the clerk said, making it clear he understood English.

"Please," I said. "We need to talk to him. It's important. Life and death."

He studied me as if he were deciding if he should trust me or not. "Fire last night. Willie house burn."

"Is Willie okay?" Michael asked.

The clerk shrugged and shook his head. "I do not know."

"Where's Willie's house?"

Another shrug.

Michael took out a twenty-dollar bill and slapped it on the counter.

The clerk snatched it. "Two miles that way." He gestured in the opposite direction from town.

"I don't have a good feeling about this," Michael said as we got back in the car.

Minutes later, we neared a clearing in the road and saw a house that had been ravaged by fire. Michael turned onto the asphalt driveway in front of the house but couldn't drive all the way up because debris blocked the path. We sat in silence gaping at the charred remains of the house.

I was certain this house had been built in the 1930s because I'd ghostwritten a book about rural homes in Québec and dug up the photos for it too. I looked upward. A large section of the shingled roof on the two-story Canadian-style home had caved in. It was hard to determine whether the shingles had been black originally or whether the fire had covered them with soot. Flames had engulfed the house all around and made short work of the exterior frame and any insulation behind it. There was nothing left to salvage but memories. The fire had extended to a cluster of trees behind the house, though it looked as if firefighters had extinguished it before it did more damage.

I looked out to the right. An adjacent bungalow more than a hundred feet away hadn't suffered any damage except for a few spots of soot. Judging from the vinyl siding, the trim around the windows, and the interlocking stone driveway, I estimated the split-level home had been built in the last decade.

Two women stood chatting in front of the house and glanced in our direction.

"Just to be sure, I'll go ask them if the house is Willie's," I said to Michael.

I stepped out. The scent of burnt wood hit me, as well as another odor—burnt plastic. As I walked across the lawn toward the women, I tried to avoid the charred fragments and soot on the ground but couldn't. I realized too late I'd have to trash my running shoes.

The women interrupted their talk and gawked at me.

*"Bonjour,"* I greeted them.

"Bonjour." The woman wearing a pair of oversized sunglasses smiled at me.

*"Savez-vous qui demeurait ici?"* I asked if they knew who lived here.

*"William Perron,"* the other woman said, her straw hat shading a face that had already had too many years of exposure to the sun. *"La cigarette, c'est toujours un problème."* She motioned with her fingers as if she were taking a puff on a cigarette. *"Pauvre Willie."*

*"Est-ce qu'il est mort?"* I asked if Willie was dead.

Both women shrugged and said they didn't know for sure. The fire had occurred late last night and it had been difficult to see what was happening, although they did notice that forensics officers transported something bulky from the house to a truck.

I asked them if Willie had lived alone.

They said yes, but his son visited often.

I asked if Willie had owned a dog or other pet.

They said no.

I thanked them and got back in the car.

"So much for my witness," Michael said after I'd briefed him.

"We don't know for sure that it was Willie's body," I said. "It could have been his son."

"Maybe, but if Willie's not dead, he's in hiding. He won't surface until things cool down. Either way, I'm back to square one. No alibi.

No videotape. No lead for my story. It's just plain crazy." He checked to see if the road behind us was clear, then backed up and drove away.

"Willie was a smoker," I said. "Maybe the fire was an accident."

"Not a chance. It's too much of a coincidence."

"You think someone found out Willie was your informant and killed him—or tried to?"

"Maybe."

"What if they come after you next?" The thought made my stomach churn.

"Give it time. I haven't published anything that terrible about them yet." He smiled.

"How reassuring," I said, tongue-in-cheek. "As if you don't have enough to worry about."

"Look who's talking? I'm not the one being stalked."

"*Touché.*"

He surveyed the road ahead. "We're going to hit the highway back home soon. I thought we'd stop to get something to eat first. Are you hungry?"

Spending too much time riding around in a car made me queasy, but I didn't want to complain. I'd agreed to come along, so this was my karma. "Not really, but we can stop if you want to."

"How about that diner up ahead?"

"Okay."

We entered a 1940s diner painted silver with orange trim around the windows. Food would only have added to my queasiness, so I opted for a ginger ale instead. Michael paid cash for our orders, slipped the receipt into his pocket, and carried the tray to a booth by the window.

With amusement outweighing repulsion, I watched as he folded down the paper around his hamburger and took a bite. No matter how dire the circumstances, one thing about him remained predictable: his appetite.

I was glad when Michael accepted my invitation to come upstairs on our return from Sainte-Adèle. I couldn't bear waiting alone for news from Dan.

Half an hour later, a knock sounded at my door. I peered through the peephole and was astonished to see Moreau looking back at me. Duchaine was at his side.

I opened the door. "Detective Moreau. This is a surprise."

"Madame Scott." He nodded. "Another tenant let us into the building," he said, as if he needed to explain why he hadn't buzzed me in advance. "May we come in?"

I didn't know what to say. He'd brought Duchaine along—not a good sign. If I didn't let him in, he'd think I had something to hide.

I heard myself say yes before I realized what was happening.

# CHAPTER 15

The detective did nothing to hide his curiosity when he saw Michael sitting on my sofa. "Monsieur Elliott, how convenient that you are here once again." He switched his gaze to me. "We would like to search your home. May we?"

"I suppose so." I looked at Michael. He'd already whipped out his cell phone. My guess was that he was calling Dan.

I glanced over my shoulder to see Duchaine snap on thin latex gloves. A word from Moreau sent him down the hall to begin his search. I hoped I wouldn't have to work too hard to put things back in order afterward.

What was Duchaine looking for exactly? Hard to tell. I later discovered he'd checked out the bathroom cabinets, kitchen cupboards, bookshelves, laundry basket, and ice cube containers. He'd even emptied the paper clip dispenser on my desk, so he must have been looking for a teensy, tiny piece of evidence.

In the meantime, Moreau stood in the hallway and in plain view of the living room where Michael and I sat next to each other on the sofa. I wondered about the detective's command post right by the door. Was he concerned that we might bolt?

"Dan's coming over," Michael whispered to me.

"You didn't have to call him," I whispered back. "They won't find anything incriminating here."

"It's for your protection."

"You seem to be doing a lot of that lately."

"What?"

"Looking out for me."

"Somebody has to."

I read more than friendship in his eyes and looked away.

Maybe our whispering stirred Moreau's interest. Or maybe he was reassured we wouldn't make a run for it. Whatever the reason, he left his post and sat down on the other sofa. Without so much as a glance in our direction, he began to scan the pages of his notebook.

For lack of anything better to do—and perhaps because my respect for the man was dwindling with each successive encounter—I studied him with a critical eye. I decided that his tweed jacket—the same one he wore the first time we met—would be outlawed in any corporate boardroom, today or even ten years back. Ditto for those flashy ties, no doubt inherited from a retired circus clown. His bowed head revealed twenty-six strands of mousy-brown hair flipped over from right to left, edging their way down his forehead. Once in a while, he'd set these strands back in place with a pass of the hand, then pat them down onto an egg-shaped dome that nature had deserted years ago.

I immediately recalled the old green couch in the living room of my grandmother's home. As kids, my cousin and I would pull out loose fibers from the back of the couch when no one was watching. We made a game out of it. By the time our mothers appeared from the kitchen to say the visit was over, whoever had the bigger ball of "yarn" was the winner. Sadly, Grandma got rid of the couch before we could finish it off. She bought a suede one to replace it, which brought our game to an end.

Minutes later, the doorbell rang. I made a move to get up, but the detective was already on his feet. He pressed the buzzer, then opened the door and remained at his former post.

Dan breezed through the door. "Detective." He gave Moreau a polite nod and hurried up to Michael and me. "Why did you let them in? They didn't have a search warrant." He yanked out a hankie from his suit and mopped his brow, then sat down.

"I have nothing to hide," I said, loud enough for Moreau to hear. "If they want to waste their—"

"Detective Moreau." Duchaine walked up to him with an evidence bag in hand. They conferred in muted tones, but it was obvious from the detective's raised eyebrows that Duchaine had located an item of significance.

Holding what appeared to be a slip of white paper inside the transparent bag, Moreau approached us. "Madame Scott, can you explain how you came to have this item in your possession?" He flipped the bag around so I could see its contents.

I'd long forgotten about the photo of Pam and Tom sitting outdoors at Pueblo's and the envelope it had arrived in with the fake Sunny Watering Hole return address. I'd tucked them in the top drawer of my dresser beneath my underwear and planned to show it to Tom when he returned from a trip. But as often happens when life gets hectic, I'd forgotten all about it.

The detective was waiting for me to answer.

"One of Tom's friends sent me the photo as a joke," I said.

The detective squinted. "A joke?"

I realized my explanation sounded out of place in the aftermath of the murders. I tried to clarify it. "Tom and his friends used to play tricks on one another. I assumed one of them sent me this photo to get back at Tom for a birthday joke he'd played on him. I meant to show it to Tom, but I forgot about it."

"What is the name of the person who sent it?"

"I don't know. If you check the envelope, you'll see that it has a phony return address. That was part of the joke too."

Dan stood up. "May I see it?"

The detective handed him the plastic bag, then gazed at me. "It appears as though someone took this photo through the window of a car. Correct, Madame Scott?"

I wasn't going to fall for his trap. I knew he expected me to admit I'd taken the picture. "I wouldn't know."

"Detective, anyone could have taken this picture," Dan said.

Moreau squinted, as if he were trying to come up with another question, one I might trip over in my haste to answer. "Madame Scott, can you tell me the names of the people your husband socialized with."

I mentioned Peter, Greg, and other BOTCOR marketing staff I'd met at company events. "He socialized with clients too, but I don't know their names."

Moreau nodded. "*Très bien.* Very well."

The topic died on his lips, but his expression revealed a lot more. I read contempt in his eyes. Or was it pity? Maybe he was wondering—as I was now—whether Tom had used his meetings with clients as an excuse to see Pam or other women. Too bad I hadn't come across Tom's appointment book earlier. Fate might have opened my eyes sooner.

Dan pursued his argument about the photo. "No purpose in exploiting this photo," he said, handing it back to the detective. "It can only be construed as circumstantial evidence."

"It is the envelope that interests me more, Monsieur Cummings."

Duchaine reappeared in the hallway. "Detective Moreau." He held a white garbage bag in a gloved hand.

I stared at him, wondering what he'd found so interesting about the garbage bag I kept under the kitchen sink.

Moreau went up to him and peered inside the bag. "Remove the item."

The officer pulled out a white shirt. It had a red stain on the collar.

"Can you explain this, Madame Scott?" Moreau pointed to the shirt.

From where I was sitting, it looked like tomato sauce or blood. I walked over to get a better look. It was lipstick...a familiar shade of red lipstick...Pam's.

"It's Tom's shirt," I said, not offering up any more details.

Moreau turned to Duchaine. "Where did you find it?"

"Behind the dryer in the laundry room," he said.

Moreau eyed me, waiting.

"I don't know how it got there," I said.

"Perhaps you hid it there," Moreau said.

"I did no such thing."

"Is it your lipstick on the shirt, Madame Scott?"

Dan cut in before I could answer. "Detective, you have no right to interrogate my client. Moreover, the shirt is hardly incriminating evidence regarding the murders."

"We shall see." Moreau addressed Duchaine. "Bag it and process it for DNA." He looked at Michael. "We would like to search your hotel suite next, Monsieur Elliott."

Dan jumped in. "Michael, I must counsel you—"

"Be my guest," Michael said to Moreau. He stood up. "I'm fed up with your innuendos. Let's get it over with."

Half an hour later, the search in my apartment came to an end. Nothing else surfaced that had the potential to incriminate me. Small wonder.

The detectives waited by the front door with Dan and Michael while I poked around in my purse for the house keys. I didn't believe in trends when it came to purse size. I only bought purses that could hold everything I needed them to hold. Because I put their size to good use, they were hard on the shoulder but so much more practical than those miniature purses that held nothing more than a lipstick and a mirror. The only disadvantage to a large purse was trying to find something at the bottom of it.

"Madame Scott, may I have your handbag, please?"

"Excuse me?" I asked, thinking I'd misunderstood the detective.

He pointed to my purse. "Your handbag. I would like to search it. May I have it, please?"

I glanced at Dan. He nodded yes.

"*Merci.*" The detective strode into the living room, holding my purse with both hands as if it contained loose eggs. He placed it on the coffee table and pulled on a pair of latex gloves.

I joined him, my curiosity changing to annoyance as he proceeded to remove the items from my purse, one by one, as if he were recording the contents in his mind. Out came a pair of sunglasses, a hairbrush, an agenda, a wallet, two pens, a notepad, a bag of chocolate almonds, a set of keys, a lipstick, two tampons, facial tissues, and a box of adhesive bandages—all lined up on the table like products displayed in a department store counter. I was mortified and didn't dare glance over my shoulder at the other three men.

When Moreau opened the box of bandages, I found an outlet for my gripe. "You won't find any incriminating evidence in there,

Detective. Paper cuts happen a lot in my line of work but not murder."

Michael chuckled.

The detective ignored my sarcasm. He hung onto my agenda, put everything else back into my purse, one by one, and handed it to me. "Thank you. I will keep your agenda for now, if you do not mind."

*Did I have a choice?*

"Suit yourself," I said, wondering why he'd want to labor through minutiae like meeting times, project deadlines, doctor appointments, and other mundane notations I'd inscribed in it. Why should I care anyway? It was his loss of time, not mine.

Then I remembered another entry in my agenda: the Pineview address and notes I'd scribbled from memory after Louise's initial call. I hadn't scratched them out, nor had I entered new details to indicate Tom was going to Granite Ridge instead. It seemed useless at the time.

A cold sweat rolled over me. I recalled Dan's concern about the similarity in mileage to Pineview and to Granite Ridge. The detective might get a false impression from my Pineview notes. A gut feeling told me he wouldn't hesitate to pounce on them. He'd try to use them as evidence against me. I prayed my slip-up would go unnoticed.


Our entourage rode in an unmarked car to the Elegance Hotel and to what I expected would be a pointless search of Michael's suite. I was eager to see the look of frustration on Moreau's face when his efforts turned up empty. His ludicrous charade against us would come to an end—once and for all.

People stared and heads turned as we crossed the lobby of the Elegance. I wasn't surprised, what with four men accompanying me—two of them with police badges around their necks. One of the desk clerks greeted Michael by name and nodded at me as we whisked by. I figured he'd recognized me from previous visits.

Upstairs in Michael's suite, Dan sat in one of the magenta

armchairs and studied his notes. Michael and I shared the royal blue sofa near the entrance and within Moreau's line of sight. Breaking from his earlier decision to stand guard by the front door, the detective settled on the matching purple sofa along the opposite wall.

Moreau leafed through the pages of my agenda at a slow, deliberate pace. Once in a while, he'd stop and frown in an attempt to decipher my scribbles and the abbreviations I used in my line of work. Sooner or later he'd relent and ask me to come over and explain a notation.

At one point, he asked me to elaborate on CMYK, an abbreviation I'd entered on the twelfth of July. I'd begun to write out the abbreviation in full during one of my anal-retentive moments but stopped after the first word: cyan.

"Cyan is a term used in the printing business," I said to him. "I wrote it down in case a co-worker might ask me about a color correction later."

"It sounds to me like an abbreviation for cyanide." He looked up at me.

Dan was at my side in two strides. He peered down at the abbreviation. "An unfair assumption, Detective. The abbreviation CMYK is widely used in the printing business."

"I am merely pointing out the obvious, Monsieur Cummings."

Duchaine had been rummaging through the front closet and now called out, "Detective Moreau, I have something."

The detective set aside my agenda and scurried over.

Dan took off right behind him.

Michael bounded up from the sofa and joined them.

I rushed over, fear rising inside me.

Duchaine was clutching Michael's leather jacket in a gloved hand. In his other gloved hand, he held out a small plastic container. It had a white label affixed to it.

At first I thought it was a bottle of pills, but as I approached, the bold black letters on the label told a different and more ominous story: CYANIDE.

Michael's eyes met mine. I watched in horror as expressions of shock and confusion flashed across his face.

"Is this your jacket, Monsieur Elliott?" Moreau asked, pulling on a pair of latex gloves.

Michael stared at the jacket and nodded as if in a stupor. "Yes." He gazed at me again. In the next instant, the astonishment on his face changed into something else—suspicion.

*Did he think I'd planted the cyanide in his jacket?*

Unable to move or speak, I remained rooted where I was standing, a barrage of questions pounding my brain as I tried to make sense of this recent discovery.

Dan dabbed at his forehead with a hankie. "Michael, don't say another word. You neither, Megan."

Moreau addressed Duchaine. "Hand me the jacket. Place the container in a bag for analysis—gently."

Duchaine pulled out an evidence bag, placed the container in it, and sealed the edge shut.

"Bag the jacket as evidence too," the detective said, handing it back to Duchaine. He turned to Michael and me and read us our rights. "You will come to the police station for questioning. Monsieur Cummings, you are invited to come along."

"Do I continue the search, Lieutenant?" Duchaine asked him.

"Yes. Who knows what else we might find. But first, call two cruisers for transport."

# CHAPTER 16

I didn't have a moment to think.

Everything moved so fast after Duchaine discovered the cyanide. Word of the police presence at the Elegance Hotel must have leaked out earlier to the media because reporters and photographers were waiting outside. With a population of almost four million, Greater Montreal had its fair share of crime, but the chance to interview suspects implicated in a double murder—and one linked to cyanide at that—was a rare occurrence anywhere. The event was guaranteed to garner media interest, if not a bonus payout, for any leads to the story.

I suspected that one of the desk clerks had called the press—maybe the same one who'd said hello to Michael earlier. He might have recognized me and made the link to my photo in the newspaper article about the murders. Just a theory, but it would explain how the reporters happened to be in the right place at the right time.

As police officers led us out of the hotel, I wished I'd put on my sunglasses beforehand. It was media frenzy out there. A fringe of bystanders had joined in to see what it was all about, adding to the buzz.

The surge of microphones and cameras gravitating toward us prevented us from advancing more than a few steps at a time toward two police cruisers parked in front. Michael and I followed Dan's advice and didn't say a word in response to reporters' questions. Dan uttered a final "no comment" before he edged his way out and hailed a taxi.

All of a sudden, Duchaine stood like a wall in front of us, his head above the crowd. Reminiscent of Moses parting the waters, he cleared a path for us through the crowd. A stocky officer with a micro haircut guided me into the back seat of a cruiser. Michael, Moreau, and a second officer drove off ahead of us in the other one.

Minutes later, the cruiser made its way down Parthenais Street and into the underground parking of the QPP headquarters—the same building that housed the morgue where I'd last seen Tom. How ironic that I'd return here days later as a suspect in his murder.

The officer escorted me out of the car and into the elevator. On the ride up, I kept thinking about Michael and the confused look on his face when Duchaine had dug the cyanide out of his leather jacket. I imagined what had gone through his mind at that moment— probably the same mixed messages that had flashed through mine.

The thick soles of the officer's shoes squeaked as we moved along a corridor and past an open area where the investigators' desks were stationed. The scent of spilled coffee on a burner and a concoction of take-out food hung in the air. A wave of nausea hit me. Just a case of the jitters, I thought, and swallowed hard.

I let my gaze wander. No sign of Michael, Dan, or Moreau. Three closed doors on my right. They were probably sitting in a room behind one of them.

The officer opened the door to Interrogation Room 1 and ushered me in. "Have a seat. Detective Moreau will be in soon." He shut the door behind me.

A musty smell permeated the air. The room held a wood table with too many scratches to count and four equally bruised chairs. I pulled out a chair and sat down. Across from me, cut into a wall that begged for a paint job, was a two-way mirror. I had the feeling that eyes were peering back at me, observing me, anticipating that somehow I'd betray my guilt. To say that I'd ever felt as isolated and exposed would be an understatement.

I shook off the feeling and swung my attention to the only other object in the room—an oversized clock hanging on the wall to my right, its thin red hand ticking away the seconds. One. By. One. Each passing moment reinforced the likelihood that I might be spending my thirty-first birthday—and decades more—in jail.

I closed my eyes and tried to block out my surroundings, but I couldn't stop the awful scenes from playing over and over in my mind:

The police finding the cyanide in Michael's hotel suite.

The stunned expression on Michael's face.

The humiliation of walking out of the hotel under police escort, cameras zooming in on me, microphones shoved in my face.

More humiliation as I got into the back seat of the police cruiser, photographers aiming their lenses at me through the windows.

I shuddered. Nothing made sense anymore. My non-threatening lifestyle had transformed itself into a roller-coaster ride with each pinnacle of chaos outdoing the last. How I'd managed to get into this predicament was beyond my most terrifying nightmare. Gone was my livelihood. Gone were my dreams of owning a home and having a baby. Gone was my freedom.

Confusion and anger swelled inside me.

I wanted to scream.

I wanted to cry.

But I held my own.

Ten minutes had gone by—although I'd have sworn it was an hour—when a female officer popped in. She couldn't have been older than twenty-one, but dark brown hair pulled back in a stubby ponytail and a thick gun belt added an austerity to her uniform and five years to her age. She asked if I'd like a cup of coffee.

I said yes. She nodded and left. I was relieved that someone had remembered I was in the room, though the notion that another officer might be watching me from the other side of the two-way mirror could refute that fact.

My hands were cold. I tucked them under my thighs to warm them up and realized I was still wearing shorts. Damn! I should have changed into pants before leaving the condo. But how could I have predicted the absurdity that awaited us at Michael's hotel suite and that we'd be hauled to a police station afterward?

The female officer returned and placed a plastic cup of coffee on the table in front of me, along with two creamers, two packets of sugar, and a swizzle stick. She gave me a quick nod, then ducked out.

I took a sip. Full-bodied flavor. Not bad for a police station. On the other hand, if one had to judge coffee, who better than the frequent patrons of doughnut shops to pick a premium blend?

My focus swung back to the grim circumstances surrounding my dilemma. On a whim, I entertained total denial of what had happened. I envisioned Dan rushing in to say the police had made a terrible mistake, and I was free to go home.

But I was no fool. Storybook endings don't happen in the real world. Common sense dictated that Dan and Michael were battling it out with the detective in another room, which would explain why Dan hadn't come in to see me so far.

I sipped more coffee. I wrapped my hands around the cup and felt the warmth penetrate my cold fingers. I tried to relax. I was innocent. I had nothing to fear. The discovery of cyanide in Michael's hotel room was preposterous. Plain crazy, as he would say. He was a crime reporter, a champion of justice and truth. He couldn't possibly have had anything to do with the murders—

The door flew open and Dan rushed in. His face was flushed and beads of sweat dripped down his forehead. If I didn't know otherwise, I'd have assumed he'd run all the way to the station behind our police cruisers.

"How are you doing, Megan?" He set his leather briefcase down. He dug out a hankie from his suit and patted his forehead, but no amount of wiping could have erased the anxiety etched into his face. Same case of nerves as me, different climate zones.

"Tell me this is a nightmare and I'll be waking up soon," I said.

He tucked the hankie back. "I wish I could, but the police are insinuating suspicion of murder here." He unbuttoned his jacket and maneuvered a chair so that he sat facing me.

His comment shattered whatever hope I had of getting through this minefield with my mental faculties intact. "Are you saying you can't defend me?"

He frowned. "I never said that."

"How's Michael?"

"Shaken up. The detective is about to interrogate him in the next room."

"What's taking so long?"

"He's waiting for Duchaine to complete his search at the Elegance." He let out a deep breath. "In case he finds more evidence."

"More evidence? Doesn't he see Michael is being framed?" I waved my hands in the air. "He's innocent. I'm innocent. Moreau is on a bloody witch hunt, damn it!"

Dan's response was guarded. "Depends on how they interpret the discovery of the cyanide."

His response disturbed me. I had doubts about the way things were progressing—or weren't—but I didn't need to hear it from my lawyer. "So what's the next step?" I asked, placing the onus back on him.

"Jane is still interviewing witnesses. We're not done yet."

"How long will Michael and I have to stay here?"

"I don't know."

I debated which was worse: spending time in jail with the most horrible offenders or evading an elusive assassin. Elusive? Who was I kidding? "Michael told you how someone pushed me into the traffic yesterday, right?"

He nodded. "Give me your version."

I briefed him on the incident.

"I'll tell the detective about your close call," Dan said. "Might make a difference."

"With no witnesses? Fat chance." My mind went off on a tangent. "The killer knows Michael's staying at the Elegance. He probably knows where I live. He can find us no matter where we are. Sooner or later, he's going to succeed in having us convicted for the murders he committed—if he doesn't kill us first." Fear tightened my throat.

Dan must have caught the angst in my voice because he leaned forward and said, "Megan, I'll do whatever it takes to prove you and Michael are innocent." His words had a determined edge to them, yet the worry lines across his forehead prevailed.

And that concerned me even more.

The door opened and the same female officer appeared. "Mr.

Cummings, Detective Moreau is waiting for you in Interrogation Room 2."

"Thank you." Dan rose to his feet and picked up his briefcase. "Hang in there, Megan." He rushed out of the room.

I thought about what Dan had said, about how our outcome depended on the police interpretation of the cyanide in Michael's suite. I tried to be logical about it.

To begin with, how many deaths by cyanide poisoning had been reported in the country this weekend? Not many, I'm sure.

So what were the chances the cyanide found in Michael's suite had nothing to do with the cyanide that had killed Tom and Pam? One in a hundred million, I'd say.

One thing was certain: if the cyanide was a deliberate drop, the murderer had to have access to Michael's suite. It meant he either worked at the Elegance Hotel or knew someone who did.

I took my rationale a step further: maybe the murderer had a motive to kill Tom and Pam but wanted to put the blame on Michael and me for some obscure reason. A double retribution, so to speak. Apart from that, nothing made sense.

Dan returned an hour later. Gloom hung about him like an albatross perched on the bow of a sinking ship.

I braced for the worst.

# CHAPTER 17

"Round one is over," Dan said. Out came the hankie. "Won't be long before the detective interrogates you." He unloaded his briefcase on the floor and took a seat on my left.

"Where's Michael now?" I asked.

"In the interrogation room." He patted his brow, then tucked the hankie away.

"How did it go?"

"He has nothing on him so far."

"So far?" I echoed. "That's insane."

"Megan, I have to caution you. Be careful how you respond to his questions. You might inadvertently give him what he's looking for."

"I have nothing to hide. I'll just tell the truth."

The door opened and Moreau darted in, a manila folder tucked under his arm. As he took a seat opposite us, the scent of cigarette smoke infused the air, and I wondered if he'd taken a few puffs before coming in. Without as much as a glance in my direction, he opened the folder and began to scan the first page.

I was still bristling from his intrusive search of my purse. For this reason alone, I supposed, I examined the man with a critical eye once again.

His shoulders arched as he leaned his elbows on the table, causing his neck to all but disappear. If I had the nerve, I'd have peeked under the table to see if his feet were touching the floor. I'd have bet they weren't. He passed a hand over his mustache. I'd come to realize this habit coincided with a theory or a new plan of attack he was contemplating. Either way, it meant bad news for me. If there was anything pleasant about him, I couldn't see it. Maybe because I chose not to.

Moreau switched on the audio video recorder and inched forward to speak into the microphone. He recorded the date, the names of those present, and other mundane details regarding the interrogation. His French-Canadian accent made his words sound forced, almost hostile. When he was finished, he looked at me. "Madame Scott, we did a search of your apartment and found a photo of your husband and Pam Strober among your possessions. You said you do not know who took this photo. Is that correct?"

"Yes," I said.

He switched his gaze to Dan. "For the record, we have verified the return address on the envelope. It is fictitious. We will verify fingerprints on the envelope, but we require those of your clients for elimination purposes, as well as a buccal swab for DNA testing."

"Agreed," Dan said.

Moreau glanced down at the file. "Madame Scott, I understand you met with a therapist last spring. Dr. Katherine Madison."

The nature of the question stunned me, but I answered it. "Yes, but only for a few sessions."

"*Naturellement*, what is discussed between a psychologist and her patient during these sessions is confidential. However, it leads me to believe you were feeling stress in your life—perhaps due to problems in your marriage. Is that correct, Madame Scott?"

Dan intervened. "My client's sessions with a therapist have no bearing on your investigation."

"I do not agree," the detective said. "The psychological disposition of your client is of critical importance."

Dan paused. "All right, Megan. Go ahead."

"We discussed stress as a reason for my inability to conceive," I said.

I saw the glint in Moreau's eyes. "And you blamed your husband's affair with another woman for this?"

"Of course not. I didn't know he'd had an affair until you told me."

Moreau shifted in his chair. "Well...would you say you had a happy marriage?"

Dan intervened again. "Detective, I don't see the connection."

"As you know, Monsieur Cummings, deep emotions often breed a motive for murder. Hell hath no fury as a woman scorned, as they say."

Oddly enough, I understood his logic. The fact that women killed their spouses had become so common as to be stereotypical. Betty Broderick was one publicized example of a woman who felt disgraced when her husband left her for a new wife. She shot and killed them both while they were sleeping. Clara Harris got into her Mercedes and ran over her cheating husband, killing him. I'd once read a story about a wife in Russia who stabbed her husband to death because he forgot her birthday. Not that I drew any comparisons to these women, but I could see why Moreau would. Because he'd made no attempt to hide his suspicions, it told me he'd already decided I was guilty.

"Detective, are you charging my client with murder?" Dan's face was flushed. "The last time I checked, this wasn't a courtroom."

"I will move on for now." Moreau switched his gaze to me. "Were you aware of a booking at the Pineview resort the weekend of—" He glanced at the file. "August 10?"

"Yes, but—"

"How did you acquire this information?"

"Louise Kirk from Pineview called Tom at home. He was out of town, so I took the message."

"Did Louise Kirk give you any information concerning the booking?"

"Yes."

"Please be specific."

Although I sensed trouble behind Moreau's question, I had no choice but to answer it. "She said it was registered under the name Scott. She gave me the date and the address, and said it was for a cottage with a Jacuzzi."

"Anything else?"

"I don't remember."

"Did you tell your husband about the call?"

"Yes."

"What did he say?"

"He said his office staff had made a mistake. He wasn't booked at Pineview."

"Did you believe your husband?"

Dan cleared his throat. I glanced at him, expecting words of advice to come out of his mouth, but he remained silent. His eyes were fixed on the detective, as if he were waiting for him to slip up on a fact or state an unfounded accusation.

"Go on, Madame Scott."

"Tom told me he was going to Granite Ridge with Peter Ewans and other BOTCOR employees that weekend."

"Do you have proof?" Moreau's eyes flickered in anticipation.

I was prepared for this one. "After Tom's death, I confronted Peter. He'd known about Tom's affair with Pam and never told me. He said he would have lied about Tom going to Pineview if he had to. If Peter hadn't covered for him, Tom would have fired him."

The detective raised an eyebrow.

"If you don't believe me, ask Peter," I said. "I'm sure he'd corroborate our conversation. Tom can't threaten to fire him anymore."

Moreau squinted, as if he weren't quite certain how to interpret my response. He turned to another report in the file. "We have evidence to show you shared the information you received from Louise Kirk. We found a note in the hotel suite of Michael Elliott. It contains details about Pineview cottage *numéro huit.*" His apparent fervor caused a French translation to slip through. "Number eight," he corrected himself. "Michael Elliott has confirmed it is your handwriting on this note." He held up a black-and-white photocopy to show me. "Is that correct?"

"Yes."

The detective stroked his mustache. "Madame Scott, I am a curious man by nature. Can you tell me how Michael Elliott came to have this information in his possession?"

It didn't take a genius to figure out he'd already asked Michael the same question. I wondered how Michael had handled it. Had he told Moreau the truth, or had he tried to cover it up and say he knew nothing about it to protect himself? I assumed the truth had won out. I maintained my resolve to do the same despite the consequences. "I left it by accident under a manuscript I delivered to Michael at the hotel. He found it and showed it to me later."

"Did you explain to him what it was?"

"No. I crumpled it up and left it with other discarded papers on the table."

"Why?"

"It was useless information."

"Why useless?"

"I already told you." I let out an impatient sigh. "Tom told me he was going to Granite Ridge. Not Pineview."

As if he hadn't heard me, Moreau lifted another report from the file. "Madame Scott, you inserted the word *cyan* in your personal agenda. We understand it is a term relevant to your job at Bradford Publishing, but it is also an abbreviation for cyanide." He looked at me.

I said nothing. I could pretend to be deaf too. Besides, it wasn't a question.

The detective went on. "We also found a memo in your agenda regarding the weekend of August 10. It included the Pineview address and other details. Since you claim your husband did not go there, I question why you did not write the particulars of Granite Ridge in your agenda instead. Can you explain this, Madame Scott?"

A glitch from my past had returned to haunt me. "I don't know. It all happened so fast." I hoped Dan would come to my defense, but he said nothing.

The detective leaned back. "You work as a ghostwriter. Do you not review content for accuracy?"

"Yes."

"It is unusual for someone in your line of work to miss such a factual error, is it not?"

"It's an agenda, Detective," Dan said. "Not a legal document."

Moreau turned to another page in the file. "Madame Scott, did you know that Pam Strober was having an affair with your husband?"

"No."

"You confirmed the shirt with the lipstick stain we found in your apartment belonged to your husband. Do you—or did you—own a lipstick of that shade?"

"No."

"How did the stain get on the shirt?"

As if I'd make his job easier. "I don't know."

"I believe you do know and you acted on it." His eyes riveted into me.

"Speculation," Dan said.

Moreau fingered another report. "There is the matter of the rental car. I question why Michael Elliott rented a car just days before the murders."

"Michael already attested he rented the car for other purposes," Dan said.

"It has yet to be confirmed, Monsieur Cummings." Moreau's eyes flitted to me. "You realize this opportunity hints at premeditated murder."

"Don't answer that," Dan warned me.

No sweat. I'd already decided I wouldn't.

"Madame Scott, would you say that you and Michael Elliott are good friends?"

"I must counsel my client—" Dan began.

"It is but a simple question, is it not?" the detective asked, annoyance building in his voice.

Dan complied with a reluctant shrug.

I took Dan's cue and exercised discretion. "Michael was my client. We had a good working relationship."

"A good working relationship," the detective repeated, nodding. "I imagine that two people working so closely would—how shall I put it—discuss matters of a more personal nature." His eyes flickered.

"Irrelevant," Dan said.

"I do not agree," Moreau said. "Madame Scott had dinner with Michael Elliott numerous times during the three weeks before the death of her husband. This fact is quite relevant to our investigation." The glint in his eyes spread, creating a strained expression as he switched his focus to me. "Tell me, Madame Scott, why did you have dinner with Michael Elliott? Did you find him interesting? Perhaps more interesting than your husband?"

"You're unduly provoking my client," Dan said.

Moreau remained silent, watching me, waiting for me to reply.

I was no fool. A candid response would incriminate me. I'd never admit to anyone how much I enjoyed being with Michael, that there was an easy rapport between us, and that the chance to converse with someone over dinner had filled a gap in my life—a gap that had grown wider with every additional trip Tom had taken.

Determined not to stumble into Moreau's trap, I calmly said, "Michael was my client. I was on a tight deadline, so we discussed his work over dinner."

With a single-mindedness that seemed to know no limits, Moreau maintained his line of questioning. "Madame Scott, I believe your relationship with Michael Elliott was more intimate than you admit."

"Do you have any proof?" Dan asked him.

"I have testimony from Eloise Speck, a neighbor who resides in the same condominium as Madame Scott." Moreau looked at me. "She saw you and Michael Elliott in a warm embrace Friday night, August 10."

*Oh no, not another minefield.* I glimpsed at Dan. His nervousness manifested itself as beads of perspiration building up on his brow. Given the scope of his legal experience, this was not a good sign.

"I was saying goodbye to Michael," I said, keeping my tone even. "He was going back to Toronto on the weekend."

"But he did not go back." Moreau stared at me. "Did you leave your apartment again later that night?"

"No."

"Perhaps to take a walk in the parking lot?"

"A walk? Of course not."

A flicker of doubt registered on the detective's face. "To repeat, Michael Elliott did not return to Toronto on the weekend. Is that correct?"

"Yes," I said.

"Can you tell me why?"

I glanced at Dan. He remained quiet. I assumed he hadn't told Moreau about Michael's trip to Sainte-Adèle to meet with his informant later that night and neither had Michael.

Frown lines gathered on the detective's brow in a sign of impatience. "Well?"

"Why don't you ask Michael?" I said.

Moreau smoothed out his mustache again, this time in two rapid strokes. "Perhaps he did not want to abandon you in your moment of crisis. Perhaps he decided to stay in Montreal because your relationship had developed into an amorous one."

"That's not true!" I gripped the edge of my chair and resisted an urge to call him the vilest of names.

"You're upsetting my client with unfounded accusations, Detective," Dan said, putting a hand on my arm.

"Time will prove them otherwise, Monsieur Cummings."

While Moreau leafed through the file, I tried to regain my composure. I knew that words said in the heat of the moment—especially to someone who was so intent on proving my guilt—could cause me regret. I had to hang on for a while longer.

The detective scanned another report. "We are investigating a statement from Emily Saunders at Bradford Publishing. It is regarding an anonymous call to your office phone—"

"Hearsay," Dan cut him off. "My client is aware of the call. It hasn't been proven to be true or relevant."

"We are working on it, Monsieur Cummings." Moreau fingered the next report. "Madame Scott, did you know your husband named you as sole beneficiary on his life insurance policy?"

"Yes," I said.

Moreau kept his eyes on me. "Did you know your husband had requested an increase on his insurance policy several months ago?"

The policy I knew about was for one hundred thousand. "An increase? Well...I'm not sure."

Dan spoke. "What figures are we talking about, Detective?"

Moreau replied, "The policy was raised from one hundred thousand to five hundred thousand dollars? Were you aware of this change, Madame Scott?"

"No," I said, stunned.

"Why did your husband purchase such a large policy?" Moreau asked.

"How the hell would I know?" I snapped at him. I couldn't help myself. He was getting on my nerves. Dan stirred in his chair, prompting me to give Moreau's question a more courteous response. "We were trying to start a family. Maybe Tom wanted to make sure we would be taken care of if anything happened to him."

"Like murder?"

*Was he kidding?* "No, like a plane crash or a car crash. Tom travelled a lot. He knew the risks involved."

The detective slowly closed the folder.

I hoped it was a sign the interrogation had come to an end. I was eager to see Michael and set things straight. Moreau hadn't said anything about the cyanide. Maybe the vial they'd found held something other than poison, like baby powder or sugar. After all, Dan did say the police had nothing on Michael so far.

But just when I thought the worst was over, Moreau surprised me. "Madame Scott, this is what I believe were the circumstances leading to your husband's death. You discovered the shirt with the lipstick stain and hid it in a garbage bag. Perhaps you intended to throw it out but you forgot to do so."

"No, that's not true," I said.

"You and Michael Elliott left the city in a rental car Friday evening of August 10."

"No, we did not."

"You supplied Michael Elliott with the Pineview address and information—"

"No, I did not."

"You asked Michael Elliott to help you take revenge against a husband who had been unfaithful to you—to even the score, as they say."

His insinuation hit me like a slap across the face. "That's a lie! You're trying to set me up!"

"In French, we call it un *crime passionnel*—a crime of passion."

I jumped to my feet. "You're wrong. I loved Tom." I remained standing, shaking with rage.

"Megan, please." Dan's hand on my arm guided me back into the chair.

"How much longer do we have to endure this ridiculous interrogation?" I asked Dan, but he didn't answer.

Moreau stared at me, as if he were contemplating whether or not I'd lunge up again. "Perhaps you had second thoughts about your murderous deed. You needed a safeguard. Perhaps you paid someone to plant the cyanide in Michael Elliott's suite to create doubts about his integrity. Or perhaps you put it there yourself."

"I...did...not," I said through clenched teeth.

There was a knock at the door and a uniformed police officer entered. He handed Moreau a beige envelope with a police insignia in the top right-hand corner. The way my interrogation was going, I was almost certain the information in the envelope would only worsen the situation.

The detective exchanged hushed words in French with the officer, but they spoke so low that I couldn't catch the gist of it. The officer stepped out, leaving the door ajar.

Moreau said, "I have asked Michael Elliott to join us."

Dan and I exchanged surprised glances.

Michael walked in and shut the door behind him. I tried to catch his eye, but he didn't look my way and took a seat on the other side of Dan.

The detective opened the envelope and pulled out two reports. A stroke of his mustache told me he was about to spring a conclusive bit of information on us of a sort we'd hoped wouldn't surface. "There is one particular matter of interest left to discuss. We have verified the mileage on the car that Monsieur Elliott rented. It was about one hundred and thirty miles."

Dan reached into his briefcase and pulled out a folder. He began to flip through its contents in a flurry of activity.

*What on earth was he looking for?*

Moreau glanced at the second report. "We have also confirmed this mileage is about the same distance as a trip to and from the Pineview resort. Interesting, is it not?" His eyebrows went up, as if some hidden revelation had come to light.

And it had.

Dan pulled out a sheet, putting an end to his search. "Detective, my clients might have known about the existence of Pineview, but they both affirm they didn't go there. As a matter of record, dozens of other resorts are located within the same distance from Montreal. Here's a list of them." He handed it to him.

Moreau took it and gave it a quick once-over. "Yes...well, perhaps your clients will claim they drove around the city in circles all night too. The reality is that they have failed to provide us with solid alibis."

"Detective, unless you have a legitimate reason to lay murder charges against either of my clients, don't make conjectures about their whereabouts." Dan pulled out a hankie and wiped his face.

His argument reassured my mind, but his unease was playing havoc with my health. My nerves were slowly ripping apart, much like the fine threads of Grandma's old couch.

I looked past Dan to Michael, anticipating that he'd jump in and defend our position the way he'd often done on matters that screamed for justice. But he remained silent, his eyes bulging in disbelief as he gaped at the detective.

My heart sank. Michael's silence spoke louder than any words ever could. It conveyed the certainty that our worst fears had begun to take shape and that he was losing hope.

There was another knock at the door and the same police officer popped his head in. In French, he apologized for the intrusion and said he needed to speak with the detective right away. Could he leave the room for a moment?

Moreau switched off the recorder. "Please excuse me." He walked out and left the door ajar.

I had the disturbing impression that he was about to call in the troops. I leaned forward and whispered, "Michael, did you tell him where you were Friday night?"

"No." He didn't look my way.

"Why not?"

"He would have asked for names. I can't break client confidentiality.

Besides, I'm still trying to prove my alibi." The way he avoided looking at me troubled me more than his reply.

"Keep it short," Dan said, his voice low. "It's in both your best interests. They have nothing on either of you to make the charges stick."

"Then why are we here?" I asked him. "Why can't we just leave?"

"We have to cooperate. It's a sign of good faith."

As far as I was concerned, I'd suffered enough in the name of good faith. My legs were numb and my rear end hurt from sitting on a wooden chair for so long. I wanted to stand up and shake my limbs to pump up the circulation. Better yet, I wished the detective would scrap this poor excuse for a police interrogation, let us go home, and concentrate his efforts on finding the real killer.

I peeked through the open doorway. Moreau was hurrying back toward the room, another folder tucked under his arm. As he whizzed by us, I peeked at the tab on the folder. It read "Scott, Thomas" in large black letters. *More bad news.* My heart hammered in my chest.

The detective sat down and turned on the recorder. "Our police laboratory found no fingerprints on the container discovered in your suite." He observed Michael with the usual caution reserved for a suspected murderer but kept me in his visual range as well. My guess was that he wanted to check our reactions or hoped one of us would renounce the other. "Did you wear gloves when you handled the cyanide, Monsieur Elliott?"

Dan blocked my view, but I could hear Michael move in his chair. "For the last time, I'm telling you the truth," he said, weariness in his voice. "I have no idea how the damn stuff got in my jacket. Someone is framing me. Why don't you believe me?"

"Your innocence is not a question of belief, Monsieur Elliott. The facts speak for—"

"Detective," Dan cut in, more forceful this time. "We're prepared to assist you as best we can. However, the evidence you have on my clients is circumstantial at best, and you know it."

The detective's left eyebrow arched in disapproval. "I do not agree. As you already know, the evidence in a criminal investigation must be weighed in the light of two key factors—motive and opportunity."

Dan sat back. "You have neither. You're grasping at straws. You're molding insignificant items your investigators tripped over to fabricate motive and opportunity. You have no concrete proof to implicate my clients in the murders."

"It is a matter of time before we discover more evidence to prove your clients are guilty."

"You're losing sight of the big picture, Detective. You've become obsessed with your own imaginary scenario. In the interim, this interview is over." Dan gathered his files and placed them in his briefcase.

Moreau grew silent, seemed to be pondering the situation. "*Très bien.* Your clients are free to go for now. Please keep in mind that we reserve the right to question them in the future. I suggest they do not leave town." He turned off the recorder.

Dan stood up, his huge frame bent over the table like an engulfing tidal wave, his flushed face within inches of Moreau's. "Detective, I told you earlier how Megan had a near-brush with death the other day when someone pushed her off the curb. It implies she's a target. And so is Michael. Why someone wants them out of the way is what the police should be investigating. I strongly suggest you focus on catching the real murderer." He straightened up.

"It is precisely my intention." The detective rose and collected his folders. Whether or not he perceived Dan's deportment as a threat, I couldn't tell. "Madame Scott, Monsieur Elliott, please wait here. I will make the arrangements for your swab and fingerprints." He left the room.

Michael stood up and, for the first time, I noticed his bloodshot eyes and the haggard expression on his face. "Thanks, Dan," he said. "You bought us some time."

"Every second counts," Dan said.

"What's our next move?" I asked him.

"Can't say yet. Waiting for info from Jane."

"I know you're going to get us out of this, buddy." Though Michael's words were hopeful, his voice had a desperate edge to it.

"We haven't been dealt the last hand yet," Dan said. "I have a couple of aces up my own sleeve." He clutched his briefcase. "You still have your suite at the Elegance?"

"I hope so," Michael said. "Most of my stuff is there. I never checked out."

"All right. After you're done here, flag a taxi and go back to the hotel—both of you. Stay put until you hear from me."

# CHAPTER 18

The lobby of the Elegance Hotel buzzed with hordes of convention-goers—an ideal smokescreen for Michael and me.

We zigzagged around visitors standing beside luggage tagged with team names that sounded as if they'd been generated during a high-tech brainstorming session: Marketing Maniacs, Disk Dorks, and Web Watchers. Each group member wore a white tag that read: "Hello. My name is..." Loud greetings echoed across the lobby as new arrivals stumbled upon the rest of their team like lost sheep that had found their flock.

Michael and I took the elevator up to the seventh floor in silence, not speaking—just as we'd done on the taxi ride over. I sensed that he still had something on his mind, but conversation didn't matter to me at this point. All I wanted to do was take a shower. Maybe it was psychological, but the hours I'd spent at the police station made me feel dirty. I prayed Michael still had access to his suite.

Luck was on our side. His electronic key worked. We walked in to discover an added bonus: room service had cleaned up and left an ample supply of fresh linens in the bathroom. They'd also left a trash bin beside the toilet. I took it as a good sign. Michael let me take a shower first and lent me a clean T-shirt.

What I didn't expect when I came out of the bathroom was the stunned expression on his face. "You have no idea what crazy messages someone's been leaving on my phone."

"Your cell phone?"

"No, the hotel phone." He walked over to it. "You have to hear this." He hit a button and held the receiver inches away from my ear. "Careful," he said. "It's loud."

"Traitor!" a thick voice bellowed. A click sounded and the line went dead.

"Oh, my God. Can I hear it again?"

Michael hit the replay button.

I listened again. "I can't tell if the voice is male or female."

"The caller must have used a device to disguise his voice. There are two other messages—all the same as this one—about a half hour apart."

My blood went cold. "It could be the killer."

"Would he be stupid enough to leave his voice on tape?"

"Don't erase the messages. We'll tell Dan about it later."

Michael looked at me. "We haven't had much time to talk about what happened today."

"That's an understatement."

"I'll go take a shower. We'll hash things out after." He disappeared around the corner.

I picked up the remote and turned on the TV. I clicked through a variety of talk shows, soaps, and home designer programs, but nothing interested me. I turned off the TV and wandered over to the window.

Heat waves and smog blurred the Montreal skyline, rendering the towering buildings wavy and hazy. Strange. The weather was as relentless as Moreau. From the beginning, his insinuations had prevented me from thinking of anything else but trying to clear my name. Even though Dan had succeeded in fending off the detective's badgering today, I sensed it was a temporary reprieve at best.

Part of me wanted to run away from the crumbling world around me. The other part craved the truth and told me the only way out of this impasse was to dig up a more worthy suspect—one that would draw closer scrutiny from the police.

I'd once read that almonds helped to clear the thought process. True or not, I often kept a supply on hand—especially the chocolate ones. I dug into my purse and retrieved the bag of chocolate almonds I'd stashed there. To think that Moreau had almost impounded it earlier. I plucked one out and chewed it slowly, then sat down to begin my analysis of potential suspects.

The most obvious contender was Peter Ewans. The loose tire on the Ford, the connection to his former job as chemical engineer, his easy access to Tom's cottage... Yes, I had to consider the possibility that Peter might have finally acted out of frustration over the loss of promotion after promotion. That Tom had climbed ahead of him on the corporate ladder at BOTCOR could have been the final blow to Peter's deteriorating ego. Add to that the loss of respect from his peers and the prospect of a career that seemed to be going nowhere, and you had a recipe for revenge waiting to happen. A sad aspect was that Pam had been trapped in his scheme—something Peter hadn't anticipated until it was too late.

I popped another almond into my mouth, letting the chocolate melt away while I put together a second theory. What if Pam was the target and Tom had been caught in the scheme instead? If so, the killer would have had a different motive. I envisioned a jealous lover or a sensitive male Pam might have dumped in her "use them, then lose them" manner. Maybe she'd pushed one too many ex-boyfriends over the edge.

And why leave a murderess out of the equation? It was now a fact that married men had not been off limits to Pam, so why discount a wife looking for revenge? Like Bill Bradford's wife, for example. What if it had been more than an employer-employee relationship between Bill and Pam? If Tricia Bradford had threatened Pam, she must have had good reason. Sure, Tricia had an alibi, and sure, she'd lose millions if she got caught, but she could have hired a hit man to get rid of Pam as Michael had once suggested. Hell, she had enough money to put a whole team into action if she wanted. Tom's presence wouldn't have obstructed her plans. The fee for knocking off one more person was no problem for Tricia.

But why stop there? From the collection of trophy gifts in Pam's office, further inquiries might reveal an army of vindictive women who were just as eager to settle a score against her for having slept with their husbands or boyfriends. Considering Pam's list of conquests, the possibilities were endless.

I felt a surge of optimism but knew better than to overreact. Dan's investigative process was far from over. Jane was still interviewing witnesses and verifying the names in Tom's appointment book. Some of the women he'd slept with might have been furious to discover he was married. It only took one, and she might have gone to great lengths to settle a score.

I chewed on a third almond, then a fourth. Another possibility lurked in a corner of my mind—one that I'd ignored until now because of denial on my part: Michael could have played an active role in the murders.

It was clear he was attracted to me. What if he'd plotted to kill Tom to advance his own interests? What if the decision to delay his trip home was an excuse to hang around and make sure his plan had succeeded? The absence of food and gas receipts from his trip to Sainte-Adèle Friday night continued to bother me. Did he forget to keep them as a matter of convenience, aware that ambiguous circumstances might work in his favor later on? Funny thing, I'd noticed he kept his receipt from our stop at the diner today.

I popped another chocolate almond into my mouth. If Michael had anything to do with Tom's death, maybe it was my fault. I'd mistaken his easygoing ways for compassion and opened my heart to him, telling him how lonely I felt with Tom traveling so much. I thought I'd kept our relationship well within the borders of friendship, but maybe I hadn't. I felt guilty for having developed an interest in another man. Intellectual adultery, I supposed one could call it. While Michael's empathy for my situation might have stemmed from a decent place in his heart, I wondered if my predicament had spurred him to take a drastic step—one he believed would set me free to be with him. It scared me just to think about it.

I crunched another almond and imagined how Michael might have proceeded. He had the Pineview information on hand—my crumpled note. A phone call would have confirmed if Tom was registered there or not that weekend. Michael could have lied about the cleaning staff not picking up the discarded papers in his hotel suite so that the police would find the Pineview note—in my handwriting—and suspect I was involved in the murders. His trip to Sainte-Adèle had given him the perfect alibi while his plan was unfolding at Pineview—if in fact he'd gone to Sainte-Adèle that Friday night. He could have lied about that too and driven to Pineview instead.

As for the cyanide, he knew little about it—or pretended not to. One of his street contacts, or even a friend in the publishing business, could have obtained it for him. With the laidback attitude of BOTCOR employees at Pineview, not to mention the non-existent security there, anyone could have slipped into Tom's cottage unnoticed and unloaded the cyanide. Michael could have walked in and planted it there himself.

Whether or not Michael spoke French, I wasn't sure, but he might have used his ignorance of the language as an excuse to ask me to go to Sainte-Adèle with him the next morning. He wanted to show me how determined he was about proving his alibi, but maybe his real goal was to beguile me. He might have had plans to take our relationship to the next level when we returned, but he had to set them aside when Moreau popped up at my door.

I thought about my near-fatal plunge into the street and bit down hard on the remaining almond in the bag. The notion that Michael might have followed me from Santino's and shoved me into the traffic made my heart pound with fear. *Had I willingly accepted a killer into my life?*

It was strange how that incident had so closely preceded the discovery of the cyanide in his hotel suite. The stunned look on Michael's face when the police found it was still clear in my mind. Would he have been so careless as to leave a vial of cyanide in his jacket? No way. He hadn't been careless at all. He'd put it there on purpose. He hoped the police would find it during their search and assume someone else had planted it—namely, me. The mistrust in his eyes, performed to a tee, had given Moreau a reason to suspect I'd planned the whole thing.

Yet how could I forget Michael's passionate kiss? Had I been so gullible as to believe he was interested in me?

On the contrary. I'd put him through hell and back. I'd be a fool to assume he'd kissed me because he cared about me. No, that kiss was his way of diverting my attention. I was vulnerable and insecure, and he knew how to gain my trust. After all, Tom had done it with his lies and I'd believed him.

I hated myself for concocting these theories about Michael. Like he'd once said, whatever happened to "innocent until proven guilty"? It was difficult but I had to be fair. I repressed my suspicions and gave him the benefit of the doubt—for now. I crushed the empty bag of almonds and stuffed it into my purse.

Michael soon emerged from the bathroom and peered at me through damp, disheveled hair. A short-sleeved T-shirt showed off muscular biceps and a trim torso. As he approached, the scent of the fresh outdoors after a rainfall permeated the air around us.

I experienced a rush of warmth and was certain that my cheeks had turned pink.

"Any calls?" he asked.

I gathered my thoughts. "No, nobody called."

"Hungry? I know I am." He smiled. "How about ordering something from downstairs?"

"Okay." I wondered where the desperate Michael I'd witnessed at the police station had gone. The cheerful version standing before me aroused my curiosity even more, if not my apprehension.

After Michael called room service and ordered up a couple of roast beef sandwiches and twelve small bottles of water, he slid into his usual armchair. "Let's talk. We have a few things to clear up." His demeanor was as relaxed as if we were sitting down to discuss his manuscript.

I couldn't continue the charade. "Damn it, Michael, how can you be so cool? Moreau almost destroyed our chances of seeing daylight again, yet here you are, acting as if you don't have a care in the world." I let my arms fall with a thud against the sides of the chair.

"That's because the pressure is off. I've had time to think things through." He glanced at a point in the distance. "I think the detective released us because he knew Dan was right. The evidence they have on us is nothing but circumstantial."

"So you're saying we have nothing to worry about."

"Not quite. Moreau suspects we had the opportunity and

the motive. Problem is he can't lay charges against us without substantive proof."

"Like what?"

"Like the means—how we obtained the cyanide, how we got it into the Pineview cottage without anyone—"

"He'll say we paid someone else to do it."

"Dan can refute it...claim it's an excuse the police use for any suspect."

A chill ran through my body. I shivered.

"What's wrong?"

I made up an excuse. "Those phone messages. I can't shake the feeling that the killer has been shadowing us all along...that he might be so close even now." I stopped, aware that my words might lead me into trouble. "Forget it. It's my imagination acting up again."

"No, it's this crazy case."

Michael's cell phone rang and he answered it. It was Dan. They chatted for a bit. "Okay. See you soon." He hung up. "Dan and Jane are coming over in about an hour."

Good. I wouldn't have to be alone with Michael for much longer. Yet I proceeded with caution. "You know what bothers me the most?"

"What?"

"I can't imagine how the cyanide ended up in your suite." I checked his reaction.

He shrugged. "I'll bet Moreau thinks I put it there."

"You wouldn't have—I mean—" Michael's eyes had a strange intensity to them. Had he caught my allusion? If so, had I put my own safety at risk? "Oh, nothing makes sense anymore."

"That's right, Inspector Clouseau," he said, smiling. "Why don't you give it a rest?"

His composure irritated me. "I can't give it a rest. I want closure. Our lives depend on finding the real killer because we can't even prove our innocence." *Our* innocence? Did I actually say that? "Michael, don't you care about anything anymore? Where's that person you used to be—the gutsy investigative reporter, determined to serve justice and get to the truth?"

He leaned forward and joined his hands, kept his gaze on the carpet. "It's not what you think, Megan. I do care—a lot. After the police found the cyanide in my jacket and took me in for questioning, I did some soul-searching. I began to have doubts...about you." He looked up at me. "I imagined the worst and I'm sorry."

Guilt raced through me. "But I—"

"Wait. There's more. I lost hope—something I promised myself I wouldn't do, no matter how tough life got. When Moreau let us go, I took it as a positive sign. Now nothing is going to stop me from getting through this ordeal. We have to believe that destiny is going to step in and put our lives back on track."

"Destiny? You're not getting mushy on me, are you? It's going to take more than high hopes or wishful thinking to convince Moreau we're not murderers."

"We're not alone in fighting this battle. We've got Dan. He's going to do whatever it takes to exonerate us. And I'm going to do everything I can to help him."

He sounded sincere, which made me feel even worse about having doubted him.

After room service arrived and we'd eaten our sandwiches, Michael sat at the coffee table and opened up his laptop. "I need to clear my thoughts before Dan arrives...check my notes on the crime story I'm been working on. Maybe I can come up with another lead."

I applauded his ability to change gears—something I couldn't do in the midst of turmoil. Instead I turned on the TV and channel-surfed, hoping it would draw my attention away from the murder investigation. After I clicked past a series of shows about cooking on a budget, washing the family dog, and living on the cheap, I hit a local news channel. A film clip spanned a row of turn-of-the-century homes on a street in a Québec town. I immediately recognized the area. "Look, Michael. They're talking about the fire in Sainte-Adèle."

The reporter went on to say how a fire late last night had destroyed the home of a resident in the resort town located north of Montreal. A badly burnt body had been found inside the home, but the identity of the victim had not yet been confirmed. Residents who were interviewed believed it was sixty-year-old William

Perron who had lived alone for the last thirty years. A neighbor confirmed he'd seen Willie that evening sitting on the front porch, smoking a cigarette.

"It might be Willie after all," I said to Michael. "What about your alibi?"

"I'll have to find another way to prove it." He frowned and went back to work.

I turned off the TV and walked over to the window. The sun had begun to set on the city core. A blue sky streaked with blurs of red and orange rays provided a superb backdrop to the skyscrapers carved against it. A breath-taking view, but it signified another day of unrelenting heat ahead. To make matters worse, forecasters had predicted the stifling and sticky El Niño influence would continue for yet another week, forcing people to seek air-conditioned places.

Moreau and El Niño—two peas in a pod. His tenacity in trying to prove my guilt left me gasping for air and waking up in a cold sweat at night at the thought of going to jail. My worst nightmare was that his persistence would far outlast that of El Niño.

# CHAPTER 19

Wednesday evening at nine, Dan set his briefcase on the coffee table in Michael's suite and clicked it open. "Sorry for dropping by so late. Information came in at the last minute." He unbuttoned his jacket and sat in the armchair Michael usually occupied.

"That's right." Jane settled in the other armchair and placed her briefcase at her feet.

Dan pulled out a document and held it out to me. "Take a look. It's a table of names and schedules from the Elegance."

I stood next to him while I examined the data.

Jane elaborated. "I succeeded in getting the names of the cleaning personnel at the hotel and their work schedules for the past week."

I noticed how she took solo credit for the task.

"How did you manage that?" Michael asked her. "Only cops have access to this kind of info."

"It's in hotel management's best interests to prove their staff is trustworthy," Jane said, looking pleased with herself for having suggested such a credible excuse.

"I knew one of the owners," Dan said with a subtle wink.

"Works every time," Michael said.

"The highlighted entries on the seventh floor are noteworthy," Jane said, steering our focus back to the document.

Michael leaned over my shoulder. "Cleanit Maid Service. Six staff, all female. Do you think one of the maids planted the cyanide in my suite?"

"It's a premise we're considering," Dan said, reaching for his notebook.

"Have you interviewed them?"

"Jane did. All checked out fine except one." Dan produced another sheet from the file. "Anita Castillo. A part-time employee in this batch of temp workers." He handed me the sheet.

The heading read: Replacement Staff—Cleanit Maid Service. "Do the police know about her?" I asked.

"Yes," Dan said.

Michael's face lit up. "Have they brought her in for questioning?"

"No."

"Why not?"

"She vanished. Didn't show up to collect her paycheck today."

"Who would work and not want to get paid for it?" I asked no one in particular.

"Someone who's getting bigger bucks to plant cyanide in my suite," Michael said.

Dan shrugged. "Whatever it takes to put food on the table."

"Do you have a photo of Anita?" I asked him.

He opened his mouth to speak but Jane answered. "No photos. Cleanit staff told me she has dark curly hair, brown eyes, and a medium complexion."

"Will the police keep searching for her?" Michael asked.

"Yes, but I doubt they'll find her," Jane said. "The personal information she gave her boss was false. The other cleaning staff didn't know much about her either, except that she waitressed in clubs on her nights off."

"Which clubs?"

"They don't know." She kept her eyes on him and crossed her legs, her short skirt riding higher up her thighs.

Michael didn't miss a beat. "You're going to follow up on it? Check out some hotspots?"

"It's a rather...sensitive situation." She glanced at Dan.

"The police are handling it now," Dan said. "It's a fraud case."

Michael frowned. "That's plain crazy. We're giving up on our best witness?"

"Not quite," Jane said. "We have another lead. Anita gave her employer an envelope and a timesheet last week. The police will do an analysis of fingerprints and DNA."

"It's a long shot. First, she might not have a criminal record. Second, there were no fingerprints on the cyanide container. How are they going to provide a match?"

"We haven't reached that point yet." Jane blinked hard, looking every bit as confident as she sounded. "We anticipate that Anita's existence alone will veer police interest in her direction. I suggest we wait and see how they proceed with this new information." She removed her jacket and placed it on top of her briefcase.

I studied Jane without being obvious. She wore a blue turtleneck top that was sleeveless and had a silky texture to it, though the high neckline would have been stifling in today's hot temperatures. Maybe her blood ran colder than most people.

"However, there's a potential downside to Anita," Dan was saying, making me wonder if we'd ever see an upside. "It's possible she's an illegal alien. Unless the police find her, they might not be able to track down the killer."

"She might have crossed the border by now," Jane said, making the situation more dismal.

"It doesn't matter," Michael said. "The cops sure as hell can't ignore this new lead."

He was right. Anita's appearance was a stroke of good luck. More than that, it dissipated any remaining doubts I'd had about Michael's integrity.

I looked back at the schedule from the Elegance Hotel and scanned the highlighted names listed under the column marked Floor 7. "Why isn't Anita's name listed on the seventh floor?"

"It's simple, really," Jane said, her half-smile making me feel as if I'd asked an asinine question. "Each maid gets a set of keys for the rooms she's assigned to. If you look carefully, you'll see Anita was one of the maids working on the fifth floor."

Sure enough, Anita's name was listed under the heading Floor 5. "She switched with another worker on the seventh floor."

She nodded. "They do that now and then to break the monotony

170

of cleaning the same rooms."

I thought about it. "Most of the rooms in this hotel have the same layout and furnishings. What would be the purpose of switching?"

"If I had a job that boring, I'd play musical rooms too." Her eyes met mine. Despite her smile, her eyes showed no emotion.

"Moving on to Peter Ewans...where's that report?" Dan began flipping through another file.

Jane spoke. "I confirmed that Peter worked in the chemicals industry for twelve years before he joined the marketing team at BOTCOR. None of the current employees at his previous workplace heard from him since he left. I'm checking out former staff. They might prove to be a valid source for cyanide."

"Maybe he has a source we don't know about," Michael said. "What then?"

She straightened her shoulders and lifted her chin. "If it ever comes to that, we'll deal with it."

A tiny muscle pulsated along Michael's jaw line, an indication that her answer didn't satisfy him. As his ghostwriter, I was familiar with the depth and accuracy of his research. He produced clear and honest facts. Why would he accept her ambiguity?

"It might be too late by then," Michael said.

"Not by my calculations," Jane said. "I still have a lot of ground to cover."

He paused. "About the loose wheel on the Ford, did Peter ever own up to it?"

"He said he knew nothing about it."

"For obvious reasons."

"In any case," Dan said, tapping a pen against his notebook, "I filed a report with the police based on your testimony, Megan. It might hurt Peter's defense if Moreau decides to divert suspicion his way."

"If he decides to?" Michael said. "What the hell is Moreau waiting for? Can't he see Peter is a more feasible suspect than Megan or me? He had the motive, the opportunity, and the means to get rid of Tom." He raised three fingers in the air, one by one, to emphasize his words. "If that doesn't count for anything, what does?"

"All right." Dan scanned a report. "Something Peter said about

Megan—"

"I'll save you the trouble," Jane said, cutting him off. "Megan, I asked Peter about the conversation you said you had with him. He denied having discussed anything about Granite Ridge with you. In fact, he said he'd never heard of the place until I mentioned it."

"I knew it," Michael said. "He's feeling the heat, so he's passing on the blame."

Jane glanced at me. "Peter substantiated his statement. He said he gave Louise Kirk your home phone number so she could call to confirm Tom's weekend stay at Pineview."

"He's twisting the facts to cover up his lies. Damn him!" I picked up my purse from the credenza, walked over to the blue sofa, and sat down. I dug out a pen and two folded sheets of canary yellow paper I'd made a habit of carrying around these days. Doodling would help me to calm down and focus.

Michael joined me on the sofa. "I'll bet Moreau thinks you made up that chat with Peter to support your alibi."

"It wouldn't surprise me," I said. "He tried to read a lot more into my answers during his interrogation at the station too." I looked at Dan. "Why would the police choose to believe Peter rather than me?"

"Your discussion with Peter can be construed as hearsay in court," Dan said. "Doesn't matter who said what." He closed the file.

"I haven't finished," Jane said. "There's more."

"Oh?" Dan opened up the file again. "I didn't see anything else here."

"It's off the record," Jane said. "And it's meant for Megan." She turned to look at me. "Peter said he couldn't believe you didn't know about Tom's affairs with other women. There were so many."

"Tom gave me no reason to doubt him," I said. "It wasn't until I discovered his appointment book that I realized to what extent he'd betrayed me. What's your point?"

Jane blinked hard, as if she were annoyed at having to explain. "Peter said he wouldn't have blamed you for retaliating against Tom."

"Peter's a jerk." I placed the canary paper on my purse and began to draw tiny circles, then hard squares around my circles.

Michael stood up. "Anyone want water?" At our affirmative replies, he took four bottles of water that room service had left on the credenza and handed them out. "The cops should be tailing Peter. All it takes is a bit more muscle to make him confess." He twisted the cap off his bottle with a snap.

Despite the logic behind Michael's argument, the image of a vindictive Peter hadn't yet solidified in my mind. "Peter might have lied and maybe he's the world's biggest asshole, but I'm not convinced he was responsible for the murders. Let's face it. Peter is a wimp."

"Pretending to pass out at the murder site doesn't make him a wimp. It makes him smart." Michael gripped his bottle so hard that water spurted into the air and landed on the carpet. "No problem. I got it." He moved over to the credenza and grabbed a handful of paper tissues from a box.

"I might have an explanation for Peter's state of health," Jane said. "His wife told me he's on antidepressants. BOTCOR co-workers said he'd had a lot to drink Friday night at the party. Mixing meds with alcohol could account for his feeling ill."

"It doesn't mean he's not a murderer." Michael patted the spill, then headed to the bathroom to dispose of the wet tissues.

"Any more witness statements regarding Peter?" Dan asked Jane, pitching the folder into his briefcase.

Either Jane hadn't had the time to enter all the information into the file or she'd held it back from Dan on purpose. I figured the latter. Maybe she wanted to appear all the more indispensible to him. Or maybe she wanted to make *him* look incompetent.

"Neighbors had nothing negative to say about Peter or his family," Jane said. "HR personnel at BOTCOR gave him an excellent job rating, though they did mention one issue."

"What was it?" Crease lines formed across Dan's forehead.

"Peter developed anger management problems two years ago. According to HR, he attended the recommended courses and seemed to have the situation under control. That is, until the day he found out Tom got promoted."

"What happened?" I asked, thinking that maybe Peter had taken a swing at Tom.

"It's simple," Jane said. "Peter lost it."

She was beginning to wear me down.

Dan came to the rescue. "Can you be more specific?"

"Of course." Jane blinked. "Peter was angry. He stormed into head office. He argued with one of the bosses and threatened to sue the company. They almost fired him."

Michael walked back into the room. "Good thing he didn't have a gun." He gave me a knowing look.

"A verbal argument is a big leap away from murder," I said.

"Peter's still at the top of my list. Nothing's going to change my mind."

Dan ignored our banter. "All right. Moving on. " As he went to retrieve Tom's appointment book buried under several files, a piece of paper slid out and fell to the floor.

"I got it." Michael picked it up and looked at it. "Who are these people?" He handed the paper back to Dan.

"Pineview staff you interviewed. Right, Jane?" Dan held it up so she could see it.

"Yes," Jane said, then asked Michael, "Why?"

He shrugged. "No reason." He sat down next to me.

Dan slid the paper back into a file. "Jane, any news on the fingerprint eliminations at Pineview?"

"The police completed their work," she said. "They found nothing unusual."

"What about the names in Tom's appointment book?" He waved the book in the air.

"No viable leads yet," she said. "The women I've contacted so far had solid alibis."

"What about Pam?" I asked her. "Any leads on the men she dated?"

Dan surprised me when he answered. "Emily came forward. Gave me a short list of her best bets." I noticed the twinkle in his eyes. "I checked them out. Each had a legitimate alibi and no hard feelings."

"What about the wives or girlfriends of those men?" I was scratching the bottom now.

He pursed his lips. "Had to tread lightly. Didn't want to break up serious relationships or intimidate potential witnesses. Nothing so far."

Michael's hands shot up in the air. "Hold it. Let's go back to Anita. If someone hired her to do their dirty work—no pun intended— why would the killer want to pin these murders on me? I have no connection to Tom. I never even met the guy."

"Based on the attempt on Megan's life," Dan said, "it probably has more to do with your connection to *her*."

Michael nodded slowly. "Okay. The killer couldn't get into Megan's condo. So he found a more accessible place to drop off the cyanide—my hotel suite." He gazed at a point in the distance, lost in thought. "Something doesn't add up. I've been in and out of my hotel room the last few days. Why did Anita wait so long before planting the cyanide here?"

I stared at him. "What do you mean?"

"I wore my leather jacket Friday evening. I left it in the car all weekend. After we met with Dan on Monday, I hung it in the hall closet here."

"That's right!" I bolted up, almost spilling my bottle of water. "The cyanide couldn't have been planted before then."

Dan jotted a note. "Narrows the timeline."

I picked up the Cleanit staff schedule and studied it. "It states here the maid service tidies up the hotel rooms before one o'clock every day." I looked at Michael. "It was later than that when you hung your jacket here, so Anita couldn't have planted the cyanide until the next day—Tuesday."

"Or today before the police search," Jane said. "It might explain why Anita didn't pick up her paycheck today."

"Talk about risky," Michael said. "Why would she plant the cyanide hours before the police searched my suite?"

"You have a point," Dan said. "Do it right after the murders. Leave town ASAP."

"So why did she wait so long?" Michael asked, echoing his train of thought.

A brief silence hung over us.

Michael smiled. "It's plain crazy. I was supposed to have checked out of here Saturday morning."

"Can you imagine what Anita would have done had she found your suite empty?" I let out a nervous giggle.

"No problem. She'd have found another sucker to pin the murders on."

"And we wouldn't be sitting here," Dan said, snapping us back to reality.

"The timing still bugs me," Michael said. "When did the news of the murders first break?" He sounded as if he'd just returned from a hiatus overseas and had lost notion of time and day. Not a rare occurrence when someone's life is turned upside down, I supposed.

"Yesterday morning—Tuesday," I said, going back to doodling triangles.

"Okay, that explains it," he said. "After the murders hit the news, the killer gave Anita the go-ahead to plant the cyanide in my suite. We all know what happened after."

"Yes," I said. "An ugly *paparazzi* scene."

Dan looked up from his notebook. "Happens often. Someone sees police cars parked out front. They call the press. Get a few bucks."

"That's sick," I said. "What kind of person takes pleasure in tipping off the media and embarrassing people like that?"

"The killer," Jane said, as if it were common knowledge.

"Why would you say that?" I asked her.

"It's simple. He's looking for attention and needs to be in the spotlight. In fact, he thrives on it. When it doesn't happen, he creates it."

"Plausible," Dan said. "Though more likely to fit the profile of a serial killer."

"I've got another one," Michael said. "How did the killer know I was still in town?"

"A call at the front desk would confirm it," Dan said.

His reply sparked a memory. "The mystery caller!" I blurted.

"What mystery caller?" Dan's pen froze in mid-air.

"The one who left messages on my hotel phone," Michael said, moving toward it. "The voice was camouflaged, but the messages were damn clear. Come listen."

Dan and Jane took turns listening to the recording, then returned to their seats.

"I'll ask for a voice analysis," Dan said, jotting a note. "The murderer—or someone connected to him—might know you after all, buddy."

"I think Emily concocted those calls," Michael said. "It strikes a familiar pattern."

"You're just looking for an excuse to drag her into this mess," I said. "She's angry and sad about Pam's death. It doesn't make her a killer."

"Oh, what the hell," he said. "We can always chuck Peter back in if you like."

I ignored him and started doodling a layer of squares around my circles and triangles.

A tap-tap of Dan's pen. "With the discovery of Anita Castillo, the police investigation might take a different direction. Swing attention away from both of you."

Convenient, but I wasn't convinced we were home free. I hadn't connected all the dots yet. "Anita, the cyanide, the phone messages... We're missing evidence that can tie this information together. Dan, do you think Moreau knows something we don't?"

"It's doubtful," he said. "His theory is basic: the killer had a gripe against Tom or Pam. He had a connection to BOTCOR or Bradford. The cyanide found in Michael's suite is the common link." He let out a deep breath. "Moreau's best guess on motive is a romance between you and Michael."

"I agree," Jane said. "It's the simplest deduction."

Her expression remained pokerfaced and masked heaven-knows-what beneath it. I couldn't tell whether she was explaining Moreau's rationale or promoting it as her own. It was a waste of time trying to read her. I latched onto Dan's last comment instead. "The cyanide drop here can't be traced back to anyone at Bradford. They thought Michael was heading home on Saturday. No one knew he was in town except me."

"Same explanation as before." Dan sounded weary, as if someone had asked him for directions to the washroom for the tenth time. "All they had to do was—"

"We know, buddy, we know," Michael said, smiling. "Call the front desk to see if I'd checked out or not."

"Those words will haunt me forever." Dan chuckled.

Michael turned to me. "I guess that puts you-know-who back in the running."

"If she really wanted Pam out of the way," I said, "she wouldn't have gone through hell and back to do it."

"What are you getting at?"

"She would have laced Pam's cup of coffee with cyanide at work."

"Too obvious. No one in their right mind would kill Pam in such a restricted setting."

"Excuse me," Jane said to Michael, a well-poised forefinger in the air. "What makes you think the cottage at Pineview isn't a restricted setting?"

"Pineview is accessible to an unlimited number of people passing through at all hours. Staff, guests, strangers...you name it. The offices at Bradford aren't. There would be fewer suspects at Bradford."

Dire implications began to zip through my mind. As far as fewer suspects went, Michael was right about Bradford, and one name rose above the rest. If anyone had ever wanted to be like Pam, it was Emily. Yet as much as she admired Pam, she was jealous of her success at work and her popularity with men. She merited our consideration, but I couldn't believe that jealousy was the only motive behind her scheme to do away with Pam. There had to be more to it.

As my doodles reverted to circles once again, I tried to grasp the logic behind the anonymous phone call at the office. Whether Emily had made up the tale about the call or not, the result was the same: she'd succeeded in diverting Moreau's attention to Michael and me. But why? Sure, she blamed me for interfering with her plans to conquer Michael. Yet she had to have acted on much more than a cold shoulder from him to frame us for murder.

In spite of the missing pieces, I had to voice my suspicions.

"Michael, let's say you-know-who had inside information, came up with the perfect plan, and knew she could get away with murder."

His eyes widened. "Are you serious? I was joking back there."

"Think about it. She was jealous of our friendship. She came on to you and you snubbed her. She smeared our names. She pointed the police in our direction—"

"Okay, okay, she was pissed off. But murder?"

"You have no idea what a woman scorned is capable of."

"You actually believe she had a hand in this?" Surprise mounted in Michael's voice.

"Yes, and she used both of them to push me into the traffic!"

"All right," Dan said. "Who are we talking about?"

"Emily Saunders, my alleged stalker," I said. "Did she have an alibi?"

"Let's see." Dan reached for a file in his briefcase and flipped through the pages until he found what he was looking for. "A note from another of my team members. It says Emily went to Toronto on the weekend. Alibi not yet confirmed."

"Maybe she lied about it," I said, recalling how often she'd lied about other things.

"I'll follow up on it." Dan wrote a note.

"I just remembered something," Michael said. "When I went to sign a contract in Emily's office last week, she took a phone call from a guy in Toronto. She mentioned his name but I can't remember it."

"How did you know he was calling from Toronto?" Dan asked.

"She chatted with him about tickets he'd bought for a baseball game at the Rogers Center," Michael said. "It sounded as if he wanted her to fly to Toronto and spend the weekend there with him."

"Did she accept?" I asked.

"Yes," Michael said.

"She used you as a witness for her alibi," I said. "She could have called him back later to cancel the trip and head out to Pineview instead."

"The police can validate the phone records," Dan said, scribbling more notes.

Jane turned to him. "Dan you have a lot on your plate. Do you want me to check out Emily's alibi for you?"

"I don't care what her alibi is," I said. "All the pieces fit. Emily knew Michael's suite number. She could have bribed Anita to make the drop. Or she could have walked over while Michael was out, arranged with Anita to let her into his suite, and planted the cyanide herself."

Michael nodded. "Which would prove the cyanide wasn't planted in my hotel suite by fluke. To make sure the police zeroed in on us, Emily told them about the strange phone call she got at the office—invented or not."

"It would certainly deflect suspicion away from her," Dan said. "Motive?"

It was a weak point, but I went for it anyway. "She was jealous of Pam and looking for revenge against Michael."

"Not enough." Dan shook his head.

"I agree," Jane said. "In any case, how would Emily have obtained the poison? It's not sold off the shelf, you know."

She was right. *How would Emily get her hands on a lethal poison like potassium cyanide?*

Michael snapped his fingers. "I've got it, and only because I have a friend who dabbled in the field. What about Ray Felton?" he asked me.

"Bradford's photographer? What about him?"

"Before the digital age, potassium cyanide was used in film processing. Maybe Ray got a hold of some for Emily."

"Another question," Dan said. "How did the cyanide get to Pineview?"

"Emily has a car," I said. "She could have transported the cyanide there."

I noticed a half-smile creep up on Jane's lips, a sign she was preparing to ask a bombshell of a question. Or maybe she was about to throw my theory out of orbit by making me look like a complete idiot.

"It's an intriguing premise, Megan," she said, "but how would you explain Emily's association with Anita?"

"What do you mean?"

"How did the women come to know each other? What was the nature of their dealings?"

I sensed a challenge and didn't know where Jane was going with this. I resorted to a bit of creativity. "Emily spends most nights hopping from club to club. Illegal aliens are known to find work in clubs. We already know Anita did. Maybe that's where Emily met her. Or like I said before, maybe she just walked up to Anita at the hotel one day and bribed her."

Michael picked up the conversation. "Megan's got a point. Extra bucks come in handy when you're living hand to mouth like Anita. Maybe Emily made it worth her while."

Jane shrugged but didn't say anything. My guess was that she was annoyed because Michael had supported my plausible explanation for her stupid question.

"What do you think?" Michael asked Dan.

Dan nodded. "Possible." He turned to Jane. "What time does the cleaning staff end their shift at Pineview?"

"Four o'clock in the afternoon," she said.

"The Bradford folder." Dan retrieved it from his briefcase and thumbed through it, glancing at each sheet until he found the report he was looking for. "No record of what time Emily left the office Friday. Her time frame might be tight."

"It could work if she arrived before Tom and Pam or later while they were out," Michael said, calling up a theory we'd discussed before.

"And walked right in if the cottage door was unlocked," I said, repeating yet another hypothesis I'd flagged earlier.

Dan shook his head from side to side in a display of hesitation.

I pressed on. "I still think Emily is the most likely suspect."

"My bet's on Emily too," Michael said.

"I thought your bet was on Peter," Dan said.

"I've changed my mind," Michael said. "What do you think about Emily as a suspect?"

Dan shrugged. "Fact remains the police investigation is ongoing. They haven't discounted Peter yet."

I didn't know why it hadn't hit me earlier. None of our theories explained the killer's connection to Michael and his hotel suite, except the one that involved Emily. She was the only person, aside from Pam and me, who knew Michael's suite number. I'd considered the likelihood she might have bragged about it to her girlfriends, but I rejected the notion. Emily wouldn't have shared anything about Michael with the competition.

"Dan, here's an eye-opener," I said. "Peter never met Michael. He didn't know Michael's suite number, so he couldn't have used Anita for the drop."

"Way to go, Megan!" Michael slapped his hands together.

The frown across Dan's forehead told me I hadn't won him over yet. "Maybe Tom told Peter that you had a client in this hotel."

"I never told Tom I was working with Michael, let alone the hotel name," I said.

Dan gave me a sideways glance. Maybe he didn't believe me. Or maybe he was surprised I didn't share client information with Tom.

"Tom and I never discussed our work," I said. "When he came home from his trips, there were more important things to talk about."

Dan nodded. "Of course."

"It has to be Emily," I said. "She's a liar and a sneak. She'll do anything to get what she wants, including getting revenge. She learned her scheming ways from the best of them: Pam."

Dan looked as if he were considering my hypothesis. "In theory, her motive is weak. If the police go this route, they'll need to prove premeditation. Show how Emily worked with Ray to obtain the cyanide. Show how she knew about Pam's plans to go to Pineview well ahead of time so she could make her move."

"Honestly, Dan," Jane said, laughing, as if it were a preposterous assumption on his part. "I don't know how the police can establish that premise without reading Emily's mind."

I did, but my instincts held me back from saying so. The last thing I wanted to do was share this information with Jane. Sure, her investigation process was as thorough as one could expect. I could easily relate to it because my job was based on verifying the accuracy of information too. Our work made us kindred spirits of sorts, but it stopped there. Whatever was behind Jane's reasoning tonight was out of whack with mine. She seemed determined to work against any suggestion I brought up, so I decided to stay mum.

"In any case," Dan said, "it's up to the prosecution to prove Emily's guilt, though her unconfirmed alibi does help our situation. Potential for creating doubt in her as a witness if she lied." He gathered his files and placed them in his briefcase. "All right, Jane. We're done here."

Jane stood up and put on her jacket. "Can we give you a ride home, Megan?"

*Damn! Michael and I had other plans.* "Well, I—"

"It's okay," Michael cut in. "I'll drive Megan home later."

"Oh...okay." Jane picked up her briefcase.

"Call you tomorrow with an update," Dan said, leading the way out.


After Michael had shut the door behind them, he slid into his armchair and stared at me. "You realize we're on our own, don't you? We have to find concrete evidence to prove Emily is the killer or we're done."

"I think I have a way. Want to go to Bradford Publishing with me tomorrow night?"

"To do what?"

"Come and you'll see."

"You're full of surprises, aren't you?" He smiled.

I smiled back. "Want to work on our plans for Emily?"

"Yes, but I'll call room service first."

Michael ordered a pot of coffee and muffins, then we sat down to put pen to paper.

An hour later, we had a framework of the strategic steps, resources, and timelines Emily might have adopted in her efforts to pull off the murders and get away with the perfect crime. At last we had a feasible theory. Best of all, we had hope—lots of it—as the prospect of closure loomed ahead.

On the drive back to my condo, Michael surprised me. "I'm going to Pineview tomorrow," he said.

I looked at him. "Pineview? Whatever for? Jane already interviewed everyone there."

"Remember the list that dropped out of Dan's file?"

"Yes, the people who worked there. So?"

"I think I recognized a name. Robert Gingras."

"That's a very common name. How can you be sure it's the same man you know?"

"I don't. That's why I loaded a photo of him on my cell to show the Pineview owner."

"So how do you know Gingras?"

"Remember the court case I attended a year ago in Montreal where I first met Jane?"

"Yes."

"Gingras was connected to that case. He was arrested for suspicion of petty theft and drug possession. Ironically, Willie had given me the lead on Gingras and his drug dealing. I wanted to see how it played out, so I attended every court session. In the end, the charges didn't stick and Gingras was acquitted."

"If Jane knew about Gingras, why didn't she mention him to you?"

"I doubt she'd remember the case, let alone his name. She only popped in the last day of the trial. She sat down next to me and introduced herself, said she had some time to kill. We chatted for a few minutes. I told her about my work, she talked about her job—casual stuff. Before I could discuss the ongoing court case with her, her cell phone vibrated and she left to take the call. I didn't see her again until two months ago."

"Don't the police have a file on Gingras?"

"Not if he had his criminal record erased since then. That's probably why Jane didn't find anything in his background check. I'll bet a clean slate got him the job at Pineview too."

"And why do you want to go to Pineview again?"

"A gut feeling. Gingras might know something about the double murders. I think he kept a low profile and didn't come forward because of his history with the cops. I want to talk to him. See if I get any bad vibes."

"I'm going with you," I said.

"It's not a good idea."

"Why? Because Tom died there, and you're afraid I might get upset?" I met his gaze.

He shrugged, said nothing.

"I'm beyond that point, Michael. I just want to prove I'm innocent so I can get on with my life."

"Makes two of us."

# CHAPTER 20

By ten o'clock Thursday morning, Michael and I were driving along Highway 243 south toward Knowlton in the Eastern Townships, or *Les Cantons de l'Est*. The fall colors of the trees—yellow, orange, and red for the most part—were at odds with the intense heat and high humidity of this late August day. Despite the comfort of our shorts and T-shirts, the air conditioning in the Mustang Coupe made breathing a lot easier.

I'd researched Knowlton on the Internet earlier and found this blurb:

"Situated on Brome Lake, Knowlton is sometimes known as the *Knamptons* (a combination of Knowlton and the Hamptons) because many residents own multi-million-dollar country homes in the area. It is renowned for its golf courses, biking trails, ski hills, Marina, and duck farming. Every September, the town plays host to the Duck Festival. Up to fifty thousand people from Quebec, Ontario, Vermont, New York, and elsewhere gather to taste the latest duck creations from world-class chefs. The streets are filled with tasting booths offering freshly cooked duck. In addition, musicians and artists perform, and local producers sell ciders, fruits, breads, jams, and honey."

Our timing was off for the Duck Festival, but I wasn't disappointed. Knowlton had everything I expected to find in a charming village and more. Boutiques, antique stores, cafés, restaurants, and B & Bs dotted this bilingual community that five thousand people called home. Although many buildings displayed New England style architecture, French influences were apparent in the names of restaurants such as *Le Relais*. Michael suggested we stop at *Chocolaterie Raphaël* to pick up some Belgian chocolates to snack on later. Who was I to argue?

"My parents used to live around here before they moved to a three-story home in Westmount," Michael said as we continued our drive through town. "I think they still own sixty acres of waterfront land on Brome Lake."

I did the math. A million dollars easily. "Did they begin their retirement here?"

"No, my Dad worked for a high-tech company in the area."

"Odd location for high-tech. What kind of work did he do?"

"Something with semiconductor technology."

"And your mother?"

"She never worked. Didn't have to."

I was glad he was finally opening up about his family. "How are they doing?"

He shrugged. "We're not that close. We had a falling out years back. I haven't spoken to them in a while."

I couldn't imagine not calling my mother whenever I wanted to. "Want to talk about it?"

A muscle pulsated along his jaw. "Not much to say. Dad got angry when I said I wanted to study investigative journalism. He thought it was a waste of time. That's when I left home."

"What did your mother say?"

"She doesn't like arguments. She stayed out of it."

"So you ran off to Toronto."

"I didn't run off. I went there to study. My grandmother suggested I go live with her and I accepted. At least she supported my career choice." He stared ahead and said nothing more—a sign of closure to the topic.

Maybe for good. Damn it, I'd pushed it too far.


Minutes out of Knowlton, we turned off the main road and drove up a gravel path that led to the Pineview resort. The charm and tranquility of the Victorian-style cottages snuggled in a thick forest seemed surreal. The imagery negated the fact that two people had been murdered here. In fact, it was the last place on earth I would imagine as a crime scene.

Michael slowed down as we approached one of the cottages situated close to the path. From the photo I'd seen in Dan's file, I recognized the door with the four glass panels and the white trim around them, the eyelet curtains in a side window, and the wood steps leading up to the front porch. I was positive it was the cottage Tom had stayed in. As if to refute any doubts, a piece of yellow crime scene tape was caught in a bush—evidence that a forensics analysis had recently been performed on the premises. Yet another painful image to add to my memory banks.

I felt a tug on my heartstrings, followed by regret that my marriage to Tom hadn't had the time to blossom.

Then my stomach knotted. *He had cheated on me with my best friend.*

Michael cut the engine. He turned to look at me. "Are you okay to do this?"

I took a deep breath. "Yes."

We mounted the front steps to the cottage. The wood beams creaked under our weight, adding a natural charm to the countryside ambiance while masking the horror that occurred here days earlier. Birds chirped in a fit of frenzy in tree branches, as if we'd invaded their space. I wondered if they'd chirped that loudly the day the killer had crept indoors with the cyanide.

Michael peered through the glass in the front door. "They haven't cleaned it up yet."

He was right. Fragments of chinaware littered the floor. Chalk marks outlined the area where Tom and Pam were found—inches from the door. A white powdery substance—probably fingerprint powder residue—covered cabinets and furniture.

Goose bumps rose along my arms, and I shivered involuntarily.

Michael put a hand on my shoulder. "Okay. We've seen enough. Let's go."

I didn't argue.

We drove further up the path and around a bend to the main reception building. Michael parked the car in front.

"My turn to take pictures." I opened the door and got out. After I'd taken three photos, I tucked the camera back into my purse and fell into step with Michael.

Indoors, a woman at the front counter greeted us with a smile. "Hello. I'm Louise. How can I help you?"

I detected a slight French-Canadian accent. No surprise with a name like Louise. I placed her in her late fifties. Her blonde hair was cut in wispy layers to her shoulders—like the Farah Fawcett hairdo of the 1980s—and I assumed she'd worn it that way for decades. It might have been outdated, but it added softness to her hollow cheekbones and lean physique. A crisp white cotton shirt and matching shorts showed off a tan and gave her a sporty yet business-like appearance. Although I couldn't see her feet behind the counter, I doubted she was wearing heels. She was about my height.

I introduced Michael first.

Louise's smile faded at the mention of my name. "Oh, my goodness. I'm so sorry for your loss, Mrs. Scott. What can I do for you?"

I glanced at a young couple leafing through pamphlets in a stand nearby. "Can we talk privately somewhere?"

"Certainly. I'll go get my husband." Louise left through a side door and reappeared moments later with a man in a blue polo shirt and shorts. He was as tanned as Louise. "This is my husband, Stewart. He can help you."

"How are you?" Stewart shook hands with us. His firm grasp surprised me because he was slim and not much taller than Louise, though the muscles on his arms told me he lifted weights or played sports of some kind—probably golf. His hair was cut so close to the scalp that it looked as if the hairs had been penciled in like so many dots. "Let's talk outside." He led us out the front door and motioned toward a table and chairs under a parasol close by. "Sorry about your husband, Mrs. Scott. Do the police know who did it?"

"Not yet," I said, choosing a chair in the shade.

Stewart's dark eyes shifted to Michael. "Are you with the media?

Cause I've got nothing more to say to them."

"This is personal," Michael said. "I need information about a man who works here."

"Who?"

Michael showed him the photo of Gingras on his cell phone.

I stole a peek. A round and unshaven face. Eyes that revealed a mix of anger and desolation. Unkempt hair that looked as if it hadn't been washed in days. The photo resembled a mug shot. Michael might have accessed it before the police allegedly erased Gingras' file.

"Robert Gingras?" Stewart arched an eyebrow. "He doesn't work here anymore."

"When did he quit?"

"He didn't quit. He took off two days ago without a word. Left all his things here."

"When did he start working here?"

"About two weeks ago."

"What kind of work did he do?"

"Basic stuff. It's peak season for us. I needed help with the washing and cleaning while I tackled repairs and upgrades."

"Did he have any references?"

"Nope. He'd been working in a manufacturing plant and was looking for work."

"No offense," I said, "but didn't you find it odd that he'd leave a manufacturing job to come wash dishes here?"

"Sorry, I wasn't clear about that," Stewart said. "He told me he was laid off."

"Laid off?"

Stewart nodded. "Because of downsizing. He begged me for a job. Said he'd work only for room and board if he had to. If the guy hadn't had a bad leg..." He shrugged. "I felt sorry for him. I gave him the job right off the bat." His expression soured. "And what did I get in return? He stole my gun. A 9 mm Beretta."

"Did you report it to the police?" Michael asked.

"Sure did."

"Any leads on it?"

"Nope." Stewart paused while the couple we'd seen inside walked out and got into their car. "Why are you looking for Gingras?" He cast a glance in my direction. "Does it have anything to do with the murders here?"

"No, " I said, not volunteering more information.

"He might be in trouble, though," Michael said.

Stewart nodded. "Wouldn't surprise me."

"Why not?"

"My employees know they can trust me with anything they tell me," Stewart said. "But Gingras, he never talked about anything to no one. Kept pretty much to himself. Maybe it's me, but I always thought the guy had something to hide. Like maybe he's done time on the inside."

Our return from Knowlton led to a reality check of my fridge. A box of baking soda. A small bottle of water. A bottle of ketchup. Half a stick of unsalted butter. A carton of milk that expired yesterday. Two eggs.

I refused to drink tap water. It tasted funny and made me wonder whether the chlorine they dumped into it was a healthier choice or not. I didn't even want to consider the presence of other unknown substances the water still contained after filtration—substances that disintegrated into particles so microscopic that you couldn't see them with the naked eye.

I reached in and grabbed the water bottle. "Source water," the label read. Regardless of the chemicals the plastic itself might contain, at least the water sounded as if it came from a clean starting place. I twisted it open and poured half into a glass, then handed Michael the bottle.

"What are your plans for the rest of the day?" He leaned against the kitchen counter and brought the bottle to his lips.

"To start with, I should pick up some groceries."

"Can I tag along? Waiting in my hotel room for Dan's call would drive me crazy."

I suspected it was his way of providing an extra layer of protection around me, but I welcomed the offer of a ride and an extra pair of arms. "Okay, but I'm warning you. I have a string of errands to run."

"No problem."

I dug into my purse and retrieved the bag that contained the last two Belgian chocolates from Michael's purchase in Knowlton. I took one and handed him the other one in the bag. "Better eat up," I said. "This is lunch."

Who was I kidding? With an appetite like his, running on empty was unheard of.

Half an hour later, I was munching on a tuna salad at Burgers & Benedicts. I watched as Michael ingested a mango burger and fries within minutes. Anyone else would have assumed he hadn't eaten in days. When he insisted on paying the tab, I didn't refuse. My bank account balance was dwindling, and I was weeks away from receiving Bradford's check. Everything I'd recently purchased had gone on my credit card.

We spent the rest of the afternoon dropping off laundry at the cleaners, picking up groceries, and buying basics at the drugstore— errands I'd often run on my own. It was much easier doing them with someone else for a change.

Michael didn't seem to mind either. Maybe he didn't have a choice. Anyone who lived out of a suitcase had to have some kind of routine going if they wanted to survive—especially if they didn't have easy access to a fridge, stove, and washing machine.

I watched as he scrutinized the labels on wine bottles at the liquor store. He helped me to select three—a Chardonnay from France, a rosé from Australia, and a Riesling from Germany. Then he paid for them, hinting that any of them would go well with homemade pasta.

I laughed. His presence comforted me and took my mind off our predicament. No man with an ounce of common sense would have stuck around to help a woman suspected of murdering her husband and his mistress. Then again, Michael wasn't just any man. All the more reason I valued our friendship so much. A sinking feeling hit me whenever I remembered Toronto was his home, not Montreal. What would I do without him?

Minutes after we'd returned to my apartment and put the groceries away, Dan called. "Sorry I couldn't get back to you sooner," he said over the speakerphone in my office. He let out a deep breath. "My contact at the Elegance just called me. They found Anita's body."

My blood went cold. "Oh, my God. Where?"

"In one of the hotel rooms."

"How did she die?"

"Possible gunshot wound."

"When?"

"Not sure. We'll know more after the forensics analysis. Okay if we all meet at your place tomorrow morning, Megan?"

Michael nodded yes.

"Sure. See you tomorrow." I pressed the off button and looked at Michael. "Anita was our last hope. Now what?"

He passed a hand through his hair. "Emily's closing in...getting rid of anyone who might talk...covering her tracks like any murderer would."

I thought about Emily and the increasing tally of dead bodies in our lives, yet a doubt nagged at me. "I can't see Emily pulling the trigger. Do you suppose she—"

"Hired a hit man? Yeah. Maybe a sleazy reference through her nightclub contacts. But he's long gone by now."

"At least we've bought a few more hours to gather evidence against her."

"For what it's worth."

"What do you mean?"

"If Emily isn't on Moreau's short list of suspects, we've got one hell of a battle on our hands."

# CHAPTER 21

Even at eight in the evening, humidity hung heavy in the air with no relief from the slightest breeze. So much for the cooling trend the meteorologists had predicted. It was a wonder they ever got it right. Pure luck, I supposed, which was what Michael and I needed right now.

We'd driven around for half an hour looking for a parking space downtown. Oddly enough, the bike lanes were more congested than the car lanes. We finally found a parking space on Mansfield Street after our fifth try around the block. Michael filled the meter to avoid getting a ticket from the Green Onions, the parking police nicknamed after the color of their uniforms. These checkers sought out empty meters with an enthusiasm that knew no leniency, and they issued a stack of parking tickets to corroborate it every year.

We were walking up Sherbrooke Street to Bradford Publishing when Michael's cell phone rang. He answered it. From the gist of the conversation, I understood the caller wanted to meet with him tonight.

"Fluky or what?" he said to me, slipping the phone back into the pocket of his cargo shorts. "Some guy wants to meet me downtown later. He has information about a drug case I'm following. He spoke French. Threw in a couple of words in English. I'm not sure I understood everything. I don't want to misinterpret anything he says, so do you want to come along?"

"Okay."

We'd reached the front doors to the building that housed

Bradford's offices. I tapped on the glass door and held up my employee ID card for the security guard to see.

Carlo pulled his gaze off a TV set tucked under the counter of the reception desk. He smiled when he recognized me and hurried across the lobby, the pant cuffs of his brown uniform gathered over his shoes like the folds of a Chinese Shar-Pei.

"Mrs. Scott, so happy to see you," he said, opening the door. He gave Michael a wary look.

"It's okay, Carlo," I said. "He's a client."

Carlo nodded and let us in. He locked the door, his key ring clattering against the metal doorframe. "Please accept my sympathy, Mrs. Scott. So young man. So unfortunate." English wasn't the Filipino's first language, but caring eyes under drooping eyelids conveyed a sadness that words couldn't express.

"Thank you, Carlo." I moved over to the counter.

"Catching up on work tonight, Mrs. Scott?" He walked back to his former location and offered me a pen.

"No, I just came by to collect a few personal things from my office." I signed the visitor's sheet. "I won't be long."

"Take all the time you need, Mrs. Scott," he said, smiling and nodding as if the building belonged to him.

In a way, it did. He'd worked the evening shift here for twenty years and made it a point to remember the name of every employee who worked here and the company they worked for. In my line of work, I could have benefited from having that kind of memory.

Michael and I rode the elevator up to the tenth floor. I dug into my shoulder bag for a set of keys and opened the oak door to Bradford Publishing.

"You have your own key to the company?" Michael asked. "I'm impressed."

"I work late hours sometimes." Inside I flicked a wall switch. A table lamp in a corner of the reception area lit up. I shut and locked the door behind us. I didn't bother turning on any other lights because I didn't have to. The building had a system that programmed every fifth neon light in the ceiling to stay on after hours on low power—part of a new administrative "green" plan to conserve energy.

"What's next?" Michael asked.

"We need to get Pam's agenda from her desk. It might contain clues that could incriminate Emily."

"Where's Pam's office?" He looked around, ready to spring into action.

"Hold on. This is where things get complicated. Pam always locked her desk when she was away from the office."

"You mean we have to break into it?" His eyes twinkled with humor or mischief. I couldn't tell which one.

"Not exactly. Kayla told me she suspects Emily had a duplicate key made because she caught her going through Pam's desk more than once when Pam was away. We need to find that duplicate key."

"Didn't Kayla ever question Emily or Pam about it?"

"Yes, and Emily said it was okay, that Pam had given her a spare key so she could check her agenda to see if any client meetings they were both attending had been re-scheduled. Pam would sometimes forget to tell Emily. As for telling Pam about the duplicate key, Kayla didn't want to cause friction between Emily and Pam, so she let it go."

"The webs we weave," Michael said with a grin.

"Tell me about it." I shook my head. "Our first stop is Emily's office. Follow me."

Our footsteps padded along the carpeted corridor. The lights hummed above and cast shadows on the walls, adding an eerie ambiance to the stillness in the place. As we walked past Pam's office, I almost expected to see her sitting at her desk.

"This place gives me the creeps," I said. "I've spent a lot of evenings working alone here, but I never noticed how spooky it was."

Michael had more realistic concerns. "What if the door to Emily's office is locked?"

"There are no locks on the doors. Company policy. The girls lock their desks instead."

"Are we going to break into Emily's desk?" I noticed that same twinkle in his eye.

"We don't have to. Emily hides a key under a *papier-mâché* rabbit on the third shelf of her bookcase. I'm crossing my fingers it's the one to Pam's desk."

"Aha! So you've done some snooping around yourself."

"Not really. I happened to see her hide it there once."

"How do you know it's not the key to her own desk?"

"Because the key to her own desk is on a keychain with her house keys."

The door to Emily's office was ajar. I pushed it open, then reached along the wall for the light switch and flipped it on.

I froze. The top drawer of Emily's desk was hanging on its edge, ready to topple. The two side drawers had been yanked out and pitched to the floor. Pens, documents, and dozens of CDs and DVDs were scattered everywhere. Books from a five-tiered bookcase lay in another pile on the floor, as if someone had leafed through each one and tossed it aside.

"Damn. Someone beat us to it." Michael surveyed the scene. "Someone in a big hurry." He pointed to the bookcase. "The books on the top shelf weren't touched. Either his search was cut short or he found what he was looking for."

"As long as he didn't find what *we're* looking for." I looked down and spotted the papier-mâché rabbit amid the stack of books. I picked it up and placed it on Emily's desk. "Can you give me a hand, Michael? The key must be somewhere under this mess."

We removed the books, one by one, and tossed them aside to form a new pile. Our efforts proved futile: no key in sight.

"What about those?" Michael gestured to the remaining books in the bookcase. "Might as well finish the job." He flipped through the pages of each book, then tossed it onto the new pile. By the end of his search, we were no further ahead.

"Maybe she changed her hiding place." I walked over to Emily's desk. I pulled out the top drawer and checked it on all sides, hoping to find a key stuck to it with tape. Nothing.

I checked the other drawers. Nothing there either.

I got down on my knees and searched under the desk. Still nothing.

I stood up and let my eyes stray around the room. Aside from the bookcase, Emily's office contained two chairs, a desk, and a computer. No filing cabinets. She had no use for them. All her work was done on computer and forwarded by e-mail to the client or put on a CD and sent out by messenger. Important documents were sent to Bradford's legal department off site.

I walked over to the bookcase. There was a narrow space between it and the wall. I pressed my face to the wall and peered into the gap. "I see something. It's on the floor, but I can't reach it."

Michael helped me move the bookcase over a few inches. I bent down and picked up what turned out to be photographs held together with a large paperclip. Bill Bradford and Pam were in the first photo. His arm was wrapped around her waist. Scratches across the photo had removed part of Pam's face, but I recognized her from the blonde hair and the low-cut red dress she'd worn that evening. I removed the paperclip and held the photo out for Michael to see. "This picture was taken at the last company Christmas party."

He peered at it. "What's with the scratches?"

"Probably the paperclip." I leafed through the others and noticed similar marks on the rest of them but only across Pam's face. "Hold on. They're not scratches. Someone deliberately rubbed out Pam's face."

"Guess who?" Michael grinned.

"How much more proof do we need?"

"Not admissible in court. You can't prove Emily defaced them. And even if she did, it's not a criminal offense."

"Too bad." I tossed them back behind the bookcase. "That key has to be in here. We're not leaving until we find it."

I stood back and zoomed in on the huge Boston fern sitting in a ceramic pot next to the bookcase. It was the only thing in the office that had remained untouched.

I walked over to it and held back its delicate leaves. "It's here!" I plucked the key from the soil.

"It probably slid off the shelf when the intruder ransacked the place," Michael said. "Indulge me. Let me try it in Emily's desk first." I handed it to him.

He picked up the top drawer I'd removed earlier but stopped

short of inserting the key. "The intruder jimmied the lock. It's damaged." He gave me back the key.

"That settles it. Let's go get Pam's agenda."

Bold and dynamic when she'd redecorated it months ago, the black-and-white 60s décor of Pam's office now seemed dated and out of place. It was as if her passing had drained the energy out of the room.

I recalled Mrs. Bradford's outburst here the other day and now wondered if her husband hadn't authorized Pam's office redo for more personal reasons. After all, it had since come to light that married men were *not* excluded from Pam's game plan. Maybe the renovation bills had aroused Mrs. Bradford's suspicions about goings-on between her husband and Pam, and that was why she'd threatened her. Then again, what did it matter at this point? As far as murder suspects went, I'd already replaced her name with Emily's.

I crossed the checkered floor to Pam's desk. My eyes rested on her trophy knickknacks. I contemplated whether things might have worked out differently had Tom added to her collection instead of inviting her for a weekend fling. But why look back? Destiny had worked its spell in the unique way that only destiny can. It had brought together two people addicted to deception and had sucked the last breath of life out of them. Ruthlessly. Sadistically. Without bias.

"You okay?" I turned to see Michael peering at me.

"Uh? Me? Sure." I walked around Pam's desk and tried the key in the top drawer. It worked! I removed a couple of contracts, notepads, and loose memos. All that remained were two pens and a box of paper clips. "Damn it! Her agenda's not here."

"Moreau must have seized it as evidence," Michael said.

I paused to think. "I'm counting on one other possibility."

"What's that?"

"Moreau doesn't have it." I closed the drawer and locked it.

"Then who does?"

"Kayla."

"Kayla? Why?"

"I think she'd had enough of Emily's snooping. Maybe she decided to put Pam's agenda in a safe place—like her own desk—after Pam left that last Friday."

"Wouldn't Kayla's desk be locked?"

"Let's go see. Her office is right across the hall."

A comfy high-back chair in a blend of organic and natural materials and a tall leafy plant hinted at the down-to-earth style of Kayla's office. Dictionaries, classical novels, and a collection of favorite hardbacks filled a mahogany bookcase in a corner by the window. A white board hanging on a wall behind her desk indicated the timeline of Bradford's projects for the next calendar year. Out of privacy concerns, Kayla used a code number for every client instead of a name.

What stood out from the rest of the furnishings was Kayla's desk. It resembled Pam's black lacquered one except it was smaller. Both desks had arrived at the same time, so it was anyone's guess how Pam had convinced Kayla to divert from natural to plastic or even if she'd persuaded Bill Bradford to cover this extra expense.

I was still holding the duplicate key to Pam's desk in my hand. What if...? I walked over to Kayla's desk and inserted it in the lock. It worked!

I opened the drawer. The first thing I saw was the faux leopard cover of Pam's agenda. "It's here!" I grabbed it. The second thing I saw was a set of keys, which I casually slipped into my pocket.

"Talk about luck," Michael said. "How the hell did the cops miss it?"

"They must have thought it was Kayla's. Looks like she found a way to control Emily's snooping problem after all." I smiled.

"Don't keep me in suspense. Check it out." He peered over my shoulder.

I flipped through the pages in July, searching for entries that alluded to Pam's trip to Pineview. "Here's a note she wrote two weeks before the trip. The Pineview address is here, the time Tom was going to pick her up... Everything we need to support our case."

"That's great, except for one thing."

"What?"

"How can we prove Emily saw this notation and acted on it?"

"We'll find a way." I shut the drawer and locked it. "I'm hanging onto Pam's agenda and the duplicate key from Emily's office too. She can fret over its disappearance for a while."

"My, my, my," Michael said, grinning. "You're finally showing your ruthless side."

"It's either our heads on the chopping block or someone else's. Right?"

"I've got no problem with that." He looked away, as if he were trying to recall something. "Yeah. About the break-in in Emily's office. If the burglar wasn't looking for Pam's key, what the hell was he looking for?"

"I don't know, but Emily is going to have a fit when she sees the mess. I'll report it to the guard downstairs in case he thinks we did it."

"Seems to be the pattern these days."

I picked up the phone on Kayla's desk and dialed Carlo's extension. My duty done, I hung up. "He's going to report it to administration," I said to Michael. "Are you ready for step two of our plan?"

"Lead the way," he said, with a wide sweep of his hand.

After I locked up, we took the stairs down to the next floor. I opened the door to the landing. Bradford's graphic arts department was straight ahead of us.

"What? No more magic keys?" Michael asked as we approached the door.

I reached into my pocket. "You mean these?" I dangled them in the air. "I took—no, borrowed—them from Kayla's desk. Oh, don't look so shocked. I'll put them back later."

"That's the second time you've impressed me tonight," he said. "If you keep this up, I'm going to start feeling inadequate around you."

I laughed. "We're not in the clear yet. If we get caught breaking into this place with a set of keys that don't belong to us, you might have to eat those words—and the keys too." I unlocked the door.

Moonlight filtered in through horizontal blinds and fell on a hodgepodge of photographic gear, Mac computers, and art tables that Bradford's photographers, illustrators, and layout artists had abandoned earlier today. Chrome and metal parts glistened in the dim light, giving the illusion they were living apparatus waiting to be assembled and put into action. In a corner, a strange human persona seemed to emanate from an umbrella, a studio stand, and a reflector. Even the camera on a tripod appeared lifelike, its lens reflecting a glint as we walked by.

I shook off a feeling of being watched and attributed it to guilt from Tom's passing—or maybe Pam's too—something I'd have to deal with sooner or later but not now. "It's dark in here, but I can't risk switching on the lights."

"That's okay," Michael said, gazing around. "All this metal. Imposing, isn't it? Like a scene out of *Star Wars.*"

*And the battle has just begun.*

We'd reached the end of the floor and turned the corner on the right when loud rap music reached our ears.

"Someone's here," Michael said, his eyes darting to the end of the corridor. The red light over the darkroom door was on.

I glanced around. "Quick. Let's hide in here." I led the way into a washroom and shut the door. Big mistake, I realized too late as total darkness cloaked us.

When I was a kid, my mother's old cedar chest in the basement had been my favorite hiding spot until the day the lock got stuck and I couldn't get out. I'd almost passed out by the time someone found me. Since then, I'd avoided entering small, dark spaces.

My pulse accelerated. So did my breathing.

I opened the bathroom door a crack and breathed in deeply. Much better.

I fixed one eye on the red light over the darkroom. Michael stood behind me, gazing over my head.

"This is the digital age," he whispered. "Bradford still uses darkrooms?"

"The facilities were here when Bill Bradford bought the business decades ago," I whispered back. "He's a photography hobbyist and uses the darkroom once in a while. Should we knock at the door?"

"No. I doubt he'd be in there listening to loud rap music. Let's wait it out."

The minutes dragged into half an hour. Michael's bits of conversation calmed me, but as time passed and silence took over, panic welled up inside me again. My chest felt tight and I began to sweat. I took two deep breaths and focused on the red light over the darkroom door. It was all I could do to keep from rushing out into the corridor, screaming.

Michael sensed my anxiety. "You okay?

I explained my dilemma.

"If he doesn't come out in ten seconds," he said, "I'll go knock at the door."

I didn't have the chance to answer.

The red light went off. The door to the darkroom opened. Rap music blared from inside.

Ray emerged. He held a canister with a symbol on it that I couldn't make out. I expected him to walk past our hiding place, but he stopped as if he'd forgotten something and headed back into the darkroom.

I whispered to Michael, "Did you notice the symbol on the canister?"

"Yes, but it's too dark. I can't see what it is."

The music stopped. Ray reappeared. He was still holding the canister. He neared our hiding place, and I got a better look at it. It had a skull and crossbones symbol on it!

Michael grabbed me by the shoulders and moved me aside. He didn't mean to throw me off balance, but I lost my footing and ended up on the floor as he charged out of the washroom.

"Hey!" he shouted after Ray.

I got up and rushed out in time to see Michael land hard against the wall. I glimpsed Ray's backside as he rounded the corner.

Michael was doubled up in pain, one arm wrapped around his chest. "Karate kick...I think...he broke my ribs."

The outer door clicked open, then slammed shut.

"I'll call the guard." I ran to the nearest phone and dialed Carlo's extension once again. My call was forwarded to his voice mail.

Michael shuffled up to me. "So?"

"Carlo didn't answer. I left a message, but I don't think he'll get it in time to stop Ray."

"Doesn't matter." He shook his head. "Poison...one more piece to the puzzle." He grimaced as he tried to straighten up. "Do you think...Ray ransacked Emily's office?" His breathing was strained.

"Only if he was looking for evidence that might incriminate him."

"Ray's connection to Emily...will support our plans."

I winced with every breath Michael struggled to take. "Try not to talk. We'll deal with Ray later. Right now, I'm going to return the keys to Kayla's desk. Then I'm taking you to the Royal Victoria Hospital."

"No...I can't go there."

"What are you talking about? You need to see a doctor right away."

He shook his head. "I have to meet...with my informant." He checked his watch. "In an hour."

"Are you out of your mind?"

# CHAPTER 22

The meeting with his informant was crucial to Michael. From reading his investigative work, I understood the difficulty of setting up a rendezvous point that was safe and neutral for both parties. Such events don't occur with frequency and a crime reporter had to grab an opportunity when it presented itself.

Michael wheezed. "I need you...to drive me there."

"But you can barely walk, let alone talk."

"I'll...manage."

I battled with my decision for a long moment. "Okay, but we're going straight to the hospital afterward. No ifs or buts."

Carlo was sitting at the front desk when we walked out of the elevator. Michael was bent over and leaning on my shoulder for support.

I told Carlo what had happened.

"Ray gone," Carlo said, concern lines deepening across his forehead. "I check message but too late. So sorry, Mrs. Scott. So sorry." He continued to apologize as he unlocked the front door and let us out.

Michael waited outside the building while I went to get the car. I drove back to pick him up but had to double-park because there was a no-stopping zone in front of the building. He spent a full sixty seconds getting into the passenger seat. All that groaning and swearing under his breath provided a viable outlet for his pain, and I couldn't help but empathize with him. It was pointless to try and change his mind again about going to the hospital, so I let it go at that.

A car horn blasted behind us. Another driver honked loudly as he shot past us in the bordering lane. Montrealers weren't the most patient people when dealing with traffic snags, especially if they materialized on a hot and humid evening.

"Where are you meeting your informant?" I asked Michael.

He grimaced as he buckled up. "Corner of...Sainte-Catherine Street...and Saint-Laurent Boulevard."

"Are you sure?" I stepped on the gas, ran through a yellow light.

"That's what...the guy said."

"Okay."

"You can wait in the car...if you like."

"Don't you need me to translate for you?"

"Oh...right."

"Does your informant have a name?"

"No."

"How are you going to recognize him?"

"Short blonde hair...yellow tank top."

"That's it?"

"Yes."

Sainte-Catherine and Saint-Laurent. The fact that the streets at this renowned intersection were named after two saints was deceptive, if not paradoxical, given that they crossed in the heart of the city's red light district.

Prostitution ranked as old a tradition in Montreal as eating a smoked meat sandwich at Schwartz's, a steamy hot dog at the Montreal Pool Room, or *poutine* at LaFleur. According to a historian whose book I'd ghostwritten, the street trade in Montreal had dwindled over the decades with the influx of escort services and massage parlors, yet one-third of prostitutes continued to market their wares outdoors. It was a risky venture, not to mention a criminal offense if the police caught them soliciting a client for money in a public place. I imagined job location was a matter of preference or convenience, as in any other profession.

I drove past Michael's rendezvous point and around the block in search of a parking spot on the street. I refused to pay hard-earned money to park in a lot for half an hour or less, so I opted for a sluggish search in bumper-to-bumper traffic instead.

I drove around the block one more time and struck out again.

With thirty minutes left to rendezvous time, I extended my search to a three-block radius and drove back along Saint-Laurent, also known as "The Main" to locals. As Montreal's oldest and most important north-south artery, it runs for six miles through the near-center of the city. This border between the French in the east and the English in the west all but vanished in recent decades with the growth of a bilingual population and the influx of immigrants— European cultures representing the bulk of them. Home to a cosmopolitan mélange of restaurants, cafés, funky clothing stores, theater, summer festivals, and cultural events, its trendy nightclubs and eateries make it a hotspot for the young and hip.

I was more familiar with the area called Upper Main, located north of Mount Royal Avenue. As a young child, I'd go shopping with my parents in the open-air Jean-Talon market near Little Italy where hundreds of fresh fruit and vegetable stands attracted throngs of buyers. We often stopped at one of the neighboring bakeries or cheese shops to purchase a special treat before heading back home.

Michael and I were in Lower Main—an area that implied pimps, hookers, punks, drugs, and thieves. Although the red light district had shrunk in size with the construction of tamer venues within it, such as art museums and theaters, people still crammed the sidewalks along Saint-Laurent, taking in the bars and explicit strip clubs, sex shops, arcades, and peep shows.

From a brochure on Montreal nightlife I'd ghostwritten, I recognized two of the clubs the author had cited. *Le Club Soda* was one of them. It held concert venues that enabled young artists and producers to make their name in the Montreal music market. The Tragically Hip, Barenaked Ladies, Blue Rodeo, and Amanda Marshall had launched their careers there. Up ahead was *Café Cléopâtre*—one of the city's first strip clubs known for its seamy cabaret shows. One after the other, the names of nightspots registered with my recollection of them.

I turned the corner on Sainte-Catherine Street and began to

circle the area again. I got lucky when someone pulled out as I was approaching. I drove into the vacated spot, grateful that I didn't have to go around the block again.

Michael expended as much grunting and swearing getting out of the car as he had getting into it. But our journey wasn't over. We had to walk two blocks west along Sainte-Catherine to the rendezvous point.

Michael trudged along beside me. His breathing had worsened, but it did nothing to lessen his determination.

Perfume and pot mingled in the air and added weight to the humidity.

Neon lights flashed from the façades of clubs and bars.

Bursts of laughter and animated chatter from pedestrians cut into music that boomed from the sky or heaven-knew-where.

Mayhem all around.

We drifted past a club that had a notice in large black letters posted on the door: "No baggy pants or flip-flops." The doorman looked as if he lifted weights three hours a day or took steroids. He scrutinized the customers waiting in line outside and made a quick selection when someone slipped a few bills into his hand.

Steps ahead, a Paris Hilton lookalike in a tube top, tight skirt, and four-inch heels stood in front of a red door leading to what appeared to be a private club. She smiled at Michael and promised him "a good time, honey." He ignored her.

Rock music thumped from inside a bar-club called *Foufounes Électriques*—French for Electric Butt-Cheeks. A gigantic black spider hung from the front of the premises over a line of alternative music lovers waiting to get inside. Across the street was Club 281, a male strip club. More people waiting in line. Up next was Metropolis, a concert hall where live bands and artists were featured. Another long lineup.

When we reached the rendezvous point at the corner of the street, Michael said to me, "Stay close." He gave me a look my father used to give me when I was a kid, then leaned against the pillar in front of a Western Union outlet and waited.

I took a position next to him and gazed up the street. I noticed a dépanneur, a hotel, and an erotica boutique. I suddenly felt conspicuous standing at an intersection known more for its notoriety than anything else. I prayed I wouldn't bump into anyone I knew.

A group of tourists strolled by. Funny how you can always tell the tourists from the locals. The men wore baseball caps, even in the evening. The women carried oversized handbags. I watched as they took turns to take pictures of their group against the backdrop of the nightlife before they moved on.

Next up was a slender young couple holding hands and dressed in identical Goth wear—black leather, buckles, lip rings. They had the same haircut and were about the same height. It was hard to tell which one was male and which one was female.

Three young girls baring midriffs under camisoles giggled as they padded by in their flip-flops, their faces painted up to make them look older. I wondered if their mothers knew where they were.

The sun had set but who would have noticed. The neon lights and car headlights just about lit up the intersection where we were standing. I suddenly became aware that my shorts were attracting stares from the men going by. I stepped back under the alcove as much as I could without losing sight of Michael.

A taxi stopped at the curb. Two women stepped out. The blonde wore a short pink dress that clung to her body like paint and revealed enough cleavage to contain a small lake. Her eyeliner was dark and thick. The redhead wore a micro skirt. Her right arm had more spiral tattoos on it than a snake had stripes. Both wore four-inch stilettos. I placed them in their late thirties, early forties. They strolled past me and dropped their purses on the ground steps away as if they'd just arrived home.

The blonde noticed me and smiled, then nudged her friend.

The redhead turned to look at me. *"Pauvre mignonne,"* she said, then blew me a kiss.

*Poor little darling?* Then it hit me. In a T-shirt, shorts, and running shoes, I must have passed for a first-year college student working the corner to pay for tuition. A friend of mine had paid her university fees this way but quit turning tricks when she graduated.

She'd gone on to become a physiotherapist. It was one way to pay the bills—even make a significant down payment on a house. No, I wouldn't go there.

When I glanced away and didn't react to their antics, the redhead told the blond it was obvious I was *une anglaise* and I didn't understand French. With that constraint out of the way, they began a conversation in their native tongue that revealed their predicament.

The blonde seemed baffled as she explained to the redhead how she'd solicited *un policier* who had posed as un client willing to pay for a good time. How could she have known he was an undercover cop? Her lips formed a pout. She'd seen him drive up to Gigi on other nights and pay up front for services in cash—fifty-dollar bills. Gigi had told her he was *un gentleman*. It was strange, though, that she hadn't seen Gigi since then.

In what was definitely not Sunday-best French, the redhead cursed at her and blamed her for the *gaffe stupide* that had led to the police hauling them both to jail. Good thing Tony had bailed them out so they didn't have to spend another night there.

Still arguing, the women picked up their handbags and walked down the block. Every so often, they stood by the curb to wave down motorists.

I peeked around the pillar to check on Michael just as someone was walking up to him.

"Michael?" the stranger asked him.

"Yes."

"I am Goldie."

Michael was supposed to be meeting with a man, but I had to stare hard to make certain Goldie fit the bill. He was slim, but the tips of his breasts protruded through a sleeveless yellow T-shirt. He wore glittering gold shadow on his lids. His hair was white blond, cut high on top, and solidified with a dollop of gel. He must have used self-tanning lotion because his skin had a bronze glow you can only get out of a tube. A gold hoop earring dangled from one ear. I pegged him at about twenty, but he could have been thirty.

Goldie gave Michael a quick once-over, then pulled out a slim envelope from his gold shoulder bag and handed it to him. "Willie."

"Willie? He's alive? Do you know where he is?"

Goldie shrugged, didn't seem to understand.

*"Une amie."* Michael said, pointing in my direction.

I didn't want to scare Goldie off, so I walked up to him with a smile. I told Goldie in French that I was Michael's translator. I began by repeating Michael's questions to him.

Goldie said he knew nothing about Willie. He was told he had to meet with Michael and say it was from Willie. He pointed to the envelope Michael was holding. "Okay?" His smile was wide and revealed a set of teeth that had benefited from a whitening treatment.

Michael nodded. "Okay. Thank you."

Another wide smile from Goldie, followed by a slower gaze at Michael from head to foot. He looked back at me and asked if we'd like to go to *Le Village* with him for a drink.

He was referring to The Village, the heart of gay Montreal located blocks east of the red light district. Gay-friendly establishments were sprinkled throughout the city, but The Village thrived as the hub of gay entertainment and had grown into a popular tourist attraction, complete with restaurants, bars, cafés, shops, and parks.

"I can't go," Michael said. "I'm busy tonight."

I translated for Goldie.

"Okay. *Au revoir.*" Goldie gave him a little wave and left.


I drove up the steep slope of Pine Avenue, a road along Mount Royal that offered a scenic view of the downtown skyline. A right turn onto a side street led even higher to the Royal Victoria Hospital, an impressive landmark that had towered over the city for more than a hundred years. Scottish Baronial, the architectural style of the early buildings, had been preserved even after a dozen new pavilions had been added to the forty acres plus of land the hospital already occupied. The "Royal Vic" was recognized as a major teaching facility affiliated with McGill University and boasted some of the best doctors in the country. Michael would be in good hands.

We joined about a dozen people in the hospital ER. Two teens accompanied by their parents had bruises and scrapes to their faces and arms. An elderly couple sat staring at the floor most of the time. A young woman held a baby that cried off and on. Other patients were in various states of discomfort, sporting bandages or slings.

An old Indiana Jones movie was playing on a wall-mounted TV. Scenes where Harrison Ford suffers a series of blows from his attackers took Michael's focus off his own pain while we waited for a doctor to examine him.

And wait we did. We had watched most of the movie before Michael's turn came up. It took another hour before they wrapped a bandage around his chest and allowed him to leave.

On our way out, I asked him about the doctor's diagnosis.

"Two broken ribs. No strenuous exercises...or physical activity for a week. Painkillers so I can sleep. I can barely move. Plain crazy."

I felt responsible for the incident that put him in this predicament. Before I realized what I was saying, I suggested he spend the night at my place. "You can use the futon in my office, if you want."

His reaction was predictable, if not amusing. At first he went through the motions of refusing my invitation, claiming he didn't want to be more of a burden to me than he already was, saying I didn't need the extra work around the house...

I reminded him I'd stocked the fridge earlier today with milk, eggs, cheese, butter, apples, honeydew melon, and strawberries. I promised I'd make him pancakes with maple syrup and apple compote for breakfast the next morning.

He smiled and accepted my invitation.

By the time we arrived at the condo, I was exhausted and would have fallen asleep in a wink, but Michael wanted to view the CDs Goldie had given him. I was about to excuse myself and go to bed anyway when I saw him trying to insert a disc in the CD player. He couldn't. The bindings wrapped around his torso prevented him from bending forward.

I conceded and popped the disc in, then settled on the sofa next to him. He'd need my help to pop in the second disc later anyway.

The first CD showed a clip that placed Michael at Willie's gas station in Sainte-Adèle. The film quality wasn't sharp and there was no audio, but it was apparent to anyone who knew Michael that it was him. He was speaking with a bearded man standing behind the counter.

"Is that Willie?" I asked.

"Yes," he said. "That was the last time I saw him."

A date and time stamp at the bottom of the screen confirmed Michael's stopover the night of August 10—the night before Tom's body was discovered.

"Thanks to Willie, you now have an official alibi you can hand over to Moreau," I said.

He shook his head. "I can't use this stuff without blowing his cover. He risked his life for me. I owe him that much."

"He's dead. What does it matter?"

"We don't know for sure. If he's alive, I don't want to put him in danger."

"What? It's your freedom we're talking about."

He frowned. "Something's not quite right. Why would someone send me this video out of the blue? It doesn't make sense. Let's sit on it for now. Okay?"

"For now."

The footage on the second CD came as a complete surprise to us. It showed a man in a short jacket entering the same gas station. He was in his thirties, stocky, and short. He kept moving, looking around in a nervous sort of way. He must have asked Willie a question because Willie shook his head to say no. The man reached over the counter and grabbed Willie by the shirt but let him go when a male customer entered the store.

"I know that guy," Michael said.

"The one who just walked in?"

"No, the guy who took hold of Willie. He's Robert Gingras."

"The employee from Pineview?"

"The same one."

"The film quality isn't good. Are you sure it's him?"

He nodded. "Same wide chest. A slight limp in his right leg. Play it again. You'll see."

I clicked the replay button. I noticed the limp this time as Gingras moved around.

"I think he's packing," Michael said. "Can you run the video again?"

I did.

"Right there. Pause it."

As Gingras stretched over the counter, his jacket inched upward to reveal part of a handgun tucked in his waistband.

"It could be Stewart's Beretta," I said.

Michael nodded. "It's starting to make sense now. I'll bet Gingras is involved with illegal drugs in Sainte-Adèle. That's why Willie sent me this video. It's a terrific lead."

I pressed play and watched again as Gingras took hold of Willie. I checked the date and time stamp. "Their meeting took place Tuesday night—the night Willie's house burnt down. Do you think he found out Willie was an informant?"

"Could be."

"Maybe Gingras torched Willie's house later that night."

"I wouldn't be surprised. Problem is: where are these guys?"

# CHAPTER 23

Dan didn't mince words after Michael and I told him about our excursion to Bradford Publishing. "Have you both gone mad? You could have jeopardized the case. Or been killed. You might still end up in jail for a number of infractions." He let his right arm drop against my kitchen table, rattling the coffee cups I'd laid out before he and Jane arrived Friday morning.

"Chill out, buddy," Michael said. "We didn't do anything illegal. We're the bearers of good news." He tried to get comfortable, but the bandages wrapped around his ribs hampered his efforts and he grimaced.

"Here's Pam's agenda." I opened it up on the page with the Pineview notation and handed it to Dan. "And here's the proof we needed."

"How did you get this?" He accepted it from me.

"With the duplicate key to Pam's desk that Emily hid in her office." I gave him the key.

"Can you prove she used it to get into Pam's desk?"

"Better. I can get you a witness."

"Who?"

"Kayla, Pam's project coordinator. She said Pam locked her desk whenever she left the office. She saw Emily in Pam's office flipping through her agenda when Pam was away." I walked over to the counter, picked up the pot of fresh coffee, and began to fill four cups.

"How can you prove that Emily actually saw the Pineview notation in the agenda?" Jane asked me. "She could have been looking for something else."

The fact that she questioned my logic made me feel as if I were on trial and had to defend myself. I milked it for what it was worth. "No one saw who murdered Tom and Pam either, yet the police suspect Michael and me."

She blinked and touched the neckline of her high collar blouse.

*Had I unnerved her?*

"Maybe we should question Emily about her eavesdropping habit." Jane looked at Dan across the table. She waited, expecting a response, but either he was too busy studying Pam's agenda or he didn't feel like answering her.

"Forget it," Michael said. "She'd only deny it." He leaned forward to reach the sugar bowl but fell short and groaned.

"Here, let me help." Jane was sitting next to him. "Two cubes, right?" She moved in closer to Michael and stretched over to pick up the cubes with her fingers.

She was wearing a short skirt. He was wearing cargo shorts. I'd have predicted her bare knee would make contact with his bare thigh and it did.

"There you go." Jane dropped the cubes in his coffee but did nothing to break the physical contact between them.

"Thanks." Michael watched as Jane picked up a spoon and stirred his coffee, over and over, in slow circles. He reached for the cup, leaving Jane holding the spoon in mid-air. "I think I've been taking too many painkillers," he said. "What was I saying?"

"That Emily would lie about having gone through Pam's agenda, let alone that she saw the Pineview notation." I set the coffee pot back on the burner with more noise than I intended, then handed out the cups.

"Yeah, it would be impossible to prove," Michael said, regaining his focus. "At least Ray's connection to cyanide turned out to be more than an illusion."

"Only if it can be proven the canister contained cyanide," Dan said as he continued to leaf through Pam's agenda.

"I'll bet it did. Ray's attack means he's hiding something. Moreau should look into it."

"I'll see that he does, buddy." Dan peered at a page in the agenda. "Megan, what do you make of this?" He showed me a note Pam had written weeks before her death. It read: *call from Mrs. B. B. linked to E.S. Fix ASAP.*

"B.B. could stand for Bill Bradford," I said. "E.S. for Emily Saunders." I put it together. "We already know Mrs. Bradford accused Pam of having an affair with her husband. Maybe Pam found out Emily had leaked word of it to Mrs. Bradford."

"Easy." Michael grinned at me as I took a seat next to Dan. "All she had to do was place one of her anonymous phone calls."

"It can be traced," Dan said. He jotted something in his notebook before turning his attention back to Pam's agenda. "Lots of names in the directory at the back. No record of Bill Bradford, though. Are you sure Pam was seeing him?"

"No, but Mrs. Bradford thought so," I said. "It would explain why she showed up at Pam's office that day and chewed her out."

"Didn't you tell me Pam denied the affair?" Dan asked.

"Yes," I said.

"She lied." Jane stared at me. "It's what any woman would do under the circumstances, don't you think?"

*Was this about Pam or me?*

Michael was gazing into his cup of coffee. Dan's attention was glued to Pam's agenda. Neither of them had caught the mistrust in Jane's eyes directed at me.

"If you're asking if I'd lie about having an affair," I said, meeting her glare, "I don't know. I suppose it depends on how much the truth would hurt others."

Jane smiled like a Cheshire cat and picked up her cup of coffee. She gave me the impression she'd won the argument—whatever it was.

I sipped my coffee and turned my thoughts to the alleged affair between Pam and Bill Bradford. My instincts told me Pam was telling the truth—she hadn't been seeing her boss on the sly. "Dan, can I see Pam's note again, please?"

Dan flipped back to the page and handed me the agenda.

I studied the spacing between the letters. It was off. "Mmm...I think I read this wrong. Maybe Pam wrote: *call from Mrs. B. Space. B. linked to E.S.*"

Michael's eyes went wide. "Bill Bradford and Emily?"

"Some women prefer dating more sophisticated men," I said, tongue-in-cheek.

"This is getting juicier by the minute." Michael grinned. "Buddy? Any thoughts on this?"

Dan joined in. "Let's assume Emily saw this note. Assumed Pam was going to fix things by telling Mrs. Bradford about her." He shook his head. "It must have terrified Emily."

"No kidding," Michael said. "Everyone knows how the rich handle the slightest threat of a scandal. When a load of money is in the balance, nest disturbers can disappear without a trace. Just like that." He snapped his fingers.

"I agree," Jane said. "Money talks. It's as simple as that."

"If Pam had one good quality," I said, "she was organized." I flipped through the pages that followed her note and found what I was looking for. "Listen to this. On the Monday after the trip to Pineview, she inserted a follow-up memo: *call Mrs. B. Fire E.S.*"

"The icing on the cake," Michael said.

"If Emily saw this memo, she could have acted on it." I kept the agenda open on the page and handed it to Dan.

"Fear of being trapped can make some people desperate," he said, taking hold of it.

"And the fear of alienation can increase it," Jane said.

I wondered what she meant by that comment but had to voice my own conclusion. "Emily could have been desperate enough to commit murder."

"It's a solid foundation for motive, isn't it, buddy?" Michael asked.

Dan didn't answer. He was peering at another page in Pam's agenda. He flipped back through the pages and forward again. "Another memo. Days after the first Bradford memo, Pam wrote: Check out Pineview. Emily's recommended number one hot spot."

I gasped. "Oh, my God. Emily had gone to Pineview herself."

"Or she casually mentioned she knew someone who had stayed there and enjoyed it," Jane said, squelching my theory. "In any case, Pam picked up on it, told Tom about it, and he made the arrangements."

"What?" I couldn't believe my ears.

Dan jerked upright. "Jane, I don't tolerate unsubstantiated remarks from my team."

She blinked at Dan. "None intended. My comments were hypothetical."

"Let's keep Pam's agenda to ourselves for now," Dan said. "It offers valuable leverage if we go to court." He put it aside. "Jane, have you followed up on Peter Ewans?"

"Yes," she said. "I told him we'd done a background check on him and his former places of employment, in particular the chemicals plant. I asked if he was aware of the symptoms of cyanide poisoning. He admitted he was. In fact, he said he suspected as much when he saw Tom and Pam on the floor. It was the reason he hadn't tried to break into the cottage."

I said, "It would have been too late anyway."

"There's more," Jane went on. "Megan, remember the picture of Tom and Pam that you received in the mail?"

I nodded. "What about it?"

"Peter sent it. He owned up when the police asked for his fingerprints. He thought you should know and asked me to pass along his apology to you."

"He was trying to warn me about Tom," I said.

An awkward silence hung in the air.

Michael tinkered with his cup.

Dan cleared his throat. "Anything else, Jane?"

"Yes," she said. "Peter admitted he tampered with the wheel on Tom's Ford."

"What?" Michael looked at her. "Do the police know this?"

"It's not what you think," Jane said. "He loosened the tire on the Ford because he wanted to kill himself on a back road by racing the car into a tree. Tom spoiled his plans when he asked him to drive the car over to the condo. Peter claims he was in a depressed state of mind at the time. He forgot about the loose tire and drove the car over to your place, Megan."

"So we can eliminate him as a suspect once and for all," Michael said, giving me a knowing look.

I was certain about one other thing: Peter's elimination as a suspect paved the way for our focus on Emily. I knew better by now and didn't voice the thought.

Dan pulled out another folder from his briefcase. "All right. The testimony I personally obtained from the staff at the Elegance regarding Anita's death."

Jane gaped at him. "When did you go there, Dan?"

"Last night," he said, opening the file.

"You should have called me or paged me. I would have been happy to interview—"

"You were busy."

"No, I wasn't."

"All right, Jane." His tone was firmer than usual.

She blinked. I could almost hear the wheels inside her head come to a screeching halt.

Dan continued. "I spoke with the supervisor of the cleaning staff at the Elegance. She was making the rounds Wednesday when she discovered Anita's body. Her statement meanders. I'll paraphrase it." He glanced down at the report. "Anita was spread out on the bed. Her uniform was torn. She was covered in blood—especially in the stomach area. I couldn't believe she was dead." He looked up. "The unofficial cause of death is a gunshot wound."

"Did anyone hear any shots?" Michael asked.

"No," Dan said.

"He could have used a silencer. Or muffled the shot with a pillow."

"Possibly."

"If her uniform was torn, she must have struggled with the killer," I said.

"Forensics is still running DNA tests on the body," Dan said.

"What about the hotel videotapes?" Michael asked him.

"Under police analysis, I assume. Which reminds me. The voice messages on your hotel phone couldn't be analyzed. Too few words. Sorry, buddy."

Michael held his hands up. "Hey, you win some and you lose some.

My gut feeling still tells me Emily made those calls."

"Dan, any news on her alibi?" I asked.

"Not yet." His cell phone rang. He fished it out of his pocket and answered. "All right. Tell him we'll be there." He flipped the phone shut. "Detective Moreau wants to meet with us at the station right away. No idea why."

My guess was that Anita's murder had thrown the detective's investigation out of whack. I smiled to myself, confident he'd have a tough time putting the blame for her demise on Michael and me. Thanks to Moreau, we'd learned our lessons the hard way. We'd kept receipts from every place we'd gone to and every purchase we'd made since the day he started to point the finger at us. If we couldn't obtain a paper trail, we took photos or videos of ourselves in our surroundings to have a digital record of the date and time it was taken. As a result, we could substantiate our alibis in case any more dead bodies fell across our path.

And Anita's was all it took.

My spirits soared. Michael and I were prepared for any new ramifications Moreau might hurl our way.

Except one.

# CHAPTER 24

It was our good fortune that we weren't escorted to another drab interrogation room to meet with Moreau. But as we stepped into a storage room at the QPP headquarters that functioned as his temporary office, I wondered whether an interrogation room wouldn't have been a step up decoration wise.

A wood desk, a table lamp, four different vinyl chairs, and a two-drawer filing cabinet looked as if they'd been collected from other offices in the building and thrown together to provide makeshift facilities for Moreau. Cardboard boxes holding archives from the 60s were stacked three rows high and six wide along the back wall.

On my left, Dan was busy reviewing his notes. He hadn't asked Jane to come along. On my right, Michael's breathing was difficult despite the support bandages hugging his chest. He'd told me it was less painful if he moved slowly or not at all—which explained why he sat staring straight ahead and motionless, like an embalmed mummy.

We waited for Moreau to arrive and then waited some more. I must have checked my watch a dozen times, swearing in silence as the minutes stretched to half an hour. Red, white, and blue pushpins secured the photos of the ten most wanted criminals to a bulletin board on the wall behind the desk. I'd glanced at their faces so often that I was confident I could pick each one out of a police lineup with no trouble.

The door finally opened and Moreau stepped into the room. As usual, he didn't say a word or make eye contact with us until he'd taken a seat and turned on the audio recorder. "I would like to discuss a matter that has come to my attention." His tone was polite for a change. I took it as a sign of weariness in his efforts to find Tom's killer—and now Anita's. "Bradford Publishing has filed a police report concerning damages to the office of Emily Saunders. Your clients were implicated, Monsieur Cummings." His gaze encompassed Michael and me.

"My clients discovered the intrusion and reported it to the security guard." Dan described Michael's physical confrontation with Ray and his ensuing visit to the hospital. "On behalf of my client, I'm lodging an assault complaint against Ray Felton."

Moreau looked at Michael. "I am sorry for your misfortune." He passed a hand over his mustache. "However, I question if the intrusion was intended to be a diversion."

Dan leaned forward. "What are you implying, Detective?"

"Someone is misleading the police on purpose. All is not what it appears to be, as they say. Perhaps your clients caused the disorder at Bradford."

*What?* I bit my tongue.

"Experience has taught me to keep an open mind, Detective. Emily Saunders might have staged the break-in to appear victimized. Or someone might have ransacked her office in search of incriminating evidence. Merely assumptions, of course." He sat back.

Moreau raised an eyebrow. "What incriminating evidence?"

"As I said, hypothetical."

"Monsieur Cummings, are you telling me how to do my job?"

Dan stiffened. "One thing we both want to avoid is tunnel vision. Another is the possibility of miscarriage of justice. Not to mention costly court cases."

Moreau seemed to contemplate his words. "If your clients are as innocent as you claim, I can only conclude that they seem to invite trouble wherever they go."

*Right. And the next thing you'll conclude is that I threw myself in front of oncoming traffic,* I held back from saying. Dan had cautioned us against speaking out of turn—if at all.

"My clients are targets," Dan said. "Until the real killer is found, their lives are at risk."

The detective turned off the recorder. "New evidence has come to light that will allow us to close in on the perpetrators soon."

"Are you saying you know who's responsible for Tom's murder?" I asked, breaking my silence.

"I cannot reveal information without compromising the murder investigation," Moreau said.

"Tom was my husband," I said. "I have the right to know."

"I regret, Madame Scott, but I cannot discuss this matter with you."

"Does Anita Castillo's alleged murder have anything to do with this?" Dan asked.

"I regret, but I cannot disclose any more information." Moreau stood up. "Our meeting is over. Thank you for coming."

That Moreau hadn't interrogated Michael and me about Anita was baffling. He obviously had no reason to link us to her murder, though I had to admit we were anticipating the challenge and were more than equipped for it. We'd brought along enough receipts and photos to validate our movements over the past week.

His mention of perpetrators threw me off, though. *Did he suspect more than one killer was involved?*

After our meeting with Moreau, Dan headed back to his hotel to catch up on paperwork. Michael and I took a taxi to the Elegance so he could get a change of clothes.

Michael's cell phone rang minutes after we walked into his suite.

He answered. "Hi, Jane... For dinner? Hang on. I'll ask Megan." He put her on hold. "Jane wants to know if we'd like to join her and Dan for dinner at seven tonight."

I suppressed an urge to laugh out loud. I pictured Jane blinking hard when Michael asked her to wait on the line while he checked with me. My next impulse was to refuse her invitation. Why would I want to sit through dinner with Jane, of all people?

I thought about it for two more seconds. At the least, it would give me a chance to get to know her better. Hell, I might even discover she possessed a warmer, more likable social side behind that glacial exterior. And Dan would be joining us. Michael would be eager to spend more time with him and catch up on "buddy" stuff.

"Okay, if you want to," I said before I was tempted to change my mind again.

While Michael went to the bedroom to change his clothes, I turned on the TV. The mid-day news broadcast was on. A reporter was talking about a man whom the provincial police considered a person of interest in an alleged murder. The picture of a bearded man appeared. He looked familiar. I was shocked when I recognized the name in the banner at the bottom of the screen: William Perron.

"Michael, come see this," I shouted. "Hurry!"

He rushed from the bedroom in time to hear the report in progress: "...burnt body discovered in the aftermath of a blaze that destroyed William Perron's home in Sainte-Adèle this week." A film clip of Willie's burnt house played over the reporter's commentary. "The victim has been identified as Robert Gingras." A headshot of Gingras appeared next. "The police are still investigating and urge anyone with information to contact..."

I clicked the remote and turned off the TV. "Now we know what happened to Gingras."

"It's plain crazy. I'll bet Gingras went there to kill him. If Willie's still alive, he's one lucky guy." Michael slipped a navy blue T-shirt over his head with one hand but groaned in pain as he tried to get his arms through the sleeves. He looked at me, exasperated, the T-shirt wrapped around his neck. "It was much easier taking it off." He smiled.

I walked over to him and pulled on his T-shirt so he could get his arms through the sleeves. "I hope they don't charge Willie with murder."

"Thanks." He tugged on the hem, letting it fall over his beige cargo shorts. "Chances are it was self-defense." He gazed at me as if some realization had just sunk in. "Gingras must have had the Beretta on him. Did the news report say he'd been shot?"

"No."

"No mention of the missing gun at all?"

"No. Maybe the police found it and returned it to Stewart Kirk."

"Only one way to find out." Michael retrieved his cell phone from a pocket. "I'll call Pineview." He waited while the receptionist transferred his call. "Hi, Stewart. It's Michael Elliott. Yes, I just saw it on TV. Tell me, have the police found your Beretta yet? No, nothing new at this end. I will. Okay. Thanks." He hung up and slipped the phone into his pocket. "No news on the gun. He'll let me know if it shows up."

"If the police didn't find his gun in the fire, maybe Willie has it," I said.

Michael shrugged. "Could be."

"The police will be looking for him. It doesn't seem fair."

"I know." He nodded. "Right now, we need to deal with that other urgent matter."

In the midst of trying to prove our alibis for that critical Friday evening, Michael and I hadn't lost sight of our impending dilemma: we were still suspects in the Pineview murders until Moreau took us off his list. The only way out of our quandary was to lure the real killer into a trap. We agreed we'd keep Dan and Jane out of our plans. They'd never consent to such a risky venture anyway. Above all, we didn't want to throw away the last chance we had of getting evidence that would clear our names. Emily's confession would prove crucial to our freedom and to her subsequent arrest.

"Okay, let's recap our reasons for suspecting Emily before we launch our plan." Michael said as we sat in our usual places around the coffee table. "Make sure we didn't miss anything."

I studied my notes on the canary yellow notepad. "Emily had a duplicate key to Pam's desk. Kayla caught her going through Pam's agenda several times, occasions for Emily to see Pam's plans to go to Pineview. Pam's note to tell Mrs. B. the truth about Emily's affair with Mr. B. was the catalyst that led to the murders." I looked at Michael. "It triggered Emily's fear and anger. Out of desperation, she decided to get rid of Pam. That Friday night, she drove to Pineview—a place she'd visited before—and slipped into the cottage to plant the cyanide."

He nodded. "The anonymous phone calls, here and at your office. All those lies she told the police about us. Moreau believed we were having an affair. We became his prime suspects."

Our kiss was still fresh in my mind. I avoided his gaze and checked my notes. "Emily was one of the few people who knew your room number at the Elegance. She was jealous of our relationship and angry with you because you ignored her, so she sought revenge. She bribed Anita to open up your hotel room so she could plant the cyanide there."

"Cyanide that she got with Ray's help," Michael added. "She was clever and covered her tracks. She had Anita killed."

"I was still an obstruction in her path to you. She tried to kill me by shoving me into the traffic." I put my pen down. "And your approach with Emily?"

"I'll get her to admit she knew about Pam's trip to Pineview beforehand. If I'm lucky, she'll reveal other details only the killer would know—like how she got the cyanide and where she planted it in the cottage."

"What about the recording equipment?"

"A reporter friend of mine—a real techie nerd—hid a tiny wireless spy camera and receiver in the plant." He gestured to the potted plant on the credenza. "It's set up to record and view on my laptop in the bedroom. We're good to go at the push of a button."

If I had any misgivings about setting a trap for Emily, it was about personal safety. Not mine, but Michael's. "You realize you're putting yourself out there, don't you?" I said. "If you have any doubts, tell me now. We don't have to go through with this."

"We have no choice. We're running out of time. I'm calling Emily right now." He reached for his cell. When she didn't answer, he left a message and hung up. "Let's hope she takes the bait and accepts my invitation for later tonight."

"She's a fool if she doesn't. I mean—" It was too late to take back the words.

Michael smiled at me. "I have something for you." He walked over to the credenza and removed a tiny blue jewelry box from behind the plant. "I want you to have this. It belonged to my grandmother." He handed it to me.

I opened the box. Inside was a diamond pendant. I recognized it as the piece of jewelry Jane had removed from her purse the first time I saw her in his suite. "Michael, I can't—"

"My grandmother believed it had the power to keep the person who wore it safe. She gave it to me after I got my first job as a reporter. I took it with me when I had to investigate leads. I wasn't much of a believer in this kind of stuff, but something kept me out of danger every time."

"What about the day Ray kicked you in the ribs?"

"I didn't have it with me." He gave me a sheepish grin. "Please, Megan, wear it for me."

"Okay." I held my hair up while he tied the clasp in the back. His hands were gentle on my shoulders as he slowly turned me around to face him. The way he stared at me unnerved me. A familiar feeling fluttered inside me and my knees went weak. I couldn't move if I tried.

"Maybe this isn't the right moment," he said, "but I'm going to say it anyway. Those weeks we spent working together, the dinners we shared..." He let out a deep breath. "If you only knew how hard it was to concentrate on my writing and keep my hands off you. But you were married then and I respected that." He slid his arms around my waist and held me closer. "I'm tired of pretending you don't mean anything to me." He whispered my name and kissed me, obliterating all real and imaginary threats from my mind.

My heart waged war with my conscience. How could I deny a bond that felt so right? I put my hands around his neck and kissed him back, feeling the thrill from head to toe that only a true connection between two people can bring.

Michael's cell phone rang but he ignored it.

"It could be Dan," I said, putting space between us.

He pulled out his phone and glanced at the display. "Private number. Could be important." He answered. There was talking at the other end of the line. Michael's eyes went wide. "Yes, sure... No problem. Okay." He hung up and looked at me. A smile stretched across his face. "You'll never guess who that was."

"Who?"

"Willie. He wants to meet with me at Berri metro station. Want to come along as my translator?"

# CHAPTER 25

It was a short ride along the green line of *Le Metro* to Berri-UQAM—the largest station in the network and the hub of the subway service. I'd always been in awe of the structural design of Berri station and rightly so. The main part is built underground in a massive cross-shaped cut-and-cover volume and spans three subway lines. At the top of the station and at its core, the central concourse is a vast open space with rows of turnstiles on four sides. The turnstiles give passengers access to escalators that allow them to transfer to the different lines within the transit system. In the middle of the open space is a circular black granite bench known as *la rondelle*, or the hockey puck. It's also known as *la pilule*, or the pill.

Willie wanted to meet with Michael at the hockey puck. I wasn't surprised. It was a popular meeting place for adults and especially students from *Université du Québec à Montréal*, or UQAM. The latter had direct access to the station through two underground corridors that linked the university to this section of the subway.

Michael and I walked up to a free spot near the puck. Small groups of students had gathered about, but Willie was nowhere in sight.

"What if he changed his mind?" I said to Michael.

"He'll show up," he said.

With each train arrival, crowds of people crisscrossed the central concourse and rushed through the turnstiles—a never-ending hodge-podge of commuters.

I spotted a man in tattered pants, a dark T-shirt with the Québec *fleur-de-lis* on it, and a red baseball cap. He was heading in our direction at a slower pace than other commuters. He had no beard, so I looked away.

"That's him," Michael said.

I followed his gaze to the man in the baseball cap. Willie's shoulders were broad but hunched, making his chest appear more concave than it was. Muscular arms indicated he was used to physical labor. A strong jaw showed resilience. A lazy eye might have given the impression he wasn't as astute as the next person, though logic told me otherwise.

"Bonjour." Willie shook Michael's hand and smiled, revealing a missing tooth on the right side of his mouth.

When Michael introduced me, Willie's eyes narrowed. He looked as if he were going to run off.

*"Une amie,"* Michael said to him. "She's a close friend."

*"Je vais traduire pour Michael et pour vous,"* I said to Willie, hoping to put him at ease by explaining I'd translate for Michael and him.

Willie studied me for a moment, then nodded okay.

We moved off to a more secluded spot along the wall.

Michael began. "I saw the news on TV," he said to Willie. "I know that Gingras' body was found in the fire that destroyed your home. Did you kill him?"

Willie said no sir, as God was his witness. He'd fallen asleep in the living room late that night—right after the news. The back door creaked and woke him up. He'd lived in the same house for thirty years and never locked his doors. Everyone in town knew he had nothing worth stealing anyway. Since his friends don't drop by in the middle of the night, he was sure that whoever had come in was up to no good.

The house was pitch black, Willie said. He grabbed a flashlight he kept by the armchair in case the lights go out—happens a lot during bad storms. Then he heard water or some liquid splashing on the wood floor in the hallway. When he smelled the gasoline, by God, he knew he was in big trouble. He turned on the flashlight and saw Gingras. The damned fool dropped the container of gasoline and pulled out a gun. That's when he jumped on Gingras. They struggled and the gun went off. Gingras turned and ran toward the back. The idiot must have knocked over the oil lamp on the kitchen table because flames exploded all around him.

Willie shook his head, said he knew he had to save himself, so he ran like the devil out the front door. Never ran so fast in his life. He kept running all the way to the phone booth at the gas station. He called a friend who picked him up and drove him to Montreal. He only found out Gingras was dead when he saw the news broadcast today.

"Where's the gun?" Michael asked him.

Willie said he had the gun. He was going to the police right after our meeting. He had to do what was right.

"It was self-defense. You have nothing to worry about."

Willie shrugged, said he hoped the police thought so too.

"I looked at the video you sent me—the one with Gingras in it. How did he find out you were my informer?"

Willie shook his head. No sir, Gingras didn't know he was an informer.

"He didn't? Why did he threaten you at the gas station?"

Willie said Gingras wanted the video from the gas station and promised something very bad would happen if he didn't hand it over. He wasn't stupid—he figured the video must be damned important if a bum like Gingras wanted it so badly. That same night, before he left work to go home, he asked a friend to make sure the video got delivered to Michael.

Michael shook his head. "I'm confused. Gingras wanted the video that showed him assaulting you. Right?"

No sir, Willie said. Gingras wanted the other video—the one with Michael in it.

# CHAPTER 26

*L'usine de Spaghetti*—The Spaghetti Factory—was located on Saint-Paul Street in *Le Vieux-Montréal*. The restaurant shared the area with dozens upon dozens of other eateries and boutiques along the narrow cobblestone streets of Old Montreal where the city was born in the mid-1600s.

Michael and I stepped inside. The wood and stone interior was rustic and inviting and reflective of traditional family values, as my mother would say. A delicious aroma of meat sauce and freshly baked bread instantly aroused my appetite, and I couldn't wait to order dinner. I hoped the service was quick. The place was air-conditioned, and I was glad I'd worn a shawl wrap over my cotton sundress.

Jane waved at us from a table off to the side. We headed her way.

She'd done her hair in large curls and pinned it up, letting a few strands fall to her shoulders. She looked good in the little black dress and chunky three-strand pearl choker she'd chosen. A bit too fancy for dinner here, but I supposed she wanted to look her best for Michael.

"Dan won't be joining us," she said as we sat down opposite her. "He's caught up with a legal case in Toronto."

"Too bad," Michael said. "Not that I don't enjoy the present company." He smiled at Jane and me.

Jane reached for her empty glass. "How about a drink? I could use another one. Any objections to white wine?"

We had no time to reply.

"Waiter!" She called out as one hurried by. After she'd placed an order for a bottle of *Sauvignon Blanc*, she lost no time in getting to what I believed was the real reason she'd invited us. "So tell me, Michael, what are your plans once the murder investigation blows over?" She smiled as she ran her fingers along her pearl choker, caressing it, openly flirting with him.

Michael shrugged. "No plans. I can't think that far ahead. Things are still in flux."

"Oh, come on," Jane said. "The investigation is almost a done deal." The tone of her voice inspired trust, but her eyes were void of emotion.

"How is it a done deal?" I asked. "The last we heard, Moreau still suspects us."

"It's simple." Jane blinked. "But you have to see it from a legal standpoint. Let me explain it to you." She leaned forward as if I were hearing-impaired as well as dim-witted. "It all comes down to motive. Whoever has the strongest motive for murder gets the detective's vote."

"You make it sound like a contest," I said.

"Trust me. I've seen a lot of trials go in unexpected directions all because of motive." She leaned back.

"Motive," Michael echoed. "So where do you think we stand on that basis?"

"It all depends," she said.

"On what?"

"On which suspect the police thinks had the most to gain." She looked at us.

She couldn't possibly be referring to a choice between Michael and me. I decided to join her senseless game and play dumb. "I thought we'd agreed Emily had won that round."

"It doesn't mean the police have come to the same conclusion, now does it?" Jane said, giving me a half-smile, which by now I came to realize was a runner-up to a blink.

"I doubt Moreau has another suspect in mind," Michael said. "We've eliminated anyone else who might have had a motive. I'm sure he went through the same elimination process."

"A real killer flies under the radar," Jane said.

He frowned. "What are you saying? That we've made a mistake?"

She shrugged. "Maybe."

"Dan didn't seem to have a problem with our reasoning," I said. "Besides, Emily's alibi is still unconfirmed."

"Trust me," Jane said, focusing on me. "He's only going through the motions to appease your little fantasy about her."

"Fantasy?" I repeated. "How can you say that? We have proof that she—"

"Stop." Jane raised a hand in the air. "We've talked shop long enough. This is supposed to be a fun night, right?" Her mouth twitched upward in a fake smile.

I was speechless.

As if another person had just sat down in her place, Jane digressed to a different topic. "Michael, remember the last time we came here for dinner?" Not waiting for an answer, she looked at me and elaborated. "It was about three weeks ago. After dinner, we went to *La Ronde* and watched the most spectacular fireworks. The International Fireworks Competition. Right, Michael?"

"Yes," he said, his tone even. "It's held every year. We watched the entry from Italy."

"They really know how to put on a show," Jane said. "We had a fantastic time, didn't we? We'll have to come back next summer. Maybe catch a performance by *Cirque du Soleil*." Her eyes got all dreamy as she waited for him to reply.

Michael gave her a vague nod and looked away as if something or someone had drawn his attention. The tiny muscle on his left jaw pulsated but was visible only to me. He was reaching a breaking point.

The waiter arrived. He uncorked the wine and poured some into Jane's glass.

She took a sip. "It's fine."

The waiter proceeded to fill our glasses. "Are you ready to order?" he asked.

I was famished. I was sure Michael was too.

But Jane had other plans. "Come back in ten minutes." She

motioned him away. "Cheers!" She lifted her glass, prompting Michael and me to clink our glasses with hers.

I took a sip and seized the opportunity to change the subject while she buried her face in her glass. I feigned ignorance and said, "Jane, Dan spoke very highly of you when he took on our case. He mentioned you were working for another legal firm before you joined his team."

"Yes, for a big Toronto law firm," she said, blinking.

"The job market is really tough these days. I've heard that lawyers who graduated last year still can't find a job. How did you manage to go from one legal firm to another so quickly?"

She threw me a half-smile. "I offered Dan a couple of big corporate accounts and the big bucks to go with them." She switched her attention back to Michael. "Which reminds me. Have you decided what you're going to do about your grandmother's settlement yet?"

He lowered his eyes. "I don't want to get into it right now."

"Why not? We're among friends." She gave me a cursory glance. "Okay, maybe I have a considerable advantage over Megan in that area, but I can be flexible. If you don't want to talk about it, we can talk about other things, like a special place we could go visit when we get back to Toronto..."

I tuned her out. Her mind games were getting on my nerves. What was she trying to tell me anyway? That she and Michael were close friends? Lovers? And what was her fixation with Michael's finances?

My stomach was growling. A waiter had just unloaded a tray of pasta dishes at the table next to ours and the aroma was making my mouth water. Other patrons who had been seated at tables at the same time as us were already enjoying their soup or salad entrées. A handful of people were lined up at the front door, waiting to get in.

Hunger overtook annoyance as I scanned the premises for our waiter. I was determined to get his attention the moment I spotted him. To hell with Jane. She could drink herself into oblivion for all I cared. I needed to eat something and soon.

As if hunger pains weren't causing me enough anguish, it was getting warm in the place, even with the air conditioning on. I removed the wrap I was wearing and hung it on the back of my chair.

"…lots to see and do along the harbor front in August and—" Jane stopped and zoomed in on the diamond pendant I was wearing. She squinted. "Michael, is that your grandmother's pendant around Megan's neck?"

"Yes," he said.

Her eyes narrowed. "Didn't you tell me your grandmother was special…that one day, you'd give her pendant to someone just as special?"

"I did," he said. "I gave it to Megan." He gave me a quick smile.

Jane's lips quivered ever so slightly. "I thought you and I had a special relationship."

"You and I didn't have a relationship."

"We dated in Toronto, didn't we?"

"For a while."

"And then we dated here in Montreal, didn't we?"

He looked down, didn't answer.

Jane raised her voice. "You stayed the night in my hotel room, didn't you?"

Michael shifted in his chair, looked around. People were beginning to stare. "Can we drop the subject?" he whispered.

"Oh, I get it. You don't think I'm good enough for you. That's why you didn't give *me* the diamond pendant, isn't it?" Anger flashed in her eyes.

The temperature in the place dropped by ten degrees.

Michael stayed calm. "Jane, you're blowing this way out of proportion."

"No, I'm not." Her body tensed. "It's apparent that married women are what you're into these days." She shot me a look of pure hate.

"What's your damn problem?" I met her stare straight on.

"You never cease to amaze me, Megan." The corners of her mouth lifted in a smile.

Her Cheshire smile rattled me more than words ever could, but I held my own and didn't look away. "What are you talking about?"

"How you manage to come across as so innocent."

"Please—" Michael began.

"Excuse me. I have to go powder my nose." Jane clutched her purse and stood up.

She moved from the table so fast that she didn't see him coming and collided with a young waiter carrying a tray of empty glasses. It toppled and crashed to the floor in a clatter.

Applause and cheers exploded around us in a gesture of understanding.

Jane wasn't as supportive. Some liquid had landed on her legs and she bent over to wipe it off. "You clumsy idiot," she yelled at the waiter. "Can't you see where the hell you're going?"

The waiter blushed. "I'm sorry, Ma'am."

"Sorry isn't good enough. You should be fired." Jane rushed away in a huff.

The waiter bent down to pick up the pieces of glass on the floor. He placed them on the tray and walked away, head bent in embarrassment.

I kept an eye on Jane until she vanished around the corner. "Now *that's* a mood swing."

"No kidding," Michael said. "I've never seen her like this."

"Well, whatever she's up to, I don't want any part of it." I stood up.

"Makes two of us." He dug out a couple of twenty-dollar bills and flung them on the table. "Let's get out of here."

# CHAPTER 27

On the taxi ride back to the Elegance Hotel, I couldn't stop thinking about Jane's strange behavior at the restaurant. It was as if a bizarre aspect of her personality had surfaced out of the blue and taken control of her mind. Maybe our double murder investigation had put too much pressure on her. That one of Moreau's prime suspects was Michael—someone she cared about—had probably put her all the more on edge.

Then I remembered the hatred in her eyes after she'd noticed the diamond pendant around my neck and the insults that had spewed out of her mouth. Her conduct had stemmed from nothing more than jealousy. She couldn't accept that Michael wasn't interested in her. Worse, that he showed a genuine interest in me. She felt humiliated and had struck out in retaliation. She hadn't spared anyone in her immediate vicinity—not even the young waiter she'd rammed into.

As the taxi weaved its way to Sherbrooke Street, Michael stared out the window and said nothing. Maybe he was embarrassed about Jane's disclosure regarding the intimacy of their relationship. Or maybe he was smoldering over her comment about the diamond pendant.

Although I'd have wanted nothing better than to vent my anger over her conduct at the restaurant, I took my cue from him and didn't say a word.

Michael asked the taxi to stop in front of a deli a few doors from the hotel. In spite of our wacky confrontation with Jane, his appetite was still functioning normally—as was mine. I glanced at my watch. Eight o'clock. Small wonder.

Michael ordered two sandwiches for takeout: turkey, Swiss cheese, tomato, and lettuce on baguettes. He paid for both and asked for a receipt.

We walked back to the hotel in silence. The lobby was filled with a fresh batch of convention-goers, their nametags plastered everywhere but on their foreheads. We picked up a bag of ice on the main floor, then rode the elevator up to Michael's suite—again in silence.

Time had done nothing to quash my anger over Jane's behavior. It had festered inside me like overheated meat sauce in a pressure cooker ever since we'd left the restaurant. A glance at Michael's calm expression made me wonder why he didn't share my resentment. Maybe he was too upset to voice his feelings.

No matter. I couldn't contain it any longer. I was going to explode if I didn't vent soon.

We stepped into the corridor leading to Michael's suite and passed a housekeeping cart. A maid was tidying up one of the rooms. Once out of earshot, I let it all out. "Damn it, Michael. I'm going to call Dan and demand that Jane be removed from our case immediately."

"I don't think it'll make any difference at this point," he said.

"Why not?"

"Her part in the investigation is over. Dan's wrapping things up... waiting for Moreau to make the next move."

"I don't care. Her behavior was rude. Unacceptable. Dan needs to know."

"I agree, but it's a personal matter." He slid his key card in the slot and opened the door to his suite. "Jane thinks I snubbed her. I swear I never gave her reason to believe we had a serious thing going on between us." He closed the door behind us.

"She obviously thought you did."

"I already told you about Jane's moods. She's Jekyll and Hyde in the flesh."

"Don't make excuses for her."

"Her mood swings make her unpredictable. The wine doesn't

SANDRA NIKOLAI

help, either. Alcohol brings out the worst in her."

"You're making more excuses."

"I'm just stating the facts." He paused. "She once told me an old boyfriend had cheated on her. She got drunk one night, then slashed the leather seats of his sports car. He never found out it was her."

I remembered how I'd thrown out the bed sheets after I'd found out about Tom and Pam. Not as violent as Jane's hatchet job but nevertheless an act of revenge. "She felt abandoned, insecure—"

"Insecure." Michael nodded. "Problem is she takes it too far."

"How?"

"She's clingy...always wants to be with me. In every way."

I assumed he meant sex. "Oh."

"She's also a gold-digger. Remember how I told you my grandmother was killed by a drunk teen while he was driving his father's car?"

"Yes."

"The kid's parents offered my family a million dollar settlement. I'd get a quarter of that amount, but I refused it. I have my own reasons. Jane is trying to change my mind about it."

"I can see why. On top of that, she's throwing insults at us. I don't want her representing our interests in court. Who knows what she'd say or do?"

"Let's get through tonight first. We'll deal with Jane later." He placed the ice and deli bags on the coffee table. He pulled out his cell phone and checked to see if there were any messages. He'd turned it off at the restaurant. He shook his head. No messages. Then he checked the hotel phone.

In the meantime, I emptied the ice into a bucket and placed a bottle of white Chardonnay in it. It would be the right temperature by the time we'd put our plan into motion.

Michael hung up the receiver. "Emily didn't leave a message."

"Let's give her more time. She'll call out of curiosity. Or she might just pop up." I set the bucket on the credenza next to two wine glasses and six water bottles. Michael had ordered these items from room service earlier, along with the Chardonnay.

He glanced at his watch. "You're right. It's only nine. We've got an

240

hour till she gets here. Let's eat." He handed me a bottle of water and took one for himself.

We devoured our sandwiches in minutes, neither of us saying a word. Michael had other things on his mind, so I didn't mention Jane's name again. I was beginning to think he was right. Our altercation with her was personal and had nothing to do with the quality of her legal work, which was above reproach and commendable. Tattling to Dan about her would be pointless. What would I gain by seeking revenge against someone who suffered from severe mood swings anyway? She had enough problems without me dumping another load on her.

As Michael got up from the chair, he toppled his bottle of water. It spilled over his cargo shorts. "Damn it! I'll go change. Be right back." He gathered the wrappings from our sandwiches and our empty water bottles, and discarded them in the trashcan in the bathroom. Moments later, he walked back into the living room wearing another pair of cargo shorts. He glanced around to make sure everything was in order. "You should get going."

"Right." I sighed and pulled myself out of the chair.

"What's the matter?"

We'd agreed Michael had a better chance of extracting information from Emily than I did, seeing as my friendship with her had fizzled but his still held a flicker of hope. Who knew what incriminating details would slip through that girl's lips after a few glasses of wine in the company of a "hot" date?

And yet... "I shouldn't have suggested setting up a meeting with Emily here," I said. "It's too dangerous. What if something goes wrong? What if she drops poison into your glass when you're not looking? What if she—"

"Don't worry," Michael said as calm as ever. He moved over to the wireless camera we'd concealed in the leafy plant and turned it on. It would capture every sound and movement in the living room from this point on.

"It's not too late," I said. "You can change your mind. We haven't put our plan into action yet."

He smiled. "Are you kidding? And waste a perfect chance to catch a killer?"

"What if we're wrong about her?"

"We're not. I'll bet she's feeling the pressure. You'll see. She's going to do herself in."

If he was feeling the least bit on edge, he hid it well, yet his brave front did nothing to quell my anxiety about the situation. He was prepared to risk his life for our freedom and asked nothing in return. I should have been the one comforting him, telling him everything would work out, but I couldn't.

The hotel phone rang.

Michael picked it up. "Hello. Hello." He frowned. "They hung up."

"Maybe Emily is getting cold feet," I said.

"Or maybe she's checking to see if I'm here or not."

"Do you think she suspects something?"

"She has no reason to."

"What if she doesn't show up? What if our scheme turns out to be one damn ridiculous mistake?"

"Let me worry about that." He gave me a reassuring smile.

I admired his confidence, but if Emily didn't take the bait, we'd never get another chance to dig up the truth. Moreau was closing in on us. For all we knew, it could be a matter of days, maybe even hours.

The phone rang again. Michael picked it up. "Hello. Oh...Emily. How are you?"

I thought he sounded stiff and unnatural, as if he'd rehearsed those words all night and forgotten what they meant. My heart was beating so loudly, I wondered if Michael could hear it too.

"Yeah, it's damned scary," he said to Emily, "but I'm in the clear. It's a different story with Megan, though... Only if you promise to keep it between us. The cops are one hundred percent sure she did it. Are you kidding? I won't be seeing her anymore. I cut my ties to her and this whole crazy nightmare."

Silence while Emily went on about something.

"You're right, I didn't give you a fair chance. That's why I called. I'm hoping I can make it up to you tonight. We'll enjoy a bit of wine, easy conversation. Yeah, in my suite. It's more private, if you know what I mean." He laughed at something she said.

Good. He was beginning to sound more relaxed.

"Yeah, a change of scenery is exactly what I need. Sounds wild. We could go there later. See you soon." He hung up and looked at me. "You'd better go. Don't forget. Take the stairs down to the next floor. You can't risk bumping into Emily on her way out of the elevator. And leave the hotel through—"

"I know. The rear exit and not the lobby. Then take a taxi back to the condo and wait for your phone call." I slipped my purse over my shoulder but didn't want to leave Michael standing there without an appropriate sendoff. I moved in closer. "Don't do anything crazy. Promise me you'll be careful."

"I promise." In spite of the pain from broken ribs still on the mend, he held me tight and kissed me.

I remembered the camera was operational and pulled out of his embrace. "I should go."

Someone knocked at the door.

"Oh, my God," I whispered. "She can't be here already."

"She must have called from the lobby," Michael whispered back. "Quick. Go hide in the bedroom."

A second, louder knock resonated throughout the suite as I rushed around the corner and into his bedroom. I left the door open a crack so I could overhear their conversation.

Michael's open laptop was on the dresser facing the foot of the bed. I turned off the volume. I didn't want Emily to follow the echo of her voice to the bedroom and find me here.

I sat on the edge of the bed—my front row seat to the live performance about to take place in the next room. I expected it to be nothing less than a nerve-racking experience. I watched as Michael stepped into the foyer and disappeared from the screen. I heard him unbolt the door.

There was a moment of hesitation.

"What the—" Michael began.

"We need to talk." Jane's voice preceded her on-screen debut.

# CHAPTER 28

I imagined how surprised and confused Michael must have been when he opened the door and saw Jane standing there instead of Emily. To describe her entrance as dramatic would be an understatement.

She'd taken the pins out of her hair and let the curls cascade to her shoulders. Gone was the little black dress. Instead a blue tank top accentuated ample breasts and a slim waist. A wraparound skirt showed off trim thighs and threatened to expose even more. She crossed the living room on strappy sandals, her wedge heels enhancing the length of her legs. A sheer print scarf wrapped around her neck flowed in the air behind her until she came to a stop by the windows where she turned to face Michael.

He'd shut the door and entered the living room but kept more than a cordial distance—an armchair—between them. He glanced at his watch, no doubt worried that Emily would arrive at any moment. "What's up? Do you have new information about the murder investigation?"

Jane shook her head. "I came here to say I'm sorry for behaving like a jealous adolescent at the restaurant earlier."

I noticed she had a hard time pronouncing her words, and a few of them were slurred. Maybe she'd finished off our glasses of wine after Michael and I had left the restaurant. Or maybe she kept a bottle in her hotel room and had downed a few swigs before coming over.

"You're sorry?" The skepticism on Michael's face was authentic.

"You're kidding me, right?"

"No." Her eyes rested on him. "I should have known better than to insult you like that." I noticed she omitted my name.

"It's too late. The damage is done."

She ignored his retort. "I also want to apologize for mentioning your grandmother's settlement in front of Megan. It was inappropriate." Her tone of voice was one you might use when asked what time of day it was.

Michael frowned. "Inappropriate? I'll tell you what was inappropriate. Your insinuations about Megan and me."

"Don't point a finger at me," Jane said. "You're no better. You and Megan disappeared from the restaurant without a word, like I had the plague or something. I didn't know what to think."

"Can you blame us?"

"Look, I've already apologized. We can stop playing the blame game now."

"Okay. You apologized. Now will you please leave?" He waved toward the door.

"Not yet. I have a proposition for you."

Michael glanced at his watch again. "I have nothing to discuss with you. I'm busy."

Her gaze drifted around the room and rested on the coffee table. "You don't seem busy to me. No laptop, no pens, no papers—"

"I don't owe you an explanation."

She gave him a half-smile. "This is about Megan, isn't it?" She gave a nod toward the corridor at the other end of the floor. "Are you hiding her in your bedroom? Is that why you're trying to get rid of me?"

My mind went into overdrive. *Had I left behind a telltale sign, like my bottle of water with a lipstick smudge on it?*

No, Michael had disposed of our water bottles along with our sandwich bags.

My purse?

No, I had it with me. It was on the bed.

*So why was Jane insinuating I was here?*

She had to be fishing. Yes, that's all it was. Fishing.

"She's not here," Michael said. "If you don't believe me, go see for yourself." He gestured toward the corridor.

I caught my breath as Jane took a few steps forward. She stopped. "Oh, forget it. I don't have time for silly games."

"Makes two of us. So if you don't mind." Michael motioned toward the door.

Good. He's getting rid of her. Emily must be on her way up by now. The last thing we needed was a face-to-face encounter between Jane and her.

But Jane didn't move. She put her hands on her hips and said, "You're in way over your head, Michael Elliott. You can't deny you could use my legal advice."

"The last time I checked, I had a lawyer and you were working for him."

She blinked. "The kind of advice I'm prepared to offer you goes far beyond Dan's capabilities."

He stared at her, his jaw clenched tight.

"Why do you think I came over here? It's because I care so much about you. You deserve the best representation you can get. I couldn't forgive myself if the police charged you with murder, and Dan lost the case because of an inept defense strategy."

"Inept? What the hell are you talking about?"

Jane's tone grew softer. "I know what you're going through, Michael. The police investigation is putting a terrible strain on you. The prospect of going to jail for the rest of your life must be tearing you apart."

"It's not over by a long shot."

"Oh, I'm afraid it is. Dan hasn't told you yet. I hate to be the bearer of bad news, but he's written off every witness as a potential suspect except Megan and you."

"That's plain crazy. Dan knows we're innocent."

Jane took a shaky step forward and steadied herself by placing a hand on the back of an armchair. "I know how much you're hurting inside. Let me help you." She went up to him, touched his face, and ran her fingers through his hair. "I can make the pain go away."

I cringed at the sound of her voice. At the way she touched him.

How her body brushed up against his.

Michael didn't budge. "It's a given the police think I'm a prime suspect. How the hell can you make that go away?"

"It's simple. I know you couldn't possibly have committed such an outrageous act, and I can prove it." She held her chin up high.

"Giving me a character reference won't cut it."

"Let me explain my alternative defense strategy. It won't take long. If you follow my advice, you'll have nothing to worry about."

He moved out of her reach and slid into a magenta armchair. He leaned forward and joined his hands. "Okay, I'll hear you out. You already have all the facts in the case, so what have I got to lose?"

*What was he doing? No, Michael, no! You're wasting precious time!*

I was on my feet and about to rush out of the room to put an end to their conversation, but something held me back. Instincts, I supposed, not to mention curiosity. I sat back down.

Jane settled in the other armchair, her left profile to the camera. "You're absolutely right. You have nothing to lose and so much more to gain. Trust me." As she crossed her legs, her wraparound skirt opened up along one side to expose her thigh, but she made no effort to cover it up. Instead, she sat there, an enticing smile on her face.

"How about some music?" Michael walked over to the credenza and turned on the radio. ABBA's "Take a Chance on Me" was playing. He'd left it on the 70s station catering to his interests.

I had to assume he'd turned on the radio to hide any noise I might make in the bedroom. Maybe it was his way of telling me to stay where I was.

He stood rooted to the spot for a few seconds but made sure he wasn't blocking the camera. Then he removed the bottle of wine from the ice bucket with one hand and took hold of the two glasses with the other.

*What? Had he lost his mind?*

This rapid shift in strategy tugged at the loose ends we'd rolled into a tight plan. Wine, music, a private setting—they'd formed part of our scheme to dupe Emily into revealing information that would incriminate her.

Only now, it was as if Michael had placed Jane in center stage.

# CHAPTER 29

I searched for the logic behind Michael's actions. Whatever Jane was up to, it wasn't based on good intentions. Maybe Michael thought so too and was playing along for reasons that, under the circumstances, he was unable to tell me. I had no choice but to trust him.

"It's chilled just the way you like it." He twisted the cap off the wine bottle.

Jane eyed him with suspicion. "You were planning on bringing Megan back here after dinner, weren't you? What happened to spoil your plans?"

"You're wrong. It's not like that between us."

"You gave her your grandmother's pendant, didn't you?"

"As a token of friendship." He poured wine into the glasses and held one out to her.

She stood up and accepted it from him. "Cheers." She clinked her glass with his and took a sip. "Mmm...very nice. I see you haven't lost your taste in wine, though you should be more selective in choosing the women you sleep with. To be specific, a certain auburn-haired widow."

"I told you. I'm not sleeping with her."

"You don't know how much I want to believe you."

"Have I ever lied to you?"

"No." She eyed him over the rim of her glass as she drank some wine. "From the first day I met you, I knew you were an honest man. I also knew we were meant to be together."

"Jane, we're not—"

"Let me finish. I want to tell you why we belong together." She took another sip and swayed but managed to steady herself. "You make me feel secure. You always did. You make me value things most people take for granted, like the romantic nights we spent—"

"We dated a few times. That's all it was."

Jane blinked. "There you go again, denying we had a strong, intimate bond from the start. We still have that bond. I know it and you know it too. Why do you keep running away from a relationship that's perfect?"

Michael shook his head. "For starters, you should start looking for someone with a fatter wallet. It'll add much more spice to your relationship."

Her lips curled upward. "That sounds peculiar coming from someone about to acquire a quarter of a million dollars."

"You know where I stand on that. Nothing's changed."

"How can you refuse to accept the settlement? It's your right." When he didn't answer, she said, "It's only because of some preposterous notion you have that it's blood money."

"It's reason enough."

"I wouldn't let that stop me from enjoying the best things money can buy." She finished up her glass as if it were water and held it out to him.

He refilled it and placed it on the coffee table. "You're missing the point. I don't need lots of money to make me happy. There are more important things in life, like loyalty and—"

"Loyalty! Of course. Even if I had all the money in the world, I'd insist on loyalty. You of all people should know how loyal I've been to you, Michael." She drew closer, her lips almost touching his.

"Damn it, Jane." He stepped away and sat down in his chair. "My life is in the balance, and all you think about is yourself."

Her eyes narrowed. "You don't fool me one bit. You're still the bleeding heart to that pathetic little widow, aren't you? I'm amazed you fell for her manipulative ways. I thought you were smarter than most men." She plopped down in her chair and reached for her glass.

"How many times do I have to tell you? There's nothing between us."

"Oh, come on. Try this for an eye-opener: the frantic young widow whose husband was murdered and the impressionable reporter who came to her rescue. What a farce!" She glared at him. "I see the way you ogle her. What is it about her that turns you on anyway?"

Michael sipped his wine, remained silent while he gazed at the carpet.

Jane's insinuations intrigued me. That she persisted in dragging them back into the discussion intrigued me even more. I remembered how she'd reacted to rumors of an affair between Michael and me during our meetings with Dan. I figured she was trying to beat out what she imagined was her competition—me. Now I was beginning to understand what churned below that icy façade. It was something vile and ugly—a jealousy that bordered on the obsessive.

I kept my eyes on the screen, unable to move a muscle as the scene unfolded steps away from me.

Jane's tone suddenly softened. "Remember all those moonlight walks along the beach? The long nights we spent together? We had some pretty wild sex, didn't we?" She laughed.

Michael said nothing, kept his gaze downcast.

Jane's expression soured. "So tell me her secret."

"Her secret?"

"Was she hot in bed? Hotter than me? Remember when..." She began to describe intimate details of their sexual jaunts, how he satisfied her every whim—no matter where and when—and left her wanting more.

The blood rushed to my face, and I was glad I was alone. I imagined how uneasy Michael was feeling at this very moment.

But he remained composed, somehow impervious to her lurid accounts of their intimate sex life. After she finished, he looked at her and said, "After what you and I had together, do you honestly think I'd jump into bed with a woman who'd just knocked off her husband?"

"Then it's off with her head! That's one way of getting the diamond pendant, isn't it?" Jane laughed at her own joke. She raised her glass, spilled some wine on the carpet, then laughed again.

My body temperature plunged. Her response shocked me, such that I half-listened while she reminisced about the time she'd met Michael in a Toronto courthouse two months ago, how they'd gone out for dinner that same night, how they'd tumbled into bed together later, how fantastic the sex was...

What a schemer! She'd say and do anything to hold on to him.

Goose bumps rose along my skin. An eerie pattern emerged, one that I had to consider, no matter how absurd it seemed. As far as their obsession with Michael was concerned, I'd say Jane was a perfect substitute for Emily. Not to mention their manipulative ways.

I turned my attention back to the screen. Michael and Jane continued to play their roles like a couple of professional actors. To the ordinary viewer, their performance could have passed for a daytime soap opera or made-for-TV movie. Jane managed to keep her hands off him, but it was just another trick to prove she was serious about getting him a get-out-of-jail-free card. She'd capitalize on something more rewarding once she hooked her claws into him for good.

"You said you had a proposition for me," Michael was saying, putting their conversation back on track.

"Yes," Jane said. "It hinges on taking on a different legal approach to your defense."

"Let's hear it."

"The weakest point in Dan's defense is that you and Megan haven't been able to provide alibis so far."

"So?"

"Here's my angle. It's simple, really. All you have to do is confess that Megan made up the whole sob story about her husband going to Granite Ridge so she could steer everybody off course. You'll admit you went to Pineview with her, but you'll play the innocent victim by putting the entire blame on her."

I shuddered. The goose bumps were out in full force now. How could she propose such an outrageous thing? She was a paralegal.

She wanted to be a lawyer. She represented justice and truth and had the respect of the legal community.

I wanted to rush out and rip her to shreds!

Who was I kidding? I was too terrified to move and too curious to find out where her proposal was heading. I stayed put.

Michael grinned. "You're kidding me, right?"

"Do I look as if I'm kidding?" Jane's face showed no emotion.

"Your premise won't work. The police suspect I had an affair with Megan...that I'm implicated in the murders."

"They have no proof either way, now do they?" She buried her face in her glass.

"What do you mean?"

"It's simple. It's Megan's word against yours."

He stared at her. "Megan's not stupid. If I try to dump the murders on her, she'll fight me with everything she's got. Besides, Dan won't go for it."

Jane waved a hand in the air. "Leave Dan out of this. I can get you a much better lawyer."

"Like who?"

"Trust me. I have top-notch contacts."

Michael hesitated, seemed to be pondering the matter. "You're forgetting a key element. The police found cyanide in my suite. What if they convict me? I don't want to go to jail for a crime I didn't commit. I'm innocent and I expect freedom. Nothing less. I need a lawyer on my side that I can trust with my life." Tension raced through his voice.

"I didn't say it was going to be easy," Jane said, her words more slurred than before. "You might get a few years of jail time. Before you know it, you'll be out on good behavior."

"Forget it. It's plain crazy."

"You have to trust me. I know how these things work."

All the while, Michael had kept pouring wine into their glasses—adding a lot more to hers than to his. I lost count. I hoped that Jane had too, and I silently urged her on with every gulp she wolfed down.

I checked my watch. Emily was running late.

As if he'd read my mind, Michael asked Jane, "What about Emily? Has anyone checked out her alibi?"

"It's been confirmed," she said.

"And?"

She blinked. "She was playing house with Bill Bradford on the weekend of the murders."

That's a damn lie! She took that information right out of Pam's agenda and created her own version of it.

"What about Ray and the canister he took from the lab?" Michael asked Jane.

"Ray wasn't involved in the murders. Trust me on that one." She reached for the bottle of wine and filled her glass, ignoring the drops that spattered onto the table. She poured the rest of the wine into Michael's glass and set the bottle down, almost tipping it over. "With these last persons of interest out of the way, the police will focus on you and Megan. You have no choice but to follow my advice. You understand that, don't you?" She gave him a pointed look.

Michael grew quiet. He'd succeeded in digging deeper and deeper, disclosing her true colors with every layer of deceit he'd peeled away. But his fixed gaze at the carpet gave the impression that he was weighing her proposal.

Jane sighed. "What's there to think about, Michael? It's a no-brainer, really it is."

He looked at her. "Anita's dead. How are we going to prove Megan used her to plant the cyanide in my suite?"

"Questions, questions. What's with all these questions? Don't you trust me to do what's best for you? I'm beginning to wonder why the hell I bothered to come here." She made a move to get up.

But Michael was faster. He dropped to his knees and placed his hands on her thighs, preventing her from getting up. He looked into her face and said, "Please, you have to help me."

"That's better." She smiled. "Come on, Michael. Think opportunity. Didn't Megan visit you here, work with you on your book or whatever it was the two of you were doing?"

"Yes."

Her smile widened. "So when you weren't looking, she planted the cyanide in your jacket." She placed a hand under his chin and kissed him on the lips. "You see? She had the motive, means, and opportunity to be a very, very bad girl."

Oh, she was slick. She had all the right answers. Given the chance, she'd rewrite Michael's testimony and blame me for the murders. Thank goodness, it was all on tape. I hated to think how her arguments might have convinced even the best jury in the world to put me behind bars. I could only imagine Dan's reaction when I'd brief him about his "brilliant" protégé later.

"So what do you say? Is it a deal?" Jane tried to kiss Michael again, but he slipped out of her reach and retreated to his seat.

He clasped his hands before him and shook his head.

"Now what's the matter?" she asked.

"Forget it. The police won't buy it."

My heart beat out of control as their conversation took yet another unexpected turn.

"What do you mean, the police won't buy it? Poisoning her husband was her idea in the first place." Jane slurped the last drops in her glass.

Michael said nothing. He kept his head down and wrung his hands, leaving his reaction open to interpretation.

His approach worked. Jane tried harder. "Look, I can get you off the hook, but I have to put the entire blame on Megan. If I show she was the instigator, the focus will be on her and not on you."

He ran a hand through his hair and appeared more skeptical than before. "I don't know. It's a long shot."

Jane paused in thought. "Okay. Let's explore a different angle. You can say Megan used her feminine ways to coax you into driving her to Pineview that Friday night. You'll plead ignorance and say you stayed in the car while the little wife ran into the Pineview cottage to sprinkle the sugar bowl with cyanide."

I caught my breath. The police hadn't disclosed the location of the cyanide. She had to be guessing.

"But I didn't—" Michael began.

"For God's sake, you don't expect the police to believe you weren't sleeping with her, do you? Do you think Moreau hasn't seen through that phony veneer of hers? I know I did. That bitch lured you into bed and into this damned mess in the first place. Just think about it." Her words were louder and more garbled then before.

"I'm so confused," he said. "I don't know what the hell I'm supposed to think anymore."

"What do you mean, you don't know?" Jane's eyes bore into him. "If you admit you went to Pineview as an innocent bystander, it'll keep you out of jail for the most part. What do I have to say to convince you this is your best defense? Look, I already have a first-rate lawyer standing by to defend you on those grounds."

I checked my watch. Ten o'clock. I wrote Emily off as a no-show. I figured Michael had too. It explained why he was playing his role with much more passion than before.

I heard a low vibrating sound behind me and turned around. The cargo shorts Michael had worn earlier were on the bed. I reached into a pocket to retrieve his cell. I recognized the name and answered. "Hello," I whispered. I tiptoed to the other end of the room, as far from the bedroom door as I could.

"Megan?" Dan asked. "Is Michael with you?"

"Yes, but he's busy." I kept my voice low. "We missed you at dinner."

"What dinner?"

"At The Spaghetti Factory."

"No one told me I was invited."

Small wonder.

He went on. "I have information about Robert Gingras. Michael remembered the law firm in Montreal that represented Gingras in a drug case last year. I called an associate there. Gingras was arrested but not convicted. He had his non-criminal record expunged. There's nothing on file for him."

Old news. Michael already suspected that much. "Okay. Thanks."

"Hold on. There's more. Jane was working as a paralegal for that same law firm at the time. She was assigned to Gingras' case. I'm surprised she didn't mention it. It probably slipped her mind."

*Like hell it did.*

"One last thing. Bill Bradford confirmed Emily's alibi. She was with him on a plane to Toronto that Friday after work." Dan heaved a sigh. "It's up to Moreau to make the next move. I'll keep you posted."

There was no time to get into a discussion about Jane. "Thanks, Dan." I hung up.

*Emily was innocent.* Michael and I had made a horrible mistake. Our plans to snare her evaporated before my eyes.

I had to make things right, but now wasn't the time to do it. It was clear that Michael didn't want to include me in whatever mind games he and Jane were playing in the other room. I'd have to wait it out until she left.

Something Dan said nagged at me. Jane had lied by omission about knowing Gingras, but why? I focused on the facts, trying to link them as best I could:

Jane knew Gingras.

Gingras stole a gun.

Anita was shot. By Gingras? Maybe. Maybe not.

Gingras was shot dead by Willie, who had nothing to do with any of this.

Damn it. I couldn't connect the dots. It was like trying to fit a stray piece into the rest of the jigsaw puzzle only because it looked as if it would fit, but it didn't fit no matter which way you tried it.

Frustration took a hold of me, such that I was considering once again if Emily could have carried out her plot to kill Pam regardless of a clean alibi.

Focus. A vital piece of information is missing. The one piece of evidence that connected the murders to Michael and me.

*Cyanide!*

I picked up Michael's cell phone and called Dan back. "Do you know if Gingras was working at the time of his drug arrest last year?" I whispered.

"Yes." The sound of paper flipping as Dan leafed through a file. "Here it is. A company in Montreal that manufactures plastic products. Why?"

"Call you back later." I hung up.

Cyanide was used in the manufacturing of plastics! I'd have to thank my mother later.

I called information and asked the operator to connect me to the Elegance Hotel. Then I asked the hotel receptionist to ring Michael's room. She had a hard time hearing me because I spoke so low, but she finally put me through.

It was with a weird sense of amusement that I heard the phone ringing in the suite. Michael excused himself to Jane as he walked over to answer it.

"It's me," I whispered. "Dan called on your cell phone." I gave him the gist of our chat and my assumptions about Gingras, then hung up and went back to view the scene on his laptop.

"Okay. Tomorrow is fine. Thank you." Michael hung up and sat down. "Sorry about that," he said to Jane. "Laundry service. They'd misplaced some of my stuff and found it."

Jane blinked. "Listen to me. This is how we're going to play it. The little wife got desperate after she found out her husband was sleeping around with her best friend. She begged you to help her. So you rented a car and drove her to Pineview. You know the rest."

I studied Jane as she adjusted the scarf around her neck. Maybe it was the intonation of her voice. Maybe it was her persistence in trying to influence Michael. Regardless, an image of the first time I'd seen her in his suite flashed through my mind again. I recalled her lingering stance by the coffee table…the way she'd hinted that Michael had another woman in his life…

*Damn it. What was I missing?*

As if she were standing next to me, my mother's words ran through my mind: "Sometimes the answer is right in front of our eyes and we don't see it—or don't want to see it."

All at once, it hit me. I understood why Michael was playing along with Jane and what he'd been holding out for all this time. He was waiting for her to reveal the tiniest scrap of evidence that would set us free: that she'd seen my note with the Pineview information in Michael's suite weeks before the murders and acted on it!

The theory alone unnerved me, but why would she want to kill Tom and Pam? It didn't make sense. Why would someone in her reputable line of work commit such a crime? What did she expect to gain from murdering two people she didn't know?

Unless she *thought* she knew them.

# CHAPTER 30

My stomach did a somersault. I would have loved to be in Michael's shoes, to tell Jane that I saw through her lies and scheming ways, and that every word she uttered was on tape.

But that was why he was sitting across from her and I wasn't. He was cool—so cool. He had the innate sense to hold back, knowing that if he didn't, it would destroy the last chance we had of clearing our names.

"What you're suggesting," he was saying to Jane, "would have taken a lot of time and effort to plan."

"Not at all. From day one, the little wife had every detail planned out."

"Like what?"

She blinked hard. "Come on, Michael. Do I have to spell it out for you? The fake alibis, the rental car, the cyanide, everything—right down to the damned Pineview details she scrawled for you on that damned canary yellow paper she doodles on all the time."

My blood went cold. Aside from the police, no one except Michael and me had seen the original note, let alone knew I'd written it on canary yellow paper. The police had shown the legal teams a black-and-white copy of it in an evidence bag.

All of a sudden, the pieces of the puzzle fell into place.

If Michael had taken in the implication of Jane's comment, he wasn't showing it. He shrugged. "I guess it could work. Premeditation. Right?"

"Yes," she said. "Do we have a deal?"

He stood up. "No damn way. I'll show you why." He turned off the radio, then pushed a button on the CD player. "The truth is I already have an alibi. A legitimate one." He grabbed the remote and pressed play.

I couldn't see it, but I knew the clip of Michael at Willie's gas station was playing out.

"Where did you get that?" Jane edged forward.

"From Willie's gas station. Where else?"

"They told me it wasn't available." She rose to her feet but was unsteady.

Michael turned and shoved her so hard that she fell back into the chair. "Sit down and stop embarrassing yourself."

Jane pushed strands of hair off her face. "Oh, we like it rough now, do we?"

He waved a fist at her. "I swear, if you try to get up again, I'll belt you one."

She remained silent, her eyes fixed on him.

"I know the truth. You hired Robert Gingras to get that tape from Willie but he failed. In fact, Gingras died while he was on the job for you, but you already know that, don't you?"

She gave him a half-smile. "Poor, poor Michael. I think the pressure is getting to you. You're inventing people I've never even heard of."

"Nice try, Jane. What I couldn't figure out was why you wanted me to lie about my alibi. But I get it now. You wanted Megan and me to take the fall for the murders at Pineview—murders that you planned and executed yourself."

She brought a hand to her neck in a protective gesture. "How dare you accuse me of such a thing," she said, sounding offended.

"Don't play the victim. It doesn't suit you."

"Come on, Michael, be logical. Why would I kill two people I don't know?" She caught herself. "For that matter, why would I kill anyone?"

"Because you were jealous. You saw the Pineview information in my suite and assumed I was going away with another woman that weekend."

"That's ridiculous. I didn't know Megan then."

261

"I didn't say Megan."

She hesitated. "I just assumed—"

"You assumed wrong—again. The same day you met Megan, you mentioned you'd seen a newspaper photo of her taken at one of my book-signing events. You were jealous. You even asked me if I had another woman in my life."

"So what? It doesn't make me a murderer." She laughed.

Michael went on. "You used your connection to Gingras and had him beg for a job at Pineview. You told him to confirm that the cottage was booked under the name Scott. Any fool could have checked it out, but Gingras was sloppy or lazy or both. He didn't dig far enough to find out more about the occupants—like their first names."

Jane blinked. "Poor Michael. You're daydreaming again."

"You believed Gingras owed you one for getting him off on drug charges last year. You forced him to leave his job at the plastics company but not before he took a supply of cyanide with him. Nothing beats calling in a favor. Right, Jane?"

"You're delirious."

"It must have been one hell of a shock to discover you'd had the wrong people bumped off at Pineview. You covered your tracks by planting the cyanide here in my suite to swing suspicion my way." He shook his head. "I knew you had personal problems, but who'd have figured you for a cold-blooded murderer?" He turned around and clicked on the remote to open up the CD tray. He reached for the CD but had a hard time leaning over.

Faster than I'd have expected from one as drunk, Jane grabbed the empty wine bottle and struck Michael over the head. He staggered and fell to his knees, his head bent forward. "Your biggest mistake was to turn your back on me," she said, "in more ways than one." She grabbed his hair and pulled his head back. "No one is going to take you away from me—ever."

My heart skipped a beat.

A loud knock at the hallway door reverberated throughout the suite and everyone froze.

*Oh, my God! Not Emily!*

The hallway door burst open.

Sergeant Claude Duchaine rushed into the living room. "Jane Barlow, I am arresting you on suspicion of murdering Thomas Scott and Pam Strober."

"What the hell—" Jane let go of Michael. She waved the broken bottle and then lashed out at Duchaine who was blocking her path to the foyer. "Get out of my way!" Duchaine tried to grab her arm, but Jane swung the bottle and slashed his hand.

"Drop that bottle," he ordered, his hand spurting blood as he advanced toward her again.

"Go to hell, you bastard!" She kicked him between the legs, causing him to double over and lean against the chair for support.

I knew what I had to do. I prayed I wouldn't be too late. I swallowed my panic and geared up for a frantic finale.

My heart pounded as I crept out of the bedroom and rounded the corner into the living room.

Jane had her back to me.

Michael had a hand on the credenza and was trying to pull himself up. I could tell he was dizzy because he kept staring at the carpet as if he were trying to focus. If he saw me, he didn't show it.

"Think about what you're doing, Jane," he said.

"I know exactly what I'm doing, you traitor," she shouted. She grabbed him by the hair. "Now I'm going to finish what I started."

I raced up to her and grasped both ends of the scarf hanging from her back. I yanked hard, but it didn't have the effect I'd hoped for.

She took a few steps backward but didn't tip over. As she spun around to face me, her scarf loosened to reveal deep scratches at her neck.

I gasped. "Anita scratched you!"

Her eyes took on a crazed expression. "You bitch! I won't miss you this time." She lunged at me, the broken bottle aimed at my face like the jaws of a piranha.

I leapt back, slammed into the wall, then ducked sideways as Jane plunged the bottle inches from my head, shattering it against the wall.

Glass flew in all directions.

263

I looked at Jane. Blood dripped from her hand, but she didn't seem to notice.

I started to run off, but she grabbed me by the hair and banged my head into the wall.

I lost focus for a moment, then seized her arms and stopped her from smashing my head into the wall again.

I couldn't hold her off much longer. She was stronger than me. She pounded my head into the wall again.

The room began to spin, go black. *Was this as far as I could go?*

No, I refused to give up. I had to find the strength to fight back.

It was now or never. I let go of her arms and dug my thumbs into her eyes.

She screamed in pain and stumbled backward, putting her hands to her eyes.

Michael tackled Jane, forcing her to the floor. She punched him in the ribs, breaking his hold on her. As she struggled to her feet, Duchaine jumped in and clutched her in a tight squeeze, only just missing her efforts to land another kick. He pinned her to the wall, face first, and cuffed her hands behind her back.

Two uniformed police officers appeared out of nowhere and took Jane into custody. As they hauled her out, she struggled and cursed at them and vowed to sue the police for a multitude of violations of her rights. Over her shoulder, she shouted, "Michael, you stinking bastard! It's not over. I'll get you for this."

Michael was bent over, grimacing in pain.

I hurried up to him. "What you just did was plain crazy, you know that?"

"Look who's talking," he said, slowly straightening up.

"I should get you to the hospital."

"Just got the wind...knocked out of me. I'll be fine."

I noticed a bit of blood on his forehead. "You're bleeding." I raced to the bathroom and grabbed a clean facecloth and wet it under the tap. I ran back to the living room, dropped a couple of ice cubes into the facecloth, and handed it to Michael. "We should get a doctor to look at that cut in case you need stitches."

He held the ice pack to his head. "This and some TLC should do the trick." His eyes lingered on mine.

Duchaine cleared his throat. "Detective Moreau would like to see you both. Please come with me."

Michael and I followed the sergeant out into the corridor. I assumed we were going to the police station to file a report. I was stunned when Duchaine led us into an adjacent suite instead.

The aroma of brewed coffee was the first thing I noticed as we stepped into Room 786. The second was that the suite was identical to Michael's but reversed in layout. It felt odd walking through a suite that mirrored his in furnishings and color choices. It was as if someone else had created a mockup of his living accommodations— something you wouldn't experience if you had your own home or apartment furnishings and visited another home or apartment.

Moreau sauntered up to us from the far end of the suite.

"What's going on here, Detective?" Michael asked him.

"We installed surveillance equipment in your suite, Monsieur Elliott. We set up facilities here so a police team could oversee the situation and move in rapidly if necessary." He motioned toward the far wall where a technician was tapping away on a keyboard at a desk. A large monitor with a split screen was positioned in front of him.

I was in awe. That Moreau had organized a covert operation without any of us knowing about it was daunting. That he might have seen Michael and me embracing earlier through the camera lens was even more intimidating.

"Why didn't you tell us about this?" Michael asked him.

"We had to follow procedure. We could not risk jeopardizing the operation."

"What operation?"

Bushy eyebrows gathered in a frown. "We have had your suite under surveillance for some time. It was for your own protection, of course."

Right.

Interest flickered in Moreau's eyes as he looked at us. "You surprised us by setting a trap for Emily Saunders."

"We had our reasons," I said. "Lucky for her, she didn't show up."

"Oh, Emily Saunders was here," the detective said. "I will show you. Please follow me."

Moreau led the way to the back of the room. He gestured toward the monitor. "The right part of the screen captures the living room in the adjacent suite. The left part captures the exterior corridor." He said a few words in French to the technician who nodded and tapped a few buttons.

I watched as a video began to play. Soon Emily came into view. She was heading up the corridor and had almost reached Michael's suite when Duchaine blocked her path, startling her. He reached into his jacket but before he could show her his badge, she turned and fled down the corridor. Duchaine chased after her, but I couldn't see what happened because that part of the corridor extended beyond the camera range. I checked the date and time stamp. It was recorded twenty minutes after Jane had arrived.

"I wish to extend my sincere gratitude to both of you," Moreau said. "Had it not been for your plans, we would not have captured the alleged suspect—Jane Barlow."

"It was Megan's idea to use my hotel suite for our sting operation," Michael said.

"It was a bizarre twist of fate," I said. "I can't take credit for any of it."

"Why not, Madame Scott?" Moreau smiled at me. "Police often fall upon suspected felons by coincidence, or fluke, as they say."

Twists of fate. Life was full of them. And it wasn't over yet.

# CHAPTER 31

Facts ultimately surfaced to reveal how a string of seemingly unrelated events had influenced Moreau's actions.

It began when Stewart reported his Beretta had been stolen from Pineview and claimed Gingras was the alleged thief. Because Pineview fell within Moreau's jurisdiction, the report landed on his desk.

After Anita was found shot, Moreau reviewed the videotapes from the Elegance Hotel. The videos showed Michael leaving the hotel Tuesday morning for a jog and returning an hour later. Jane arrived afterward—within minutes of one Robert Gingras—but Moreau had no reason to suspect a link between her and Gingras at the time.

Moreau assumed I'd hired Gingras to kill Anita. His theory was that I'd paid her to plant the cyanide in Michael's suite and wanted to eliminate her as a witness. However, the gun used to kill Anita was nowhere to be found and Gingras had vanished, so Moreau couldn't prove his theory. On pure speculation, he arrived at my condo and asked to search the premises, then followed up with a search of Michael's suite. Taking possession of evidence that Dan upheld was circumstantial at best, a persistent Moreau put Michael and me under police surveillance.

Moreau's focus changed when Gingras' burnt body was identified and Willie turned himself in, along with the Beretta, a copy of the gas station videotape with Gingras in it, and a signed statement corroborating Gingras' threat on his life and the destruction of his home.

At that point, Moreau hadn't yet made the connection between Gingras and Jane. He continued to keep an eye on Michael's suite and observed our scheme to snare Emily. As luck would have it, Jane walked right into our trap instead and supplied Moreau with first-hand evidence that established her guilt and proved our innocence in due course.

It came as no surprise when ballistic tests later showed a match between the bullets found in Anita's body and the Beretta. DNA tests performed on skin cells under Anita's fingernails confirmed she'd scratched Jane on the neck before meeting her fate. It explained the high-neckline tops, thick necklace, and scarf Jane had worn in the days following that altercation.

I kept picturing how Jane might have stalked Michael and me, how she'd seen him leave his hotel to meet me for dinner so many times. It must have driven her crazy with jealousy. How fortunate that Michael hadn't opened the door to her that Tuesday before he left to meet me at Santino's. I imagined how unstable her state of mind must have been just minutes after Anita's murder. I trembled at what she might have done to Michael, especially with Gingras at her side holding the Beretta. That she'd pushed me into the traffic was horrific enough to grasp, but our physical confrontation at the hotel would haunt me longer than I'd care to admit to anyone. Anyone except my shrink, Dr. Madison, who helped me to deal with the trauma of it all.

I read Tom's obituary in the weekend newspaper with a peculiar detachment, as if it had been written about someone I didn't know. My indifference lingered right through the funeral service on Monday morning at St. Paul's Church. My mother sat beside me, crying for both of us. For reasons that didn't need explanation, I couldn't shed a tear.

Michael didn't attend. We'd decided it would be in our mutual interests if he stayed away until the press coverage died down.

My co-workers from Bradford Publishing showed up. The notable absence was Emily who was on extended sick leave due to "deep personal grief."

Peter Ewans was there, pale and in a daze. Ann greeted me warmly, offered her sincere condolences, then took Peter by the arm and led him off.

I placed a white rose at Tom's gravesite. I forgave him for deceiving me and for taking advantage of my tolerant spirit. I finally had closure, so why hold a grudge? He'd have to answer to someone with a lot more influence than I ever had over him.

A final autopsy report found that Tom had an inoperable brain tumor. It was difficult to determine how much longer he would have lived. It could have been the reason he'd decided to increase his life insurance policy. No one will ever know for sure. Only when my clinical tests for STIs and HIV came back negative was I able to turn the page on this part of my life.

I dropped into Bradford weeks later to meet Kayla for lunch. I owed her one for having safeguarded Pam's agenda. As useless as it had been for our initial purposes, it was the catalyst for the sting that nabbed the real killer. I didn't bother explaining its disappearance from Kayla's desk. She'd assumed Emily had found a way to get into her desk but couldn't prove it.

Kayla had good news, bad news, and so-so news.

The good news: she'd been promoted to Pam's job. She asked if I'd work freelance for the company. I said yes.

The bad news: Ray Felton had been arrested and fired—all on the same day. The police had searched his apartment and found hundreds of photos and CDs of nude women, including Emily. Ray had sold the photos without the women's consent. He admitted he'd ransacked Emily's office looking for photos she'd swiped from the office lab. She'd planned on turning the evidence over to the police, but they'd beaten her to it when they'd searched Ray's apartment.

The so-so news: Emily left the company. The fact that Mrs. Bradford had found out about her affair with Bill had driven Emily over the edge. It hadn't helped that she'd lied to Mrs. Bradford about Pam and Bill in the first place, then bribed her for a considerable sum to keep it "between them." Emily later believed Mrs. Bradford had sent a goon after her. I didn't say anything to Kayla, but it explained why Emily had fled when Duchaine stopped her outside Michael's suite. She must have thought he was a thug reaching for a gun instead of his badge.

Before Emily left, she confessed to Kayla that she'd snooped in Pam's agenda to keep tabs on her social contacts. Emily swore she only dated the men whose names Pam had crossed out at the back of her agenda to indicate she'd lost interest in them.

When I'd scanned the directory in her agenda, I'd noticed Pam had drawn a line through Tom's name. She must have had second thoughts and decided to have one last fling with him at Pineview. Emily didn't know how lucky she was.

A year later, Michael and I made our appearance at the courthouse. Even the sun filtering through the clouds on that September morning couldn't defuse my trepidation about seeing Jane face-to-face. Although Dan had run us through the process, I was sure I'd pass out from the sheer stress of it all before I even opened my mouth on the witness stand.

The time I spent in court was a blur. I couldn't remember a word I'd said if my life depended on it. Nature's way of protecting me from mental and emotional anguish, I supposed.

Jane was diagnosed with Borderline Personality Disorder, but a psychologist and lead witness for the prosecution testified her BPD was at a high-functioning level and didn't impair her work. He also stated Jane felt no guilt in breaking the law to attain her goals. He explained how Michael's rejection of Jane and his interest in me had amplified her lack of control over him and presented a recipe for psychopathic behavior.

After a jury of six women and six men deliberated for two days, Jane's guilty verdict came in. She turned to look at Michael and gave him a weird smile—the sort that gives you chills and keeps you up at night thinking about it. Then she puckered her lips and blew him a kiss before she was escorted out.

Dan had a hard time dealing with repercussions from the legal community. He had regrets about not having picked up on Jane's "bad character" earlier—a legal requirement he promised he'd adhere to more closely in the future. He said goodbye and promised to keep in touch after his return from a two-month vacation in Nassau.

The arms of justice extended as far as Sainte-Adèle. The facts Michael had pooled from informers helped the police arrest a drug producer who operated an ecstasy lab there. The lab had evolved into a drug-trafficking operation linked to other criminal conspiracies and to Montreal-area street gangs. Two local newspapers honored Michael for his article covering the incident.

I often wished I hadn't implicated Michael in my problems, though trusting him saved my life. As he'd often pointed out, destiny steps in to deal with matters we can't resolve or refuse to resolve. It was life's way of putting us back on the right track.

Destiny played another role in Michael's life. He had initially refused to accept the monetary offer from the parents of the teenager who had killed his grandmother. He changed his mind after he found out the teen's parents were doctors and that their only son would live out his life in a wheelchair. As a condition of his acceptance, Michael donated his share of the proceeds to medical research—two hundred and fifty thousand dollars.

He was three times lucky when destiny stepped in again to balance things out. From his grandmother's estate, Michael received his cut—a quarter of a million dollars. He invested the funds and told me it would in no way change his commitment to his day job. I believed him.

"What should we drink to?" I offered Michael a glass of red wine and sat down next to him on the cushy sofa in our new home.

"To the future." He smiled.

I smiled back. "To the future."

Michael glanced away, as if he were looking for the right words.

I hoped it had nothing to do with marriage. Of course, I couldn't negate the chemistry that had existed between us from the start. Our love for each other had passed the test of time and survived the dilemmas that had come with it. Michael was everything I wanted in a man and I valued our relationship—as long as there were no strings attached. In truth, I appreciated my newfound independence now more than ever.

"Have you thought about what you wanted to do in the next while?" he asked.

Uh-oh. Here it comes. I wanted to discourage him before he made a fool of himself. I fingered the diamond pendant around my neck. "Long-range plans don't work for me."

"Okay. Then how about going on a short trip with me?"

Totally unexpected. "Where to?"

"Portland, Maine. A reporter friend at a newspaper there asked me to step in for him while he's out of town."

I did the math. With the proceeds from Tom's insurance policy, I had the start of a decent nest egg for retirement. I shared the mortgage payment on the two-story house in the west end I co-owned with Michael. I worked my own hours as a ghostwriter for Kayla...

"Traveling is therapeutic," he said. "It gives the soul a freedom of sorts."

Freedom. Now there's a worthy destination.

## ACKNOWLEDGMENTS

I want to thank everyone who provided invaluable feedback and encouragement, especially author Colleen Cross and editor Catherine Adams.

Warmest thanks to family and friends who inspired me to follow my dream. I am extremely grateful to my husband, John, for his patience while I disappeared for long stretches of time into the pages of my novel, and to my daughter, Carolyn, for designing and bringing my book cover to life.

## ABOUT THE AUTHOR

Sandra Nikolai is the author of the Megan Scott/Michael Elliott Mystery series. In addition to her novels, Sandra has published a string of short crime stories, garnering awards along the way.

A graduate of McGill University in Montreal, Sandra held jobs in sales, finance, and high tech before leaving the corporate world to pursue a career in writing. She likes to think that plotting a whodunit reveals the lighter— yet more mysterious—side of her persona.

Visit Sandra's website at www.sandranikolai.com to read her blog posts and sign up to receive her latest book news. Follow her on Twitter: @SandraNikolai or connect with her on Goodreads or Facebook at www.facebook.com/SandraNikolaiAuthor

Books in the Megan Scott/Michael Elliott Mystery series:
*False Impressions*
*Fatal Whispers*
*Icy Silence*
*Dark Deeds*